Barque Whisper

Barque Whisper

ALUN RICHARDS

ST. MARTIN'S PRESS
NEW YORK

Library of Congress Cataloging in Publication Data

Richards, Alun.
  Barque whisper.

    I. Title.
PZ4.R513Bar   1980   [PR6068.I244]   823'.9'14   79-23069
ISBN 0-312-06707-0

This yarn is for my friend

W. Cyril Rogers

with my thanks for the constant avail-
ability of his unrivalled knowledge of
the port of old Swansea and its ships,
fevers, mutineers, scoundrels and saints
of long ago.

Author's Note

I would like to express my debt to W. Cyril Rogers, Robin Craig of University College, London, Dick Richards, and to the librarians of the City of Cork, the London Library, the Swansea Public Library, and the University College of Swansea for their help in researching material relevant to this tale, and also to acknowledge an award from the Welsh Arts Council.

For information relating to the *Caleuche*, I am indebted to *The Nitrate Clippers* by the late Basil Lubbock.

Chapter One

From the beginning, there were complications. Very little was clear. There were so many things left unsaid, matters that would be explained later. The whole story, he was led to understand, would only unfold as time went on. There was so much he would have to see for himself when they got there, out around Cape Horn and up that arid west coast of South America with its windless deserts and treeless slopes. There was bad luck, he had been told, coincidence, superstition, mutiny, double-dealing, shipwreck, desertion and – as ever in any seaman's tale of woe – bad weather. There was a good deal about to be uncovered that certain people would not want to know about; in short, a past best left alone. There were also those who must be kept in the dark from the beginning, which had meant that meetings were held in secret, voices were lowered, and there was not always time to answer questions in full. It was to be, as he had told the Mate, a mouth-shut job, and that just about summed it up as far as everybody was concerned except himself. For himself, the news brought by Senhora Felipa Salaverry, the Brazilian woman of colour with the Peruvian name, was nothing less than the return of the dead from the grave.

Such was the substance of the thoughts of Captain Jack Hannah, Master of the barque *Whisper*, on the night before sailing. But it had all begun three weeks before.

On 1 September 1858, the year of which I write, he, Jack Hannah, recently discharged Chief Officer of the Liverpool clipper *Pass of Erinmore*, had been polishing an empty brass shell canister in the house of his aunt overlooking the village of Ennal's Point at the end of Sveynton Bay where the family had always lived. He was twenty-seven years of age and had been at sea, man and boy, since he was fourteen. He had recently returned to Sveynton since he had hopes of obtaining a command on one of the copper ore boats which regularly plied from the port to the west coast of South America. It was a famous trade based on one simple economic fact. To smelt one ton of copper took a hundred tons of coal, and the proximity of the

7

rich Welsh coalfield with the mining valleys running down to the sea like the fingers of a glove meant a continuous supply of cheap coal. It made sense to establish smelting works near the supply and when the demand grew for copper, and Cornish ores were exhausted, ships went ever further afield and this in turn meant the establishment of a fleet. The vessels themselves were copper bottomed, as strong in rib and planking and as well found in gear as any of their bigger sisters, and Jack Hannah, clipper trained, had every qualification for command. It was work for young crews and young masters, with regular voyages around Cape Horn, deep loaded both ways, coal out and ore home, and the prospect of promotion and profit at a much younger age than in the larger vessels sailing from the English ports. In every respect save one, his expectations were correct, his qualifications were impeccable, his ambitions eminently realisable.

The one haunting flaw in the case for his advancement was what might be called the family connection, for in the eyes of Henry Chauncey-Vernon, the proprietor of the Vernon Smelting Works and most substantial shipowner in the port, he, Jack Hannah, was very simply his father's son. And his father, Captain Joshua Hannah, late Master of the Sveynton barque *Avalon*, lost with her Captain and all hands nine years before, was forever associated with an affair which had become known as the *Avalon* Mutiny, an occurrence which ended with the hanging of an unknown Greek seaman. The attendant disrepute on that occasion, the rumours and counter rumours which surrounded his dead father's name, fixed him for ever, it seemed, under a cloud of suspicion which not only hovered about him, but actually preceded him, darkening the eyes of clerks, sending mere tallymen and book-keepers whispering down gloomy corridors, bringing limp, apologetic and lying smiles of regret upon the faces of marine superintendents here in his home port. It was as if his late father's reputation as a hard task master, too fond of the fist, hard-cased and hard-mouthed, remained after all these years, taking on some amorphous shape from which harbingers of doubt and misgiving drew sustenance still, inevitably causing second thoughts to become first thoughts. Wherever he had gone in search of the employment for which he was so eminently qualified, he had met with reservations and hesitations. His homecoming, like his expectations, was a mistake.

Until the change came, as unpredictable as a squall in the doldrums, arriving suddenly and unexpectedly – and at night – in the presence of one Senhora Felipa Salaverry. And then once more he sat in the front room of the little house, polishing that empty brass shell canister, brooding upon her offer, seeing the reflection of his large, plank-jawed face, his flaming mop of untidy, carrot-red hair, while his massive frame filled his badly cut serge suit so that the very length of his arms and the rippling power of huge biceps pressed the sleeves of his jacket as tight as silk hose upon a stout leg. He was a very large young man, awkward of gait, sullen of brow, his physical strength the most noticeable thing about him. He was all shoulders and hands, a frowning man of buried thoughts with a quickness of temper he had learned to control, a man who led by example, as his references stated, and there was a lot more to him than his captains had perceived. Deep, they said of him in the fo'c'sle; a horse of a man, a man not to be contradicted, but a man too, who could cheat the sea and was never afraid of it. Had he not gone over the side in Pabellon de Pica to save a ship's boy when a tidal wave lifted the old *Annesley* on to her beam ends, and parted her cables after her chain cut through the wood planking to below the load line? Three hours he'd held on to that lad, lashed him on to a plank and brought him ashore safe and sound when the number of dead ran into hundreds. He'd taken his sea boots off under water and bitten through the straps with his teeth, they said – a gold watch job that! – and there wasn't a real seaman who wouldn't go anywhere with him, up aloft in any weather or any vessel, when it was a look-alive, handy jack you wanted. With him aloft, or conning the ship, or getting off sail smartly in a snorter, you were sitting royal, for he was a real down-easter. Hard, mind, but the real stuff, a right down-east johnny-cake, and a very hard man to shave! So spoke the fo'c'sle.

But there was more than this again. The fo'c'sle like his captains saw the outer man, but he was a more complicated man than the simplicity of his shipboard actions suggested. The sea was what he had attempted to understand. It had a kind of private meaning to most and to Jack Hannah, like his father before him, it was something to be learned, winds, tides, currents, channels, shoals, races, rips, a variety of maritime laws. A star-dogged moon was bad weather, he used to say. See one, experience the weather, you learnt that for ever. One voyage they called him star-dogged Jack, meaning a jonah, but that was a scurvy trip and no fault of his. No, the sea was something to be watched and respected, but it could be

9

mastered, given the luck. You didn't *have* to be a star-dogged jack and the sea, the ever untrustworthy sea – he would grant it that! – was to be survived upon and used. It did not trouble him. What troubled him was himself.

The bunched rag which traversed the cylindrical brass canister went round it for the twentieth time. There was a blemish near the base and he pressed his extended forefinger against it, manoeuvring the improvised pad so that it scoured a dent in the brass. He wanted no encrustation of dirt to show. He was aware that he was making more of this unnecessary task than he needed to, but he was also very grateful for it, the simple reason being that he was not alone and there was a particular pair of sharp green eyes which he wanted to avoid. Seated across the room in the single window which overlooked the shelter of the headland of Ennal's Point in whose comforting lee the nodding masts of a dozen moored oyster dredgers were to be seen, was his fiancée, Beatrice Trevoake. Her face was tearstained, her hair awry where she had patted it, curled it, twisted it in her fingers until finally she had clasped her hands together and now sat limply in the corner, her own tall frame slumped, her normal composure reduced to a mute silence. But it was not a silence such as any engaged couple might face. How did you comfort a man who had learned what Jack Hannah had just been told?

At twenty-three, Beatrice, a capable young woman with every expectation of marriage to a man she had known for most of her life, could not reasonably be expected to express sensible thoughts about the re-emergence of the dead. Then the business proposition recently put to her fiancé was itself unusual. So was the bearer of the news, this Senhora Salaverry, and so too were the people the stranger's mysterious presence had aroused. One day in the port and she had shaken up the sediment of the most undesirable elements in the whole of Sveynton. And the news she brought was all so incredible that Beatrice wanted to test every statement, hoping to find an echo in Jack Hannah's voice of the distrust she herself felt, not for him, but for the people she must now think of as his associates, the flies the stranger had shaken out from their crevices. You throw a stone into a pool, the ripples continue to the very edge. You throw a stone into a muddy pool, the dirt rises, clouding what was once so crystal clear; an apt description of her misgivings, Beatrice thought. Presently she spoke, anxious to recapitulate and re-examine every detail. It was a veritable morass of confusions, of lies, half truths,

10

words with double-edged meanings, she was sure. The pool grew muddier as every second went by.

"Whom did she first approach, this woman?"

"She came to enquire of the owners of the *Whisper* if she was available for charter."

That was simple enough. Except that the *Whisper* was one of the few copper ore vessels not owned by the omnipresent Henry Chauncey-Vernon. And it was a woman enquiring. That in itself was extraordinary. Beatrice would not forget that. Senhora Felipa Salaverry, a mouthful, a handful, a baggage, and only a would-be charterer then. Nothing was agreed for some time.

"A woman of colour?"

"She is a Brazilian."

"She went to the port authorities then?"

"No, she went to a chandler. The chandler sent her to Belasco. She said her instructions were to be discreet."

"A woman of colour?" Beatrice had all the prejudices of her time and ours.

"She's not a negress, creole maybe," Jack Hannah said.

"Belasco has a coloured servant," Beatrice said. She had good reason to know the *Whisper*'s part-owner.

"Does it make any difference?" Jack Hannah said irritatedly. He had stopped his polishing and looked moodily at the distant headland. These were the least important facts. A stranger had arrived. The stranger had money and a proposition. None of these things bothered him, nor that the stranger was a woman. It was the news she later gave him which had ended his sleep, the fact . . . the fact . . . the fact that had stopped his framing coherent thoughts. If anything was sinister, it was that a man like him could be struck dumb by a thought. For the news had made his very knees tremble and his stomach heave. But then it was not so much news as a blow in the face of all his hopes, and like the news, was a threat to his pride as much as anything.

But it was the Senhora that bothered Beatrice, the Senhora and the man she went to first, Belasco. Then there was also this colour business. Sveynton, although booming, was small. It had a population of forty thousand odd, including villages like Ennal's Point spreading out along the coast, and most of them were Welsh or of mixed Welsh and West Country stock like herself, with the usual smattering of Irish immigrants who lived in hovels along the sailor

11

town bordering the dock. There were few parsons of colour, much fewer than at Bristol across the water which had prospered with the slave trade. But Belasco, the self styled Baron Belasco, a metropolitan immigrant, recently domiciled in the town, was a quack doctor, a speculator and man of parts, well heeled judging by his showy appearance, but still a man about whom few positive facts were known. He was said to be worshipped by the colliers in the mining valleys for his manipulative skills in the healing of injured backs. He was both masseur and adviser and had achieved wonders, people said, as people will. The Chauncey-Vernons sent for him when their groom had a leg crushed in a fall; then when the leg mended – it was the leg of a very young man – he had been summoned by Henry Chauncey-Vernon when a racehorse had actually broken a leg and astounded everyone by devising a splint when all opinion, medical and veterinary, had advised shooting. The horse, too, was a very young horse, but it had survived, Beatrice knew. There was no denying that, but then others said that the leg couldn't have been broken in the first place, and this incident, like other miraculous cures of croup, fits, gout, nervous headaches – he was a hypnotist as well – led Baron Belasco to greater success, and there was only one proviso, a simple condition of treatment, coins on the table first. Cash down. What was more joyous to the healer than the glint of gold? His title was, of all things, said to be a Norman title – which meant that it wasn't verifiable – but he had certainly prospered and although he was only on what might be called professional terms with Henry Chauncey-Vernon who practically owned all he saw, with Roderick Chauncey-Vernon, Henry's profligate and idle brother, there was a much closer relationship: the gossip about it – Bristol women of ill repute up to the house, theatricals, some said, doings behind closed blinds, the servants discharged for the night and savage dogs let loose in the grounds and the aromatic smells of incense clinging to the blinds in the mornings – none of this reported intelligence had escaped Beatrice. Nor had Belasco's deep-set, hooded eyes, eyes that undressed you, that lingered upon you and caressed you, and hands that might not be as chaste as they were said to be; and as for that silken voice, his habit of standing so absolutely still as he surveyed you that a nervous flutter of apprehension inevitably followed – it was unmentionable! Of the whole Belasco persona then, Beatrice stood in total disapproval. In exactly the same way, she disapproved of Roderick Chauncey-Vernon who, in her eyes, was weakness personified, from knees to chin to clammy hand-shake, and to the very trilling notes of his light musical voice. They were both very definitely fast, Beatrice thought, unlike Henry Chauncey-Vernon of whose respectability she had first-hand know-ledge since she was governess to his children.

She had studied the family and knew that the father, a shrewd Cornish metallurgist, had created the fortune, established the smelt-ing plant, bought the ships and developed the docks. The hyphen-ated name came with the fortune and Henry carried on to prosper, the family originally as strange to the port as the Scottish Butes were to neighbouring Cardiff. Henry, bluff, inscrutable, a man of habit and industry, troubled her little apart from his refusal to employ Jack Hannah, but the other two, his brother Roderick and Belasco, were joined in their ownership of the *Whisper* by two others who divided the traditional sixty-four shares in the vessel between themselves. The other partners were equally shady, equally questionable in her eyes: one Cornelius Lewis who advertised himself as a painless tooth extractor – satisfaction guaranteed! – the inventor of Hudson's Botanical Toothpowder – "teeth as white as ivory tho' never seen so black or yellow"; and lastly, the Reverend Elias Evans, a noncon-formist preacher, temporarily without a calling who was also said to lie in wait for servant girls after chapel, girls whom – the Henry Chauncey-Vernon servants said – he had worked up into a warm and willing emotional state by the full flight of his Welsh oratory, a much used sermonising process known as the *hwyl*. In a sentence, the sixty-four shares in the *Whisper* were held in one hand by the agents of the devil himself and Beatrice could not help but dwell upon it. ("Dirty devils too!" as the Welsh kitchen maids said, with a licking of the lips and much head-shaking.)

And these were to be Jack Hannah's employers!

There was Belasco with his large yellow landau (and his large hypnotic eyes), his four horses in splendid trappings, each with postillions in brilliant cockades and a black fellow standing beside it in green livery, gold shoulder knot, silk breeches and white stock-ings to boot, and there was Cornelius Lewis, shifty-eyed and wet mouthed, the Reverend Elias Evans bringing up the rear, a hand-wringer that man, soulful and effusive, a prophet's beard reaching down to his midriff and the dark glittering eyes of a greedy peasant burning into you, when he could face you at all. Add to them, the swarthy Senhora Felipa with her bustle, her ostrich feathers, her

13

flashing teeth and above all a ripeness of figure that rippled beneath her gaudy clothes – she would put on weight eventually like the Italians did – and who carried a gaudy parasol *in September*! – and you had about the most conspicuous figures imaginable. And how they could proceed about any business with discretion, Beatrice simply did not know. Poor girl, she had met nothing like them in her life. Nor indeed had Sveynton.

"When she went to Belasco, this Senhora, what exactly did she tell him?" (Like had met like, she wanted to say, or the devil would find his own, but then the Good Lord – who was more Welsh than metropolitan, naturally – did not decide exactly who was fitted to own the one unemployed vessel in the dock on this blustery September day.)

"She was looking for a vessel to charter," Jack Hannah said, repeating himself. "It must be a strong vessel capable of a voyage around Cape Horn. There was a cargo of best anthracite to be delivered to Talcahuano. That was the outward cargo. Then the return load was off a neighbouring island. She wanted a master, she wanted a crew, and there was a need for secrecy."

"And the return cargo," Beatrice said, "is guano – it's bird droppings, isn't it?"

"Yes. As a fertiliser it's fetching upward of thirty pounds a ton, the richest manure in the world. A substantial deposit and you can name your own price. A ship reaches Falmouth with a cargo, it's sold twenty times before she reaches Liverpool, the price increasing every day. They even ship it out again to America."

"Then why the need for secrecy?"

"I told you, every discoverer of guano deposits is anxious not to reveal the source. Masters sailing out of Liverpool do so under sealed orders. They're only allowed to open them when they reach latitudes that prevent them speaking to homeward bound ships."

All this, she supposed, was the everyday commerce of the sea, and certainly not a matter upon which she could express an informed opinion. There had been rumours of guano deposits to be prospected in the port before, but principally by men who told of prospecting on remote African islands like Icheboe to which they gave the romantic name of the Coast of Dead Ned. What was now unusual was that the Senhora had her cargo already loaded into a vessel aground on a Chilean island, and the *Whisper* was to off-load this cargo into her own holds. Nearly six hundred tons lay in this broken backed ship whose name Beatrice had forgotten.

"The vessel is . . ."

"The *Gazela*. She's broken her back, but quite dry and safe."

"And all these months will wait for you with her precious cargo?"

"I told you why."

She repeated it, the phrase which had caused them such consternation. It was the very nub of the matter.

"Because she has a shipkeeper on board?"

Now for the first time he looked at her and the pain in her eyes was apparent. Whatever else they had in common, these two, they had the same height and colouring. Both were six foot. Ginger looked at ginger. She had the most perfect of ruddy complexions, her lips were full, her hair which she wore piled above her head was auburn, rich and luxuriant in texture, and her nose – she described it as aquiline – although larger than a perfectionist might have wished, was a further mark of character. Like her height, it set her apart from the crowd. She was full bosomed and straight backed, but all the better to bend, he'd thought. And of course, with her education, she had a splendid hand and such a head for figures that he was sure that together their fortunes would be made if ever he could raise the capital for a ship of his own. All this he'd thought for a long while and he had no cause to change his mind now, except that the news, the still unspoken horror of what he had kept to himself – save for the one blurted utterance when Beatrice had first entered the room – that horror remained.

After sensing his confusion, she drew back from the definition of the expression "shipkeeper".

Instead, she said, leading him on to it, "You were suspicious?"

"Of course I was suspicious. I couldn't understand why she had come here to Sveynton of all places. The guano trade's a Liverpool trade, what there is of it. It was said to have blown itself out by the middle of the 'Fifties. Of course, people came across new deposits all the time, but I wanted details of where the *Gazela* got her cargo, how she went aground. If she drifted ashore, she could drift off again. With a cargo like that, why would it be kept there all these months waiting – waiting for what? For Senhora Felipa Salaverry to come back to Liverpool, and when she got to Liverpool to find she'd better come to Sveynton!"

"Then again, it's not a deserted coast. They'd be in hailing distance of northbound ships. A vessel in ballast or with a part-cargo – what was to stop her master hailing one and making off with what they could shift themselves? The *Gazela*'s a Brazilian vessel so why didn't they get a dago to get her off? Why come here? That was the first thing. The second was how she went aground in the first place. What happened to the crew? The place is practically uninhabited. There's hardly any fresh water on that coast. Then she said – when I asked her – they had English sailors, or some of them were English, and where were they, I said? They wouldn't stay aboard, was all she said. It was all in the air. I couldn't get details, or enough details, just that she was here with her cargo and her charter out and she knew where there was more of the stuff to be got. And that's what interested Belasco, not one voyage, but twenty. 'Young man,' he said, 'this is your future. You have it in your hands. You wish to acquire capital, your ambition is a ship of your own? Very well, you have your answer here this morning!' And that was all."

It was her ambition too, for herself and for him, Beatrice thought, but try as she might, she could not bring herself to raise the question which concerned them most. That would have to come from him. Again, she concentrated on the details, the half-understood things which bothered him. (He would come to the matter of the ship-keeper, no doubt.)

"What did she say when you asked her about the grounding of the ship?"

He had picked up the empty shell case once more, now he put it down again and folded up the cloth. The metal polish had stained his fingers and on his palm there was a black-edged line like the border on a bereavement notice and although not a great believer in omens, a thought came to him immediately. Deaths there had been, deaths there would be again. He flexed his shoulders uneasily and then, avoiding the central fact once more, began to go over the questions and answers that offered a remote possibility of understanding. They were offering him a command, Belasco, Roderick Chauncey-Vernon and the others, but eager as he was – and furious and frustrated as he was after weeks of evasions and abortive interviews – he wasn't jumping at anything he was offered. Being a shipmaster was a responsible business. You did not sail anywhere in any vessel without the whole thing being above board, and the proposition brought by this baggage sounded very rum from the

16

start. Lock, stock and barrel, it was fishy, no doubt about that. First of all, there were the questions that were not satisfactorily answered, and there were so many of those so eloquently evaded that for all his suspicions, he had to guard against weariness in the effort it took to challenge each one.

He remembered the Senhora's voice again, ever prompted by Belasco, their two voices silken, the one accented, rich and melodious, the other deeper, playing an accompanying refrain. The Senhora's lips were kept slightly apart most of the time, now amused, now serious, as she ran her eyes over him with a frank interest that was almost impolite. His ginger mop of hair had attracted similar interest amongst the shoreside girls in Shanghai and her first look at him had put him in mind of sailortown women around the globe. Meet her in 'Frisco in the Bella Union or Madame Lucy's Whore Shop in Sacramento Street and you wouldn't be surprised to hear her calling, "Sixty-nine, Jack?" or "Rompay the cooler!", the whore's call all over the Barbary Coast. Come to think of it, there was something of the Chileno about her, and·before she opened her mouth, these memories had already stirred his embarrassment for he knew that American seaboard well, and the last trip there had ended with him hurtling along Dupont Street blushing furiously at the memory of one choice call: "Two bittee look-see, four-bittee feeley, six-bittee doey!" But then he was a puritanical young man and these disturbing reminders once put down, he'd addressed himself pointedly to the matter in hand. He'd questioned her, all right – questions-questions-questions!

"Are you telling me, Senhora, that this shipkeeper has been left on board alone these last three months?"

"No, there is a pantry man with him and they have friends ashore," said the Senhora flatly.

"But when the vessel put ashore, you had a full crew?"

"No, we were shorthanded. We had been in a tidal wave, and instead of rising with the wave, her bows were drawn under. She was swept clean from stem to stern. That accounted for six, the Mate and some others. All the boats were gone."

Oh, she had such a nautical turn of phrase, she might have been coached, he thought. And expertly coached at that.

"And the damage was made good and you proceeded, I take it?" he sounded like an assessor at a marine enquiry.

"Somehow or other, yes. There is no word to describe that

17

voyage. We were beset with difficulties, incidents from the start."

"And desertion?"

"Yes. Desertions and death. It is so hard to explain, seated here all these miles away."

"Quite," Belasco said with a reassuring nod. Baron Belasco understood, he implied. Belasco didn't seem bothered with any difficulties. But Baron Belasco did not intend to risk any more than his two pennyworth of sixty-fourth shares.

The Senhora continued, found an eyebrow to raise, now spoke apologetically, as if half-incredulous at her own story.

"Some of the crew were my own countrymen. They are so superstitious. After the tidal wave, the carpenter thought he saw the *Caleuche*."

"The *Caleuche*?"

"She is a legend of Chilote sailors, a phantom ship. She precedes, then follows disaster. An apparition, you understand?"

"No," Jack Hannah said.

"They were exhausted, nervous, at their wit's end, surely you can understand that?"

"No," Jack Hannah said.

Belasco spread his hands wide, smiled.

"Simple peasants imagine, ignorant minds run riot, bad luck, bad weather, isolation. It's a tale of woe, Mr Hannah. You've heard of the Flying Dutchman? An illusion of exhausted minds."

"Bunkum! When did the crew desert?"

"They put off to a Chilote ship."

"Mutiny?"

She shrugged her very handsome shoulders, gave another insolent lift of her arched eyebrows. This was a woman who was afraid of nothing, he'd then understood, a new kind of woman. And all the time those eyes continued to regard him with faintly amused approval, as if to say, "You're very young, you're very slow on the uptake, forgive me but trust me and I'll have patience with you. And it won't be unrewarding either!"

"They feared they could not live in those seas. There were days – weeks – when it seemed as if nobody could live."

"And those who died?"

"Nine by drowning."

"Nine?"

"The wind is terrifying in any west coast gale. They call it the *terremoto*. Nothing can live in its wake, no building can withstand it. Ships can be thrown half a mile above the high water mark. Half our men went with one wave."

Jack Hannah kept to the facts, head down and glowering still; such facts as they were, he said to himself. His carrot head was aimed towards her like a firework.

"Nine by drowning and the rest deserted?"

"Yes."

She did hesitate once, he noticed, and the smile slipped from her full moist lips.

"It would be wrong of me not to be frank at the outset. There was a certain amount of fever on board."

"Ah," he'd said. Oh, yes? he thought. Fever! Splendid! Anything else? Apart from the Flying Dutchman! And why not throw in a vengeful albatross?

"Fever of an undiagnosed kind," said Belasco carefully.

"Two, three, four cases," said Senhora Felipa.

"How many cases?"

"Three certain, then then the deaths by drowning, then . . . Well, I've said we had superstitious boys on board, *mestizos*. After the *Caleuche*, the carpenter jumped screaming from the foretop in his madness. It was not an amusing occurrence."

"Hm . . ." Jack Hannah said. "There's not a mark on you, Senhora Salaverry?"

Her reply was very simple.

"I am a business woman."

"To be more precise," Belasco said, "the cargo is worth thousands of pounds."

"And you must understand, Mr Hannah, there's an element of luck in finding large deposits of guano. It is all profit, free for the taking, a fertiliser as easily dispensed of as gold dust when nitrates are in short supply. And so rare."

"Quite," said the Reverend Elias Evans sagely from his corner. Now, hiding behind that bush of beard, he was as unsuspecting as his own deaconate must have been.

"Luck and information," she added lightly. "Neither holds good for ever, and speed and secrecy are essential to the matter."

"Well, Mr Hannah?" Belasco said. He spoke for the others, the absent Roderick Chauncey-Vernon, Cornelius Lewis sitting in the

19

shadows with his ears popping and the Reverend gentleman who had hardly spoken at all. "You've come to us with every recommendation. Your past captains cannot speak too highly of you. You'll be given a free hand with your officers and crew, and the *Whisper*'s a fine vessel. What d'you say?"

He did not answer immediately. They hadn't come to him with every recommendation. They'd simply sent for him. He hadn't gone to them previously because he'd never heard of them. One ship did not make a shipping company. All he knew of the *Whisper* was that she'd been purchased for a song after some local chandler's financial collapse. He hadn't even inspected her then. No, it was all too fishy, he'd said to himself. Calling it a whore's tale was putting it mildly. *Caleuche*, he thought sardonically, Flying Dutchman . . . What did they think he was? Some wide-eyed shop girl? So he'd made up his mind at once. That red head shook, the huge shoulders heaved. The firework fizzled out.

"No," he'd said again. There were too many unexplained things. And central to the tale was the idea – he was sure it was no more than an idea – that a ship could drift ashore and deposit itself high and dry on a remote Chilean island and just remain there as conveniently as an abandoned hansom cab – all this while the buxom Senhora traversed half the globe to come here to Sveynton in order to collect him to solve her problems. It would take him three months with the best weather and all the good luck in the world to get back there, so that in all, six months would have elapsed since she had last made any contact with the vessel, and in this time, half the world could have looted, pillaged and burned their prize, never mind what the sea did. State it like that and the proposition was ridiculous. And if it was not ridiculous, it was a thieves' deal, all my eye and Betty Martin, he said to himself. If he could have fathomed a motive, he would have suspected Belasco of procuring the woman to get at him for a more obviously sinister purpose. Perhaps it was a cock and bull story, simply destined to get the *Whisper* to sea, heavily insured all the while, *with the specific intention of losing her*. It would be only too easy to blame a young captain with his first command, and since there had been one or two cases of this sort of late, the underwriters looked sardonically at captains who had ever lost a ship, so that a man who had been on their black list would obtain no insurance, whereas he, with his clipper experience and a clean record, would not cause a single eyebrow to be raised. Perhaps this was a part of their game.

They wanted a presentable young man to take the vessel to sea, then lose her! But then the Senhora was determined to accompany him, she said. So he couldn't quite see how she would risk herself on such a venture and this likely explanation had to be dismissed for the moment.

They asked him again, but he still refused, growing redder all the while.

"No," he'd said once more. He wouldn't be specific. He had nothing to be specific about. Except that he didn't like the smell of it. Another thing was that the meeting had taken place, not in Belasco's premises where you'd have expected it to be held, but in the surgery-cum-workshop of Cornelius Lewis, the painless tooth extractor. These premises above a gloomy damp-infested stairway in Salubrious Passage were badly lit with an actual barber's chair, the gloomy walls showing a number of lurid posters advertising various preparations, including one which showed a whiskered man pointing to a set of teeth which might have been designed for a horse. This prescribed a purifying and beautifying agent known as SOZO-DONT which was described as being an antidote for gum boils, swelled face and a scurvy-curer into the bargain. Here in this unsalubrious atmosphere above Salubrious Passage, Cornelius Lewis, a small, buck-toothed little man with startled eyes and large protruding ears, had said absolutely nothing, as had the Reverend Elias Evans, save for a nod or a grunt, both men leaving Belasco and the Senhora to do the talking. To make matters worse, below the chair which the maker of dainty teeth had indicated for Jack Hannah, there was a mound of hair clippings. If he had done nothing else in his life, apart from acquiring a few shares in the *Whisper*, Mr Cornelius Lewis, the painless tooth extractor, had put the barber downstairs out of business! Such were the owners of the *Whisper*.

"No?" Belasco said. "Come, Mr Hannah . . ." His eyes were hurt, as if he had personally been let down by a patient whose gratitude he had taken for granted.

"No sir," Jack Hannah said. All this when Beatrice knew nothing of the matter.

Then Belasco smiled as if to say, "There was good in all really. The sun would shine again. Reason would prevail."

"I was afraid you'd say that," said Belasco.

"The port is not empty of shipmasters."

"We are aware of that too."

"There we are then," Jack Hannah said.

21

He'd been about to leave, half-furious with himself – how he wanted a command! – but glad that common sense had prevailed in the end. Then the Reverend Elias Evans finally spoke, implying by his aggrieved tone that he should have been at the centre of the discussion from the beginning. Now another element seemed to enter the already seedy atmosphere of the shabby dental parlour and it was one which Jack Hannah was to remember all his life. For the voice of the Reverend gentleman – he had not yet unfrocked himself – had all the cadences of the country Welsh. It was rich, sibilant and musical. Above all, it had a tone of utter sincerity. There was something warming about it. Hearing it, you felt that voiceless people had found a spokesman. But now, leaving the divine concerns for which it was best equipped, it addressed itself to all of them with simple reproachful charity. Oh, good works! Now was the time for them!

"We should have told the boy at the outset," said the Reverend Elias Evans feelingly. The mistake was theirs, he implied.

Cornelius Lewis lisped his agreement. They looked from one to the other. Belasco, receiving the Senhora's nod, cleared his throat, his own voice now of a grander order, belonging to no place, metropolitan Baron Belasco, healer of all ills.

"Perhaps you are right," said Belasco to the Reverend.

"It is very difficult," said the Senhora to all of them.

"But it will go no further than these four walls," said Belasco.

"Upon our word of honour," said the Reverend Elias Evans.

"Very definitely," said Cornelius Lewis.

"For everybody's sake," said Belasco.

In concert, they sounded like the forerunners of all the corrupt city councillors who would ever disgrace the port.

Jack Hannah sat there dumbfounded, noting pertinently as he stared from one to the other, that there were not four, but five walls in the odd shaped building. Dimly, he realised that there was more to be told that concerned himself, much more, a something they knew that he didn't, a something of shattering importance and as intimate as the Senhora's glance. The silence then was electric, a tropical silence, and he felt the sweat icy under his armpits.

Perhaps he should have known all along, he thought later. He should have seen something on the woman's face. After all, even a whore's face spoke volumes. She was about thirty, he guessed, perhaps a year or two older. Her English, although accented, was excellent, text book stuff. Her attractions . . . well, they were not for him (he thought then). There was a drawing-room air to her, for all her colour, a sophistication that belied poverty, or indeed, her quite remarkable adventures. Perhaps there was English blood there, French or American, he did not know. Save for the intentness of her gaze, she might have been one of many others he had seen in their carriages along the Levee in such places as New Orleans. She had a dual persona, that of a showboat lady with the air of a young waterfront madame. But this was not all. There are certain faces which immediately get to you, he thought. Their very bones speak. You see them in a crowd and feel an immediate response. His response was to run from that secret, hiding mouth. And her eyes were too knowledgeable. He could see at once she was a match for Belasco. She'd mastered him, and the others stood in awe of her. That face, that brow, the swell of those breasts – she was poured out of copper, immobile now like an Indian waiting in the darkness. And her scent . . . she brought the exotic aroma of forbidden foreign places into dingy, puritanical Sveynton. But the silence could not last.

"It is not accident that Senhora Salaverry has come here to Sveynton. She was sent here to see you," Belasco said.

"To see me?"

"Yes, Mr Hannah, I am afraid so."

He stared at her, and immediately a part of him knew what news she had brought. He could not be precise nor quite articulate his feelings but he knew he was a wounded man and of one thing he would always be sure, he was his father's son. From that he could never escape. Else why was he shunned by every reputable shipowner in the port?

"It will come as quite a shock to you," the Reverend Elias Evans said gravely, nodding as usual, about the Lord's work as usual, sincere as usual, lugubrious as usual.

She – Senhora Felipa – was suddenly gentle, intimate; suddenly a different woman again. Now she was concerned, apprehensive. She almost stretched out her hand to him. The showboat lady, the madame, had vanished. He could almost feel her pulse quickening. There was a slight delectable huskiness to her voice. It was like a lover's.

"The shipkeeper of the *Gazela* is your father, Captain Joshua Hannah."

He'd just stared at her, his heart pounding, stared and stared and in those soft brown eyes he saw a reflection of his pain. She understood him then, he was sure.

"No . . . Not possible. Not . . . not . . ."

"I'm afraid so. He sent me. I am his messenger. He begs you to come. Believe me, I am telling you the truth, Captain."

She was the first to promote him, he thought.

And that was how it had gone, the interview in the shabby parlour, although months later when it ceased to have any importance, he found it hard to understand how he had felt any sympathy at all in those liquid eyes. The messenger . . . But ten minutes later, supporting himself against the pillar of those grubby premises in Salubrious Passage, he'd vomited in the street. It was all too much to take, even for a man of his capabilities and massive strength. But nausea was nothing to what was to follow.

"Will you put that canister down and look at me?" Beatrice Trevoake said.

For answer, he put his hand inside the shell case and drew out the screwed-up press of papers that was inside. They were papers, including newspaper cuttings which his mother had preserved there. As a child he remembered two such canisters on either side of the mantelpiece in this same room. One was used for storing bills – paid; and the other – debts outstanding, and after his mother's death, only receipts were kept, but the screw of papers he now produced were faded newspaper clippings relating to his father's missing ship and the trial of one Emmanuel Eugene Bombas, charged with the murder of Captain Joshua Hannah on the high seas. Among them was a gruesome account of the hanging, given to reporters by a certain Dr Flynn at the assize court in the City of Cork where survivors were landed. He had read it over and over again.

"In my judgement, the rope was placed too soon around the Greek's neck for it slipped above the cartilage tending to produce a more violent convulsion of the limbs and trunk than was usual. Death was not instantaneous, due to the Greek's wearing of a beard and being short and stout necked, and his mouth was much distorted. Drippings were observed . . ."

"It is over and done with!" Beatrice said loudly. "If you believe nothing else, believe that. Oh, Jack!"

"There are other things," Jack Hannah said wearily. "They are most concerned that no one in this port knows of my father's existence. They say it might cause such a commotion that it would reduce the profit of the venture and cause others to stop us sailing."

24

"What others?"

"The owners."

"Of the *Whisper*?"

"Of the *Avalon*. She was very heavily insured and substantial sums were paid over after the trial."

"What are you saying?"

"The *Avalon* was worth more at the bottom of the sea than lying idle against Henry Chauncey-Vernon's dock wall. This was nine years ago, remember, and there was a great slump in shipping in this port and every other."

She did not take in the full import of what he said immediately. Indeed, Beatrice's mind had missed half the details of the proposed voyage, never mind the lost *Avalon*, but she could not help herself snapping, "That woman!" It was a phrase which would remain on her lips for an eternity, even cloud her dying thoughts. That woman . . .

"Yes," Jack Hannah said. Between them already there was a feeling of another presence mocking them both, their honour, their chastity, their littleness, the puny scale of their humble ambitions. In that moment he knew too, in his very bones, that this other one had been his father's baggage. He should have guessed that all along, guessed it years before in the crow's lines about his mother's haunted eyes. Like the whalemen of Nantucket, solemn, church-going, family men, his father was another who hung his puritan conscience on the tip of Cape Horn, paying with the foresail for the debts he left behind him. And what debts, Jack Hannah thought, his fingers crumpling the newspaper cuttings which his mother had so carefully preserved. How could he not look again? And why had she preserved them? Or were they retained by chance? And why had he himself not destroyed them? Oh, why did they all have this capacity for opening self-inflicted wounds? He read on.

"*I Emmanuel Bombas emphatically declare that I am innocent of the crimes for which I have been convicted and stand to hang. I took no part in murder or mutiny upon the barque* Avalon."

"You mustn't go," Beatrice said. "Oh, please, Jack . . ."

But he knew that her pleas were hopeless, frail whisperings in the cavern of his vengeful heart. He would have things to say to this father. There were so many unanswered questions, old scores to settle.

"I must," he said. And that was all.

25

Chapter Two

"Name?"

"Bones, sir. Billy Bones."

"Rating?"

"Able seaman."

"Last ship?"

"*Pathfinder*, sir. Cap'n Bowen from this port."

"You're a liar!"

"No, sir, Cap'n Bowen can speak for me, sir. And I was on the *Mona* with him, all on the West Coast run. You can ask Cap'n Bowen."

"Captain Bowen's as dead as mutton. Haven't you got any papers, seaman's book? – nothing at all to show for yourself save for what you stand up in?"

"Ah, that's it, sir. The knacker's got all my tabs ashore. Sorry about the niff on me, sir."

"The knacker?"

"Well, it's on account of his daughter, sir – a difficulty. He's got me strapped on account of my papers, his daughter bein' four months gone and it beginning to show large, like. Twins by the look of it, that's why it's a pierhead jump, sir."

"Are you God-fearing, sober, a hardworking seaman willing to give your all for your Captain and shipmates?"

"As Gawd is my judge, sir!"

"Make your mark there. Next!"

"Excuse me, sir, next man's a dummy. Built like an ox, but no roof to his mouth. I generally speaks for him."

"No roof to his mouth?"

"Not since he was dropped, sir. A Dutchie, he is, but he understands what you say to him, and work, sir? Well, there's horses have been put out of work since he came off his last ship, sir!"

"No roof to his mouth . . . Well, he'll not answer back! Name?"

"His name's Flohr, sir, Flower Flohr, he goes by."

"Where was he born?"

"Saint Pauli, Hamburg, sir."

"How old?"

"Thirty-nine, sir. Address – the Mission."

"Any advance?"

"Yes."

"Next!"

"Twomallow, sir. William Twomallow."

"Rating?"

"Able seaman."

"Last ship?"

"*Star of the Isles*, Waverley Line, Liverpool."

"Where were you born?"

"Ennal's Point, sir, like yourself. Excuse me, sir, my father went down on the old *Avalon* with your father."

"We're not here for a family gathering! Any advance?"

"Yes."

"Next! What is your name?"

"Grail, sir. Harry Grail."

"Rating?"

"Able seaman, sir."

"Where were you born?"

"Appledore, sir."

"Last ship?"

"*Pathfinder*, sir. Cap'n Bowen from this port."

"You haven't been talking to that – "

"Yes, sir. But I told him Cap'n Bowen was dead!"

"What is your address?"

"Ennal's Point, sir. Like yourself. I got relations just come over from the other side."

"Make your mark."

"Excuse me, sir. I can write."

"Next!"

"Scuse, sir. Samuel Scuse."

"Last ship?"

"*Locksley Hall*, sir, Cap'n Maclean."

"Rating?"

"Cook, sir."

"What is the matter with your face?"

"Warts, sir, had 'em all my life, but it's nothing malignant. I got a book, sir. Conduct's marked, sir, all 'very good'."

"Any advance?"

"Yes."

"Next!"

"Morgan, sir, Morgan Morgan."

"Where do you live?"

"This port, sir."

"Rating?"

"Able seaman."

"Last ship?"

"*Sophia* of Cardiff. Excuse me, sir. I had a relative on the *Avalon*."

"I don't want your relatives. What is your age?"

"Twenty-four, sir. I got a book, sir."

"There is a 'Decline to Report' for your conduct on this page."

"That was on the *Gunford*, sir, a blood boat if I ever saw one."

"Why were you disrated?"

"Refusing duty, sir. Scurvy off Cape Stiff. Ten men down and the Mate at loggerheads with the Captain to put back into Port Stanley."

"Have you learned your lesson, Morgan?"

"Yes, sir. I've been on the beach six months."

"Are you a God-fearing, hardworking seaman willing to give your all for your Captain and shipmates?"

"Yes, sir."

"You'll be rated ordinary seaman until you prove yourself. Make your mark. Next!"

"Breeze, sir. Jackie Breeze."

"Rating?"

"Able seaman, sir."

"What happened to your hand?"

"Lost two fingers, but I can pulley-haul with the best."

"Frostbite?"

"No, sir. Stabbed by a pimp in Marseilles."

"You'll be rated ordinary seaman until you prove yourself."

"Next! What is your name? State your place of birth! Rating? Any advance?"

And so it went on, big men, small men, large men, tall men, half without gear, some the worse for drink, but jacks the lot, and was it ever different? Captain Jack Hannah thought. One crowd of seamen is much like any other and the haste which attended the departure of the *Whisper*, as well as the need for secrecy about her destination, had made Jack Hannah take the best he could get. He was well familiar

28

with the recruitment problems and with crimps foisting anything moving upon helpless captains whose crews had skipped. Once in California he had seen a shrewd captain pay good blood money over for a corpse, one solitary dead body lying in a heap of drunks in a dank fo'c'sle where they had been thrown. Rats had been sewn into the sleeves of the corpse's tightly strapped reefer jacket, a shrewd move to cause movement enough to give the illusion of life and eventual labour. But the *Whisper's* crowd were better than that, the majority good men with papers, men he could rely upon, Sveynton jacks with good records, and a young Second Mate, Harry Waters, with whom he had sailed as an apprentice. In every respect save one, Belasco, acting for his partners, had kept his word in the matter of provisioning and victualling the *Whisper* and Jack Hannah had been allowed the freedom promised.

The one exception was in the matter of the Mate and here, Captain Hannah, seated in the saloon with glistening braids marking his new authority upon his sleeve, felt yet another reservation. Belasco had not insisted. Nobody had insisted, but there was nevertheless just the slightest pressure. There was a Mr Handel Evans, an excellent man, well tried on that Cape Horn run with his papers all in order, a man a little down on his luck and although in his forties, not the kind of man to challenge the young Captain's authority. Far from it. It just happened that he was a brother of the Reverend Elias Evans and Belasco would regard it personally as a favour if . . .

And so it went. He'd said he'd see him, nothing more. To tell the truth, he was getting a little worried about the crew then. Secrecy meant scouting the taverns, the dives, and along the wharves, and as every day went by, there was a further risk of leakage and gossip, but then Handel Evans arrived, damp and oily in a September drizzle. Belasco arrived with him, but only stayed long enough to make the introductions and enquire about the provisioning, and then Jack Hannah had spent a mealtime watching this Handel Evans. He was taller than his soulful reverend brother, a leaner man with cadaverous cheeks, an altogether more mournful appearance with a habit of leaning forward to pay special attention to what his superiors said. Noticeably, amongst his papers, there was a temperance certificate. He was time-served enough, a graveyard man for the graveyard watch in short, and if there was one word to describe him it was dutiful. And he had his answers pat, a worrying soulful man who would present no threat. You did not reject a man for his tombstone look. Graveyards had to be dug and ships fussed over.

"We're carrying coal, Mr Evans."

"Yes, sir. You'll not want her tender."

"These barques are strong enough. The keelson's raised above the skin and there are strengthened trunks for ore."

"If I may make a suggestion, sir?"

"You may."

"I've some experience in this trade. If the coal's been standing in the rain, there's always a danger of the liquid causing slurry, sir – and if you're not careful you'll have the wings full of water. Coal dust plays the very devil with pumps, sir. Oh, they need watching, these dockyard mateys."

"I'm aware of that."

"And another thing, if she's too heavily loaded aft, she'll pitch heavily in a seaway and tend to ship water from fore and aft. Then there's ventilation, very important with coal in case it overheats, as I'm sure you know, sir."

"Indeed, I do. You know your business, Mr Evans."

"We all have our strengths and weaknesses, sir, and cargo's always been a special interest with me."

Could you fault a man who spoke like that? Unctuousness was no barrier to employment. Goodness knows what servilities the man had been brought up to practise. The town Welsh were ever different from the country Welsh where the squirearchy and the landlords demanded the touched forelock. Perhaps Evans like his brother had been brought up in this workhouse-fearing atmosphere and was a little chapel-touched to boot. Perhaps he'd try him on his navigation. Jack Hannah tried to like the man. It must be hard selling yourself to a younger man. He'd had enough rejections himself lately. A few more questions then.

"What course would you lay for Talcahuano, Mr Evans?"

"Well, let me see, sir, the West Coast? On leaving the chops of the channel, I should make a westing, say 10°W to avoid getting milched in the Bay of Biscay."

"And after?"

"I'd shape to Madeira and the Cape Verde Islands."

"Landmarks?"

"If I'm well to the westward, I'd keep a sharp look-out for St Paul's Rocks."

30

"And for Cape Horn?"

"I'd look for the Brazilian current first, stay out about one hundred and fifty miles and then down to the Horn, of course."

"And after the Horn?"

"I'd stand up into the southeast trades."

"Hmm . . ." The man was right enough, but these were generalities. It might take them a month to beat around Cape Horn. "You don't mind me questioning you, Mr Evans?"

"Not at all, sir. It is your duty."

"Supposing you were in a barque like this, five hundred tons burden, going before the wind, and it suddenly hauled out to the port quarter, what would you do?"

"If the sails were lifting, I should keep her off a bit whilst I trimmed the yards."

"Which yard first?"

"Foreyard first, following with the main, and then the mizzen."

"Let's say you're running before a moderate breeze in thick weather and you suddenly see land close to – ahead we'll say?"

"Which bow, sir?"

"Port."

"Well, sir, I should bring her up to the wind as quickly as possible."

"Which tack?"

"Starboard."

"And your helm?"

"A-port, bracing up the afteryards for the starboard tack. Then I'd set the spanker and any other after sail I could."

"Anything else?"

"Of course, sir, I'd have called you, the moment we made a landfall, I'm well aware of where the responsibilities lie, Captain."

Jack Hannah had one further question.

"Mr Evans, you said you were a man of strengths and weaknesses. It's a hard question to answer, but what are your weaknesses?"

The pale blue eyes looked back at him ruefully below the balding forehead and the lank sideboards. Now his thin lips assumed a mournful smile. This was a man who went by the book. You could not see him aloft exchanging yell for yell in a roaring headwind. He was more housekeeper than shipmaster.

"It's hard to admit, Captain Hannah."

"I should find it hard myself."

31

"Well sir, I was very strictly brought up and I'm a man of conscience. I worry too much. Perhaps it is my lot in life to follow rather than to lead."

It was this answer that engaged him. The chief officer must complement his captain. This was not the Royal Navy with a remote, gold laced figure of fear strutting along his quarter deck aft, and ships so crammed with men that they could not be occupied without elaborate drills and punishments, one man in ten being needed to devise employment for the remainder. This was a working barque which had to pay its way. Trade did not only follow the flag in Jack Hannah's eyes, it ruled it and was the whole reason for their continued existence upon the seas. Whatever you said about Evans, with his obliging shopkeeper's air, his eagerness to please, he was of the stuff of commerce in a way that Jack Hannah was not. He'd also very likely be a good book-keeper and this was another point in his favour. He did not particularly like him but they were not there to like each other. They were there to complement each other. Let Evans do the worrying. He would employ him for that and let the devil take care of the rest.

So he'd engaged him. Young Harry Waters, the Second Mate, was an imp, a little monkey, nimble and cheerful, a jollying way with him and active as a cat – they'd complement each other and he himself would oversee them all. Let Evans be the ship's wife.

When it was fixed, the articles closed, the manifest and all the Custom House impressments complete, the cargo stowed and only the hatches needing to be battened down, Evans came silently into the saloon and remarked for no reason at all: "I was very sorry to hear of your father's death. I knew him when I was an apprentice in the *Coquimbo* years ago."

"A bit late for condolences, Mr Evans?"

"A manner of speaking, sir. No more."

Why on earth should a man offer his condolences after nine years? Why mention it at all? He could understand the crew seeking to ingratiate themselves, but this Evans had such a sidling way to him. What did he know? And why were the riggers, the harbour master, the pilots, even some of the crew, giving him such strange looks at times? No one had told him of the isolating barriers of authority. And then, he was such a young captain with this midwife of a mate haunting him. He was in his cabin which, like the ship, could not disguise a fine rime of coal dust when Evans came again, huffing like a charlady, a small smug smile in his face now.

"Beg pardon, sir. A young lady . . ."

"Which young lady?" Not the Senhora yet, he hoped. She had definite instructions to join at the last possible minute. And Evans did not know about her yet.

"In a hansom, sir. She sent the driver aboard to summon you personally. A Miss Trevoake, smart by the look of her."

"Tell her I'll be down presently."

"Aye, sir."

"And Mr Evans."

"Sir."

"Tell her it's too dirty for her to come aboard."

"Very thoughtful of you, sir."

The Mate left, noiselessly padding up the steps of the companionway. Lugubrious was the word for him, but the crew already had a better description. Old Grease, they said, the bumscrew that would never finish tightening!

Jack Hannah, aware that he had neglected Beatrice Trevoake shamefully, made haste to wash his hands. He smelt of tallow, of kerosene, of rope and hemp and tar, all the multitudinous smells of the *Whisper*, and the quick wash he gave himself in cold water was little better than a lick and a promise. Coal dust covered everything inside the ship, and when the wind came from the north, the stench of the copper works could be smelt miles out to sea. Ashore it fouled the vegetation, changing the colour of the very leaves of the trees and there were even reported cases of sheep dying as a result of recent experiments in trying to convert the copper smoke into sulphuric acid. All in all, the Chauncey-Vernon profits had debits which affected the people of Sveynton with mixed blessings, Jack Hannah thought. Now still grimy, his face a grey pallor beneath that flame of ginger beard and hair, he went ashore at a run without a single instruction to the simpering Evans. Let him wonder. And the men too.

Beatrice remained in the hansom cab. When he put his weight on the step, the whole vehicle lurched.

He sat beside her heavily, frowning as usual. He could not help his next remark. Economy was part of his entire nature.

"A cab?" he meant to draw attention to the expense. It was not a thing they did every day.

33

She raised that long nose of hers and drew back a little from him. "We will only be parted for half a year!"

"I thought we agreed to save."

"We will have six months of saving! Tell the driver to go along the coast road to Ennal's Point," Beatrice said. She had evidently taken pains with her appearance. He was evidently determined not to notice it.

"The coast road?" he said. "We could have taken the tram there?"

"At this time, there are workmen travelling on it, and most of them in a filthy state."

He looked at his hands which were still ingrained with coal dust.

"I'll call in my aunt's and wash."

"It will add to the evening's pleasure," said Beatrice.

"Madam!" said he.

"Tell him to drive."

He did so and very soon they made their way across the tram lines to the curve of Sveynton Bay where he now concentrated his attention on the weather for a moment. He'd noticed earlier that a September gale was beating up the channel, forcing the pilot cutters and the oyster skiffs to hug the shelter of Ennal's Point. They would have to beat down channel when they cast off their tug. He noticed the sea, then he swivelled his eyes back to Beatrice. There was weather in the offing and in her eyes too, he thought. He could see it in the flush of her colour, the heaving of her breast, the way her eyes avoided his, and he sought for some pleasantry at the back of mind; and not finding it, suddenly remembered his manners and removed his uniform cap. Oh, what a clumsy fellow he was! He'd forgotten this was one of the last nights they'd spend together. And he hadn't even bothered to change out of his coaling suit. Now he flushed and stumbled for words.

"Beatrice . . . er . . . My apologies for not er . . . being . . . er . . ." What could he say? "Er . . . ready for you."

No answer.

"A quick wash will remove this er . . . stench of the ship." He was suddenly reminded of the seaman, Bones, apologising for the niff from the knacker's yard about him. But at least Bones's engagement had some reward, Jack Hannah thought. The extraordinary thing about his own courtship was that he and Beatrice had scarcely brushed lips together. At her house, her mother seldom left them alone. They'd shared a settee once on the night of the solemn

34

handing over of the ring, but they'd barely had a moment to themselves for Beatrice's mother was an inveterate cake and sweetmeat deliverer, a mincer, always in and out of the best room of the house. Privacy there was not to be, and the Trevoakes guarded their four daughters like Arab potentates. And now it soon seemed as if there'd been gossip enough in the harem. While Captain Jack had been busy, Miss Beatrice had been brooding and it was not long before she came directly to the point.

"When is *that woman* to join?"

Senhora Salaverry had momentarily slipped from Jack Hannah's thoughts, but in Beatrice's mind, there was already a private noose forming, it seemed.

"In the morning, shortly before we sail."

"And you have not clapped eyes upon her since that first meeting?"

"Not once. Belasco has attended to all our provisioning."

"I see," said Beatrice, never once looking at him but staring ahead or out of the shoreward side of the carriage window as they proceeded. "Still, you will have three months to rectify that misfortune."

"Six," he said. He had already made a calculation about food since he was acting as his own purser and had done his best to add in six months' supply of delicacies. He'd also ordered hogs, chickens and a porker. So he had calculated the voyage precisely. "Yes, six months. She's coming back with us. But you know very well what I think of her."

If Beatrice did know, it was just not enough to know. She required massive confirmation. After all, the little *Whisper* was about twenty-eight feet wide, and a hundred and sixty-odd feet from bowsprit to stern post. The royal dogs were kept in a less confined space.

"You will be very confined together."

"I mean to clap her in the Mate's cabin, put her in his charge and keep myself to myself. They will think they have a post captain from a ship of the line with silk breeches and scented hose by the time this voyage is over. I'll have nothing to do with her."

"And what about the crew?"

"They will have to behave themselves, naturally."

"You will not allow them to wash naked on deck?"

"No, only her!" he said, making a joke without really thinking of

35

the consequences. "It will take their minds off the salt horse junk I've got for them!"

She flushed. She did not, as he should know, like remarks of that kind. They very definitely verged upon the improper. So she changed the subject as a young lady should.

"Mr Henry Chauncey-Vernon stopped me in the corridor today. He is very curious as to your employment and your destination."

"He's showed precious little interest in me before."

"He made it his business to ask me the cargo you carried."

"*And?*"

"There is only one phrase in this port, coal out and ore home."

"What did he say to that?"

"The market's dropping! Baron Belasco is also coddling him, saying that if he is as successful with ships as he is with horses, he will double his fleet in a voyage."

"Belasco told him . . ."

"Belasco is very clever. He calls it his speculative venture and makes a great joke of it. Naturally, the customs men have reported Belasco's presence along the dock so he tells Mr Henry he had better watch out for he is the shrewdest of the *Whisper*'s sixty-fourthers, and if they are lucky, he will found a rival line."

"And no mention of my father's ship?"

"None."

"Nor the woman?"

"None. She has disappeared into Mr Roderick's house. Our servants don't even know she's there at nights and they seem to know everything."

"Has Mr Henry said anything specific about me?"

"Only generalities, glad that you are at last in employment."

"Does he know that I've haunted his own offices?"

"Presumably."

"Presumably!" he echoed. A benevolent employer might have done more than that. He owned over twenty ships. "He hasn't overburdened himself with thought upon the matter."

"No," Beatrice said drily. "But we have been into all this before."

The cab dropped them at his aunt's house. Now they entered it alone for the second time, a circumstance which was verging on the 'fast' in Beatrice's eyes since it would certainly cause comment amongst the neighbours. What disturbed her more, however, was the haste with which he made for the brass shell canister on the

36

mantelpiece once inside. He was going to take those cuttings and papers with him. Once again his first thought was not for her and she began to catalogue her woes. First, it was his failure to obtain a command which stood between them. Now, having obtained one, it was the past, his past and the murky aura which surrounded his father's name. Would she herself never figure first in his thoughts? It was as if she too had a mere sixty-fourth share in him.

Putting down her mother's warnings – she would come to those presently – she said: "I thought we might take a meal, then visit my parents?"

"A meal?" he said over his shoulder. His large hand still scoured the inside of the brass canister as he rummaged among the newspaper cuttings. "A restaurant meal?"

"Dinner, yes. And my father wanted a word with you."

"What for? You haven't mentioned . . ."

"To congratulate you, silly! Upon your captaincy."

"Ah . . ."

"But if you would rather not . . ."

"No, no, no," he said again. "I mean no offence, but I have to be aboard again quite early."

"Aboard?"

"Yes, there are a hundred and one things to do still."

He still busied himself with that wretched canister and, dimly, she thought came to her that as usual she was in the way again, as usual an obstacle.

"Perhaps you would prefer me to leave you now so that you can pursue your real interests in this life?"

He turned slowly, flushing. Carrot-top looked at her once more, she thought.

"Listen," he said – as if she ever did anything else. "A man was hanged, men disappeared off the face of the earth. My father was blamed. First he was victim, then he was criminal, then dead, now alive. With all this . . . all these occurrences . . . lies, half truths – whatever – do you expect me to dance?"

"You will have six months to devote yourself to these matters."

He blushed. "Don't you understand what I'm saying? It's not some problem in book-keeping, a matter of long division, or some tricky sum!" The enormity of it, he thought. Getting at the truth of it was like trying to fist your way through a smoke cloud. It was endless and weightless. It gave him headaches and crowded out his brain. It was a growth. His father alive, but better dead and disgraced than alive, for the dead were perforce silent, he thought. But now there could be no silence, not until they sat face to face upon that stricken ship. The *Gazela*, he thought. Not a record of her existed as far as he could trace. Oh, what was the truth?

"At the moment," Beatrice's voice cut in amongst his thoughts, "I am waiting for you to wash. I spend my day with children expecting the same thing. Surely, it is not too much to ask that our last evening together should be just a little different?"

He stuffed the screw of papers into an envelope, conscious of the asperity in her schoolmarm's voice, while she saw the headline turn over upon one of the newspaper cuttings, Avalon *Mutiny – Plea of innocence*.

"Then there's my father," she said. "He wants to warn you."

"I can hear his grocer's voice!"

"He says Roderick Chauncey Vernon would do anything to upset his brother. He feels this venture is part of such a scheme and that you are being used."

"Then you *have* spoken to him?"

"I merely told him you were appointed master of the *Whisper*, no more."

"Hm . . ." Jack Hannah said. "I'll go and wash."

And now she thought of what her father'd said of Jack Hannah in particular.

"He's too bluff. There's not a courtesy in the man. And I'll tell you this, a man that can't get on with his employers, can't get on with his men. You have to respect authority before you can dispense it."

That was her father. Then there was her mother.

"He is so awkward, dear. I shudder every time he sits on those cane chairs. And his hands . . . they're like plates. And with that hair, he must have a dreadful temper. You make sure you have a long engagement. And be sure in your own mind, dear, that's all we ask. Myself, I should be frightened if he ever touched me."

There was another voice which intruded into her thoughts, that of a certain Miss Annie S. Swann who gave weekly advice to the lovelorn in the pages of the *Ladies' Home Companion*, a journal which she studied regularly.

Girls of a certain age, wrote Miss Annie S. Swann, *are very susceptible, too apt perhaps to take a man's attentions seriously. If I were asked what I considered the greatest drawback to married happiness, I should unhesitantly answer, bad temper. It is a blight which nothing can remove, a continual cross not to be got rid of in a day, or many days.*

"What's the weather doing?" said Jack Hannah entering the room once more and staring out of the window. "Ah, wind's come up and veering as I thought. There'll be east in it by the morning."

Then he turned and looked down upon her, his hands clenched upon that envelope of newspaper cuttings – she knew he had been examining it again outside the room – and now his huge sausage fingers were whitening at the knuckles as he looked at her.

"Look, your father – his questions – there've been enough questions. D'you know, I couldn't keep a civil tongue in my head if I went there? You understand? I couldn't."

"But I promised my mother!" Beatrice said

"Yes . . . yes . . . yes, but in the circumstances . . . surely, you understand?"

"No," she said.

"Beatrice . . ."

She stared up at him. He seemed to want to say that he did not belong in a house. Even his normal speaking voice had a boom to it. But what was most overpowering was not his immense toppling height but his total ignorance of her feelings.

"It's like this," he said. "I have to get back on board sooner than I expected. This man Evans, he pads around. It's the ship, you understand?"

Her hand went to her ring, that solitary garnet stone in the single band of gold, the most reasonable ring they could choose between them. ("It would do for the maids," her mother had said, "especially if they were getting married in the vestry!" – meaning advanced pregnancy forbade the altar.) And now Beatrice began to remove it.

"Look here . . . no need for that. Can't you see. I'm preoccupied?"

"It's hopeless," she said, "hopeless!" But she still could not remove the ring. The knuckle had swollen.

And he, typically, now expressed a professional interest. "Try a little lard."

She could have hit him with it!

"Look here," he said. "I can't go off leaving things unsaid. In this state, I mean. Have we an understanding, or not?"

What could she, or anybody else, say to him?

39

"I am," she was about to proclaim, "not accustomed . . ." she had not actually completed the sentence when, like the very arrival of the Brazilian Senhora in the first place, there was a further act of melo-drama punctuated by the stamping of horses' hooves as they were brought up short in the street outside. A coachman's shout drew them both to the window.

At first, she thought it was her father. She was aware of the impropriety of her entering the house alone with Jack Hannah. It was not her father, however, but her employer's messenger, Henry Chauncey-Vernon's footman sent on a message with a sealed envelope, an envelope what is more, which was written in her employer's own hand and addressed to Captain Jack Hannah.

Perhaps it was in some way an answer to her prayers, she thought. All the spirit had been drained out of her by his insensitivity, his oafishness, his brute lack of understanding of her feelings. But now she had a moment's hope. He brought the envelope into the room, tore at the seal.

"What is it?"

The coachman has been instructed to wait for a reply.

"An offer," Jack Hannah said. "He's offered me a captaincy in his own fleet. The *Mangosteen* – she's laying off Falmouth with orders for the Baltic."

Beatrice clapped her hands together. "At last! Perhaps he was just waiting for a vacancy to occur?"

"Perhaps . . ."

"Well, aren't you grateful? Surely you'll take it? He's a substantial employer. Isn't it what you've wanted all these months?"

"Take it?" he said. "How can I take it? I am already committed."

"Committed . . . to Belasco? D'you think he would not drop you at the slightest sign of advantage to himself? A month ago an offer like this was just what you wanted."

"Yes," Jack Hannah said. "And a month ago, Mr Henry Chauncey-Vernon had no reason for wishing me well out of his way."

"Reason? What reason could he have?"

"We shall see."

"You mean you are rejecting him?"

"Of course. I am already committed."

"And me?" she said. "You make this decision without the slight-est reference to me?"

40

"What is it to do with you?" he said. "I have agreed. A bargain has been struck."

But later when his reply had been sent and at last her precious ring had been removed and lay upon the mantelpiece, he had another explanation. Nothing was simple about the Hannahs nor the *Whisper*. Present one layer, remove it, you met another, equally off-putting. Now it was his father; a nine-year-old layer, dead skin come alive. Further explanations now, all equally unsatisfactory.

"On the night before my father sailed, my mother begged him not to go. 'We have enough,' she kept saying over and over again. 'We have enough.' Then when the news came that he was lost and most of his crew with him, 'I knew it,' she said, and she said that over and over again too. I asked her and asked her what she meant, but she would never tell me. I was at sea myself when she died and there was no message. She had not spoken for weeks and all my father's papers had long been cleared away, save for these she overlooked," he pulled the envelope in his pocket. "And these anyway are public knowledge. There were so many questions unanswered, I thought they would never be answered, but now, don't you see, the answer is before me?"

"No," Beatrice Trevoake said. "It only shows that your father had as little feeling for your mother as you have for me."

"And that is all you have to say to me?" he said, mortally offended now.

"Yes," she said. Her eyes wandered to the ring lying on that dusty mantelpiece and she rubbed her swollen knuckle ruefully. If only she could cry, if only abject tears could have moved him! But she could not. He had received his answer, and now she added to it, white-faced.

"You can keep your appeals for your Senhora!"

And that, he thought, was very much in the run of things too, as what sailor ever went to sea with a woman's blessing? He looked at the solitary red stone of that little ring on the mantelpiece, and somehow he knew it would lie there gathering dust for an eternity. "And that is your answer?" he said finally. But by now she did not even bother to reply.

Their engagement was over.

Chapter Three

A showboat piece was how Jack Hannah described this Senhora Felipa to himself and the phrase has travelled down through the years in the family so that I, his relative, have a certain indication of the state of his feelings at the outset of this eventful voyage aboard the *Whisper*. A showboat piece, a flouncy madame, a real waterfront jane – that was how he saw her then and it is not hard to imagine the comic opera side to her arrival at the dock. As to what Jack Hannah actually thought, there is no reason to suppose that his feelings would differ much from those of any other young captain at that moment. There will be historical certainties later, facts beyond all dispute – these are the most incredible, needless to say – but at this time, it is not hard to imagine the stir caused by the arrival of Baron Belasco's ornate landau with its four horses picking their way across the tramlines, the black fellow and the postillions in all their finery very much in splendid attendance. The *Whisper*'s owners were with the Baron and they descended like a small posse alongside the ship and the sight they presented to Jack Hannah and the amazed Mr Evans was as gaudy as a theatrical event. First came Mr Roderick Chauncey-Vernon, well wrapped up in a plaid cloak against the chilly morning air and wearing a sporty three corner hat with a Tyrolean feather in it. He descended in haste to assist the Senhora, Baron Belasco in his own tall hat and black cloak racing from the other side to dispossess him of the lady's gloved hand, while behind these gentry, came the reserve sixty-fourthers, the Reverend Elias Evans, sombre in fustian black, and little Cornelius Lewis, shabbily unobtrusive except for his protruding ears and teeth. The servants struggled with the Senhora's trunks and hat boxes, and from above on the *Whisper*'s poop deck, the ensembles resembled some seedy gnomic chorus clustering around its leading lady regally ablaze in green.

Only the clanking of the paddle tug's wheels as she fussed at the entrance of the dock waiting for the *Whisper*'s warps to be passed reminded them that they were within minutes of putting to sea and

42

the thick towing hawser lay along the deck in readiness. But, for the moment, the charade dominated and held everyone's attention. Senhora Felipa wore a turban toque of some frilly material and the rest of her was a small sea of movement, a frenzy of frills and flounces. Jack Hannah had already announced his philosophy to all aboard. Like his father's, it was concise. Work, he believed in, fingers to the bone was his motto, and every man aboard had better remember that. There were other homilies. A hand for yourself, a hand for the ship – and the hand for the ship would be a size smaller by the time they docked again, said he. But now it seemed a goddess of pleasure was coming aboard in pantomime trappings. He should have known then. Work and pleasure did not go together.

"Bless my soul!" said Handel Evans. "Are they your connections, sir?"

He had not for the moment recognised his own brother who was occupied with the black fellow at the rear of the coach.

"They are our owners, Mr Evans."

"The lady?"

"Our passenger."

"*Passenger?*"

"And charterer."

"Good gracious me!"

The sailors, already picked in watches, stood about the deck in various attitudes of incredulity. The idea of secrecy was laughable for now a small crowd of coal trimmers, black as colliers, the whites of their eyes glistening, appeared, bound for another ship, and they paused, adding to the gaping crowd of longshoremen which had begun to assemble. The landau with its four handsome horses was attraction enough, but the *Whisper*'s owners standing about the Senhora were the strangest quartet imaginable. You felt as if one pipe on a flute, and they would break into a dance, Jack Hannah thought. It was as if the last day of September had found a wind which had scoured the cracks and crevices of the port, producing left-over bluebottles of the most exotic hues to add to the disgrace of the poor *Whisper*'s dockbound suit of coal dust and grime. Her crew were suddenly frozen to the deck with awe. Only the rasp of Jack Hannah's voice represented anything like the normality of a workaday morning.

"Send two hands for the baggage!"

43

"The baggage, sir?" said Mr Evans as dumb struck as a stage door johnny.

"The woman's baggage! You will take the Second Mate's cabin, Mr Evans, and Mr Waters will mess with the carpenter. The lady's name is Senhora Salaverry. She is to be given every courtesy."

Mr Evans had difficulty in speaking at all. ("Pewce, he was, boyse," said Able Seaman Morgan Morgan later, "Pewce indeed, oh deuce, pewce as a set of drawers his face was, her drawers if you sees what I mean!") Young Mr Waters, the Second Mate, with a grin like a melon, had already darted to the head of the gangway and presented himself as the chief charmer on board at the earliest possible moment.

"You men there!" bawled Jack Hannah at the huge speechless German and Billy Bones who were standing on the coiled warp so as to get a better view. "Clear that warp from the gangway!"

"Aye, aye, sir!" said Bones, and presently Mr Waters soon darted down the gangway, and now, like a page boy at a wedding, took the dusky bridesmaid's hand and led her on board, Baron Belasco following.

Jack Hannah was next to move, stiff now with a resolve to present the face of unbending authority. Start as you mean to finish, he'd said to himself (one of his father's phrases), and he had taken some pains with his appearance. He wore a stiff, starched wing collar and black tie above his brass buttoned reefer jacket and that untidy red mop of hair was mostly concealed by a narrow grommetted blue serge cap whose stiff poke slanted down over his eyes. Now his bulk blocked her path completely and there began the first of the inscrutable stares with which he would attempt to keep the baggage at her distance. A naval officer would have saluted – the gloves and visiting cards and scent brigade! – but he lifted his cap one inch like a railway guard, the most cursory of gestures as to a second class passenger.

"Senhora Salaverry!"

"Captain Hannah."

"You are on time I see. I am anxious to make haste."

"Which is why I am on time, Captain!"

Mr Waters appeared behind her, still showing all his teeth. He wore faded and grimy dungarees since he it was who would attend to the passing of the warp to the waiting paddle tug, but from the sparkle in his eyes, you could see that the new arrival was the making of his voyage. Evans fussed up behind like a porter.

"Mind your gown there, Madam. Pardon me, we haven't had time to hose down yet."

"Would you show the lady to the saloon, Mr Evans?"

"Am I not to be permitted the luxury of waving to my partners?" said the Senhora.

"No," said Captain Hannah. It was to become his favourite expression. "We shall be hauled alongside the coaling yard presently and the air will be thick with dust. The saloon is the best place for you until we are clear of the dock wall."

"But . . ."

"If you please, Mr Evans?"

"This way, Madam."

"Senhora, Mr Evans, Senhora Salaverry," said Captain Hannah. "And Mr Waters, perhaps you would remove that grin from your face, take up your station at the capstan and get those jackasses off the rail!"

"Aye, aye, sir!"

A hubbub of movement then, Captain Hannah was pleased to see. Belasco came aboard next, while behind, Billy Bones and the German struggled with the leather trunks, and down on the dock, Roderick Chauncey-Vernon stood a little apart from the two most bizarre of the sixty-fourthers, the tooth extractor and the Reverend who continued to stare up at the *Whisper*'s yards as if they had never seen them before. Indeed, there was an asylum air to them all as if a lunatic's dream had come to life and reality. All their departure lacked was a pierrot's band. And what was it all for? Bird shit, Jack Hannah said to himself, answering his own question. The romance of the sea boiled down to what you could carry and what you got for it when you could carry it. It was as mundane as that.

Belasco said, "I understand approaches have been made to you by another interested party, Captain?"

Jack Hannah scowled once more. Would nothing ever be kept secret?

"I regarded myself as already under orders, sir."

"We are most grateful."

"Then if there is nothing else . . ."

"The Reverend Elias Evans would have liked to have said a prayer."

"That won't be necessary."

"I think he is also anxious to have a word with his brother."

"The tide is on the turn, sir. Every minute that tug fusses about us costs money. The Reverend can say his prayer on the dock as we are warped out."

"Thank you, Captain. There's one more thing. Mr Cornelius Lewis has brought a gift for you."

"A gift?"

"A tarpaulin muster. You have a slop chest, Captain?"

"Ah, no sir."

"It can be brought aboard then. It only remains for me to wish you God speed and *bon voyage*."

"Thank you, sir."

Evans appeared, fussing again.

"Excuse me, sir, gentlemen. The Senhora would like very much to watch our departure from the poop deck."

"I have already addressed myself to her on that matter. She'll be out of the way in the saloon. Now sir, if there is nothing else?"

"Only to wish you good luck once more."

"Thank you. Show Mr Belasco off if you please, Mr Evans!" Baron be damned, Jack Hannah thought. "And have the gangway brought in and secured."

Evans went off like a courtier while Jack Hannah turned his attention to the foresail which had already been rigged to steady their progress down channel once the warp had been passed to the waiting tug. Now at last they were ready, and on the dock the Reverend Elias Evans actually knelt in prayer and although they could not hear the words, their leave-taking was thus attended by the blessing of the Almighty. Mr Waters had his watch running the coiled hawser forward and soon the grunting of the hogs in the sty beneath the fo'c'sle head and the cackling of the chickens in their pen aft was joined by the clanking of the capstan.

"Single up aft!"

"All ready aft!"

"Single up for'ard!"

"All ready for'ard!"

"Let go aft!"

"All gone aft!"

"Stand by to pass the warp."

A heaving line hurtled over from the stern of the tug and presently the large towing hawser was taken aboard, the forward springs removed, and soon, aided by the tide, they were drawn slowly past the dock wall and the outer pier and, once free of the landward protection of the wall, they felt the lurch of the open sea. Jack Hannah did not cast a further glance ashore and his first thought was to test his men aloft, but at the last moment, as they swung past the pierhead, out of the corner of his eye, he just saw a solitary figure huddled in the shelter of the little light tower. There was no mistaking her exceptional height, or the strands of auburn hair coming awry in the breeze, but no hand was raised, nor was there any final gesture at parting, and Beatrice Trevoake who must have roused herself early, with or without her employer's permission, stood there a mute and unresponsive witness of their departure.

He swallowed, undecided what to do himself, but then he remembered that single gold band with its simple garnet stone and the gesture she had made, and turned his back. As if the circus act of his owners were not enough, now she had added her presence further to distract him. Enough of her! Enough of the land! Although they would be under tow for hours yet, he lost no time in getting ready.

"All hands make sail! Loose all lower and upper topsails, foresail and jibs!"

And to the helmsman: "Follow the tug. And watch your steering!"

Land quit, Beatrice Trevoake quit, there only remained the Senhora.

In the saloon, Senhora Felipa had evidently made herself at home. She had removed her cloak and laid it carelessly across the back of *his* chair, he noted, along the handsome mahogany piece at the head of the fixed table which was, by time-honoured tradition, the captain's chair. Ignoring her for a second, his eye noted that everything was in perfect order, the glistening woodwork, the cupboards with their inlaid whitewood panels and polished brass handles, the leather-bound horsehair cushions and the brass skylight, even the fiddles on the table had been brought to a perfect shine by the ship's boy, little Tommy Dance. The saloon was also free of coal dust – in a better state than his cabin – and the moment he stepped into it, he felt a glow of satisfaction. There was nothing wrong with the *Whisper* that a month's labour would not put right. By the time she made her landfall, he'd have her back to her Appledore trim. He'd have her

47

spars painted white too, add a little dash to her appearance, he determined.

But now the green swell of a full blouse and a dusky complexion added an exotic touch of colour to the overwhelming masculine aura of polished wood and brass. There was a perfume too, a fragrance he could not describe – what did he know of perfumes? – and as he removed his cap – never ever had he been able to stand upright in any vessel with the complete certainty of not knocking his head – he glowered once more at what he saw next for she had in front of her, spread along the saloon table, an ancient blue-backed chart of her own. It was as if, from the moment they'd quit the land, she had produced credentials for her own command. He might have been ducking in there for an interview!

He picked her cloak up and deposited it disdainfully on a nearby chair and sat down heavily glaring at her.

How amused her eyes were!

"I hope I am not to be confined here for the entire voyage, Captain?"

"You will have your cabin presently."

"Poor Mr Evans has not had time to vacate it yet?"

"He is where he should be – at his duties."

"You did not think to tell him earlier?"

"My instructions were secrecy."

"Splendid! But soon I shall have to unpack my traps."

"As soon as we quit our tug, I'll send the boy to you."

"Thank you."

He squinted at the ancient chart. It was old and pencilled upon, something vaguely familiar about it.

"None of the men aboard was aware of your coming. I thought it best not to tell them."

"Then their tongues will be buzzing now!"

"I daresay, but some of these men might not have sailed otherwise."

"If they knew our destination, you mean?"

"No, no. If they knew a woman was to be aboard."

Her smile came frankly now, teasingly, with a pink sliver of tongue as a complimentary bouquet.

"Superstition, Captain?"

"Exactly."

"And you doubt my story of the *Caleuche*?"

"The – what?" he had forgotten.

"The apparition I spoke of?"

"I doubt it, yes. There are superstitions and superstitions. By and large, they do not like women on board trading vessels. They are not used to it. It confines them."

"And you?"

"My concern is the ship, a fast passage and a profitable one. I don't like . . ." he hesitated again. Frills, he wanted to say.

"What, Captain?"

"The unusual."

"Ah," she said. "Well, I expect we shall have plenty of surprises when we encounter your father."

That set him back. He felt his stomach heave, his embarrassment becoming total, and below the surface flush a chill of permanent dread, a stone cold part of himself frozen to protect his vulnerability. He wanted to run then, just to absent himself from what he feared most of all, a total exposure of his sense of hurt and betrayal.

"I would like to talk to you at length upon that subject," he said hoarsely. "But for the moment, I hope you will not mention it." Captain! he thought; five minutes on board, she had him pleading.

"Of course."

"Nor our destination, except in the general direction. The crew naturally assume we are going to Chile for ore and I have not disillusioned them. As for my father, his reappearance is also unknown, I hope?"

"That was our agreement. Believe me, I do understand how painful it is for you and I have insisted upon secrecy with your owners."

"Yes," he said. "Quite." But then he came out into the open. "Myself, I've never seen a more untrustworthy lot in all my life."

She smiled again, shrewdly this time.

"Greed will silence them."

"I wonder?"

"I know!"

He fingered the chart upon the table. "There's another matter. By tradition, there is one set of charts on board a ship engaged in voyages around the Horn, one set only, and the ship's position is known to the master only. That is why the log-book is kept under lock and key unless an entry is made that has to be witnessed."

She stared at him, frankly incredulous.

49

"So I must ask you for the charts until we reach our destination."

"You are not serious?"

"I am perfectly serious."

"But why?"

He actually smiled. For once, perhaps for the first time, he was being asked a question and now, suddenly, he seemed to have found a new articulateness and spoke without embarrassment, with all the confidence of his position and authority.

"You have already given me the answer."

"I have?"

"Yes," he said. "Greed! The men are signed for a voyage between specific latitudes. If we traverse these latitudes they are entitled to more money. Then again, we will be rounding Cape Horn. There may well be situations when a fo'c'sle crowd will want to put about, or run back to some port for repairs or shelter. If they know a port of refuge is near, it is sometimes an incitement to mutiny. That is why they must have no precise knowledge of the ship's position."

"You keep them in ignorance?"

"They were born in ignorance, and they will die in ignorance. If you please, your chart?"

The chart, old, cracked, and blue backed, was only half unfolded. Her hand lay upon it. He thought for a moment that she was going to refuse him, but the smile did not leave her lips as she brought the stiff-backed blue covers together. At that moment, the ship's bell struck, there was an accompanying distant toot of the paddle tug's siren, a rapid clambering of footsteps outside and young Waters, the Second Mate, entered.

"Beg pardon, sir. We're beginning to overrun the tug. There's wind enough and we're ready to make our own way."

It was the news he so much wanted to hear.

"Very good."

"Sir?"

"I'll be up presently. Have the watch stand by to hoist the upper t'gal'nt yards. We'll want to get off at a lick."

"Sir."

Young Waters left, but not before noting the fixed expression on his Captain's face, for Jack Hannah had noticed a faded but firm copperplate signature upon the front cover of the folded chart. Masters, by tradition, bought their own charts and took them from ship to ship and the signature upon the Senhora's chart was quite decipherably that of Joshua Hannah, his father. It seemed to reach out at him with an evil luminosity. He could not help blurting out: "It's true, then?"

"Of course it's true. Why should you doubt me? Do you think I should have come all this way over all these months for my own benefit alone?"

He did not answer. He had asked himself questions enough and the answers – all the answers – were improbable. From start to finish, the mutiny upon the *Avalon*, his father's ship, made nonsense of the expectations of reasonable, logical people. Pick up a meat cleaver, disembowel an eighteen-year-old steward, remove his heart and drag him to the ship's rail with his entrails half-hanging out and then pay regard to his last and dying words, "Tell my mother how I died!" And that was recorded, sworn to and testified. So what could he now say? The paddle tug's final toot marked his sudden collapse into incoherence once more.

But they were not being inarticulate along the decks or in the fo'c'sle. Working the yards or tailing the halliards, the chanteyman had raised a chorus.

> *"Sally Brown, she's a black mulatter!*
> *She drinks rum and chews terbaccer!*
> *Way – ho! for Sally Brown!"*

"Keep silence there!" shouted a flustered Evans. But it was a shanty, known the world over. It did not specifically refer to Senhora Salaverry. Although Sally Brown she became known as, a judy spotted from the first day. They had their first main meal of fresh beef stew, flavoured with onions and carrots, but once this was eaten and the watch below settled down for the night, they got the bogie stove going and in the ripe sailor-fug of the fo'c'sle, there was only one topic of conversation.

Who was she?

Where was she bound?

And where did she hail from, by Christ? Nothing like her along the Strand in a month of Sundays!

See the gear she brought? See the clothes she wore? Musical comedy wasn't in it!

And the bandboxes, the leather, a bit of quality stuff that. And the other big box – the boards – the easel, was it? A hartist, by God. paints an' all!

But why was she aboard? That was the point.

The statements were what you might expect in a crowded fo'c'sle. Normally, they would have concentrated their attention on the Captain and the mates. Was the old man a driver, a cracker-on of sail? They wanted to know that for the simple reason that they would have weather enough to face, and a man who fought the Horn, going forward every chance he got, would cause them bleeding fingernails enough. Then there were the mates, the sailmaker and carpenter, and above all, the cook. A good 'doctor' could make a voyage and the unfortunate wart-encrusted face of Old Slushy the cook was so off-putting that the man must excel at something. But these matters, even that bumscrew Evans, Old Grease himself whose nature they had soon divined were put upon by this, the first night, when by tradition immemorial, the First Mate kept the deck. The same questions were repeated over and over again. Who was she? Where did she come from? What was her purpose on board?

"She's a Chileno, by her colour. Chile way, you can bet!"

"No, a *mameluca*. See the sloe eyes on her. Come-to-bed eyes, or a quick one on the park bench if you haven't got a bed. Ten-a-penny round the joints in Bahia. A *Brasilliana* if ever they saw one."

"Too tall," said another, "and not fat enough for that." Didn't they know the *mamelucas* run to fat in their twenties? Married at twelve, they were, old women at nineteen with their dugs reaching down to their knees!

"Maybe, there was Indian in her, a splice of the up-country stuffing in the *chapados*? That straight back said horses."

"Give or take a continent, maybe she was a Creole?"

"You might as well say a chee-chee, an eight anna girl!"

But they could not agree. Only one thing was certain and that was that she was unlike anything any of them had ever seen before. There must be English blood, some said, otherwise at thirty the figure would have gone and about this there was finally agreement. Hot climes and a stiffening of the old ramrod, it was, boys, the tarbrush adding to her curves, moistening the quim, feathering the nest, whichever way you liked to look at it – as every man jack there would have liked to do just that! The conversation indeed was ripe. And the smell on her too, a rare perfume, boys, enough to make a man swallow Paddy Murphy's goat, hook, line and sinker until the horns was sticking out through his lily white arse! Oh, but they

52

would have given their all to get at her, and if they couldn't get at her, well, then let them learn all they could about her.

Little Tommy Dance, the fourteen-year-old ship's boy, lean and swarthy himself, had already spent two years on the Sveynton pilot boat and shared his job of ship's peggy to the fo'c'sle and the cook with the delectable task of personal servant to the Senhora. He it was who'd helped her unpack those commodious trunks and boxes.

"Hi there, Peggy, what's she got up her shift? Seen her drawers, have you?"

"What's she got stowed in all that gear?"

"Well, clothes," said little Tommy.

"We've seen them. What else?"

"More clothes, laces, frills, fine things next to her skin."

"What else?"

"Letters and parchments in a leather case."

"Is it treasure, we're going for?"

"And books, books and magazines."

"Jesus, she can read!" said one with disappointment as if this last fact put her out of his dreams. "A proper Seraphina!"

And before they reached the chops of the channel, they had a new song going, a fo'c'sle chorus that lasted all the way to Chile.

> *"Sera . . . phina!*
> *Seraphina's got no shimmy.*
> *I bin down and yes, I seen her!*
> *Sera . . . phina!"*

That ended Sally Brown for a while. Sally Brown became Seraphina while Senhora Felipa remained the same.

Chapter Four

"From the day she came aboard," Harry Grail said, "I knew there was going to be trouble. I was in the *Pathfinder* with Captain Bowen on three voyages around Cape Stiff and never once would he take a woman aboard, not even his own wife, not on that Cape Horn run. Days, weeks, months, we were, making a run at the Horn with the best captain that ever sailed out of this port, days when you opened your mouth to speak and your spit froze and cut back against your face, drawing your own blood, boys, your own spit and your own blood, days when you couldn't see nothing in front, nor behind you . . . pulley-haul weather, boys, the lee rail running under for weeks at a time. I knew she'd have to be confined, d'you see? You couldn't have her up on deck, it was a cabin job, week after week of it. And somebody'd have to go down to see to her, and you know what Jack is, it would have to be the officers, and that was trouble again, even with that old grease-pole, Evans.

"No, I knew it was trouble, and I was against the very idea of it from the start. I would never have signed aboard in the first place if I'd have known and that was bloody Jack Hannah for you, and the owners. Well, enough's been said about the owners, but from the start there was two things that bothered me, the chief being a woman aboard at all, and none of us knowing, not even the officers from the day we signed. Not right, it wasn't, this not knowing, for not one of us could get off her once we'd signed without the threat of the magistrate's court over our heads. Not that we had a chance of skinning out, for the moment she was aboard, the gangway was up and we was all let go in a flash. He practically bundled the owners off like they was bum boat men, and even when we was passing the pier, he turned his back on his own fiancée. Three years bespoke they was, him and one of the Trevoake girls, and a chain of shops to be split between them when old man Trevoake died – and turned his back on that he did – so you can tell what was in his mind from the minute we sailed. You don't have to tell me what got in his eyes . . . his bloody ginger john willy!

"No, the woman was the first thing, a doxy, I knew as soon as I clapped eyes on her, but that wasn't the chief thing. The chief thing we was to realise later, and what I knew then, I don't mind admitting. I never told anyone at the time, and that was, my brother Walter sailed on the old *Avalon* with Jack Hannah's father, and there was other men too who'd known men, or who had relatives lost with him, our Walter, Willie Twomallow lost his father as did Taffy Morgan, and more than that, old greasepole Evans had served with Joshua Hannah on the old *Coquimbo* – and d'you mean to tell me that was all an accident – that Jack Hannah didn't know the connection when he signed those men? He knew all right! And I'll tell you this, I've not a good word to say for Jack Hannah, but by Christ, compared to his father, he was a lemon by all accounts, and there were letters to prove it that they never brought out at the trial of that poor old Greek, letters from all over to testify what kind of man he was. And not one of 'em was ever read at the trial.

"No, you can't tell me nothing about Joshua Hannah that's bad enough, and his son not much better, but the real trouble started with having her aboard from the first day, and that I stick to. From the first week, she even began to strip to her shimmy in front of the poor peggy boy – hardly a stitch on her when he went in there – a boy only fourteen. Downright disgusting it was, and whatever is said of seamen in general, I tell you that woman was evil – pure evil – right through to the poxy marrow – and I knew it from the start. Even when we had weather avoiding the Bay and they was all fussing about seeing she was well wrapped up, 'You wait until we get to the bloody doldrums,' says I; 'You wait until we're stuck there like a fly in treacle, by Christ! Then you'll see what harm she'll cause.'

"No, before we ever rounded the Horn, before we even sighted the *Gazela* – *Gazela*, my arse! – I knew, d'you see? I felt it coming. Trouble, boys, and all because of her bit o' fancy.

" 'What is it like, Peggy?' they kept on asking the poor lad. 'How is the barometer this morning? Let's have a look! Rising or falling?'

" 'The only ship I ever had to cross my legs on before breakfast,' says another. 'There's half of us can't go aloft when she's on deck,' and such remarks.

"Oh yes, pure filth from the moment we slipped the tug. The only good thing was the food, I give him that, well vittled we was, and the cook a bloody marvel, but that didn't last. And if you asks me,

the good food led to the other, the this and that, that went on all the
time."

LOG OF THE BARQUE WHISPER OF SVEYNTON.
Jack Hannah, Master.

Wednesday 22 October:
Towed to sea 7.30 a.m.   Midday SW ½W   Lundy Light.

Thursday 23 October:
Noon Lat. 50° 46N.   Long. 5° 44W.   Distance run – 64
miles.   Fresh SW winds. Men scraping the poop, painting the yards.

They were soon looking for the *Nortada* once they cleared the Bay
of Biscay, the breeze that wafted across the Atlantic towards the
Equator, the same breeze that had taken Columbus and marked the
routes for ships innumerable ever since. There were days of plain
sailing, of finding their feet; in general a feeling of well-being, fresh
mutton and taties while fresh supplies lasted, tighteners of bread and
ship's biscuit, and once, duff and treacle pudding which followed a
delectable sea pie, served in layers. And Jack Hannah, well pleased
with the *Whisper*'s performance, had so far managed to avoid the
Senhora by contriving to stand the night watches, busying himself
with the ship and allowing the mates to join her in the saloon while
he himself followed his plan and stood aloof. For a week or so, he
had ample excuse for his self-imposed confinement. There was
always the ship, the hands to be watched, behaviour checked, the
natural apprehension of taking a strange ship with a strange crew to
sea. But within a week, these apprehensions had gone. There was no
logical reason for his behaviour and in the confinement of the
Whisper, it was beginning to be noted.

The Senhora meanwhile, behaved herself perfectly (it was
reported).

"Makes all the difference in the world having a lady of quality
aboard," said Mr Evans. "I mean, it takes the roughness out of
things. I mean, you have to mind your Ps and Qs, I admit, but in my
view, it has a very beneficial effect all round, sir."

"You're not eating in your cabin again, sir?" said Samuel Scuse,
the cook. "There is *room* in the saloon, sir. We've got the fiddles up
and it's like a Christmas party in there, sir. Lunch they're calling it
now, a little bit o'lunch with the Senhora."

But he'd heard the crew and somebody had a mouth organ going in the evenings.

> "Sera . . . phina!
> Seraphina's got no shimmy,
> I bin down and, yes, I seen her!
> Sera . . . phina!"

He had also observed the bantering which little Tommy Dance, the ship's peggy boy, got on deck. But of the Senhora, little more than a glimpse, a curt 'Good morning', a brief 'Goodnight'. Once when taking a sight with his sextant, she'd approached him on deck and he'd choked her off. That was noticed too.

"My view, boyce," said Morgan Morgan, "is that the man have suffered a haccident. Honly hexplanation – caught himself somewhere delicate on a bit of barbed wire when he was small, like!"

> "Sera . . . phina!
> I bin down and yes, I seen her!
> Sera . . . phina."

The truth was, of course, that he'd just brooded. Night after night, pacing the cramped deck or seated alone in his own cabin, he gave his mind again and again to the facts which surrounded the loss of his father's ship, the *Avalon*, and the hanging of that solitary Greek. What had happened, according to the testimonies, was unusual enough in that the Greek had been tried for the murder of the Captain and officers 'with others unknown', as the charge read. No bodies had been found, the *Avalon*, it was said, had been set on fire and was never recovered. Quite simply (the prosecution said) one day a ship's boat bearing the name *Avalon* had put into a remote island on the bar of the Paranahyha River, on the northeast coast of Brazil where another British ship, the *Glanely*, was loading hides. It was unusual for any vessel to be there at all and since the ship's boat bore the name of a British ship, curiosity had been aroused, and three men in a state of destitution were taken aboard, a Maltese, the Greek, and a British seaman, Theodore Yates, the only man to have been shipped originally in Sveynton, the *Avalon*'s home port.

They had a melancholy tale to tell. All three were survivors of the

Avalon whose cargo of coal had overheated, the vessel had caught on fire and been abandoned, the crew dividing into two lifeboats. There had been a hard voyage with some loss of life in violent weather and soon after the vessel went down the two lifeboats had separated in the night, the survivors having no knowledge of the Captain's boat, or what had happened to it. It was a not uncommon story of loss at sea, and since the island was uninhabited, the Captain of the *Glanely* had taken the survivors aboard and thereafter to his destination, the port of Cork. In passage, Yates who was already in an advanced state of tuberculosis, asked to see the Captain alone, and reported that far from being helpless survivors, his companions were mutineers who had murdered the Captain and his officers and deliberately set the *Avalon* on fire.

In the trial which followed, one of these three men, the Maltese, had turned Queen's evidence and his testimony, together with that of the dying Yates, had been sufficient to convict the Greek. There were so many unanswered questions, so many men unaccounted for, and in particular, the character of Captain Joshua Hannah was called into question, adding to the doubts. No one had fully understood why the vessel seemed to have lost half her original crew for it seemed the mutineers were newly recruited men, Captain Hannah having shipped them in Buenos Ayres, a port that was never his destination. The other witness, the Maltese, had soon disappeared, and apart from the accusations that were made about the dead Captain's behaviour – "a blow first and a curse later" – the matter had faded into oblivion, one of those poorly explained happenings at sea.

Except for a letter which arrived too late to be considered in that remote Cork courtroom from Scranton, Missouri which was later printed in the newspapers alongside Yates's testimony, itself particularly damning, a chilling description of a riot of blood-letting. A seaman had got back to Pensacola from Buenos Ayres with a tale to tell.

Bombas told me to go down on my knees in the blood of the victims and I had to swear that I would help him to the best of my ability. When the Captain was thrown over, I saw him clutch his injured arm. After this, all the bodies were thrown overboard, Bombas gave me an order to wash down the decks and on the poop, I saw a human heart. It was that of the apprentice Morgan. His dying words were, "Tell my mother how I died." Those were the last words he spoke.

There was this, then there was the steward's letter.

Scranton, Miss.
USA

Gents and Sirs,
I, C.O. Wilkins, beg most respectfully to say that I sailed aboard of the barque Avalon from 1 February to 4 October 1851 under Captain Joshua Hannah and no greater pig of a man ever existed. Earlier that year, he was arrested for cruelty to sailors and was placed under 500 dollars bond but he pulled out, leaving his bondsman to settle. In passage, there was no mutinous conduct, the crew being composed of quiet, inoffensive Sveyntòn men from his home port, but hard men to shave as he soon found out.
On crossing the bar, there was never a chantey sung on her and on the third day out we went off in a body and complained about the food which was of the worst any of us had ever had, but he said of his own men that they were nothing but a lot of Sveynton jacks and waded into them with a belaying pin. In passage, three men were knocked insensible because they were half a point off course and it was the general impression that the Captain and the Mates were behaving in such a way that all the men shipped would skin out without their wages at the first port we touched. There were fire arms and weapons constantly on show, and we never came on deck but that someone was forcibly chastised. The only man to reason with him was the cook, Emmanuel Bombas, a Christian soul who treated all the men for cuts and abrasions and was himself struck by the Captain and the Mates, but only responded in prayer, turning the other cheek, and this made the Captain worse, acting more like an animal as each day went by.
Gents and sirs, when we put in to BA with five men down with scurvy, I swear it was in order to recruit men who would do his bidding for no master ever treated a crew worse as if his sole intention was to lose the ship . . .

And so it went on. Oh truth, Jack Hannah thought, where was it in all this morass? Was it in these bloody, gory, impossible details – that human heart, that "tell my mother how I died", or was it in the simple statement read at that gallows?

"I, Emmanuel Bombas, at the moment which I depart this life, express my deep gratitude to the Dean of Cork and the two Protestant clergymen who took such a kind and humane interest in me, to Mr Hourdi, the Consul, and all those Greeks and Britons who have tried to save me from the gallows. Finally, I forgive those who have borne witness against me, as I hope to be forgiven by God and received into His Holy Kingdom."

59

Such were the known facts which must have occupied Jack Hannah, and while a biographer likes to pretend that he knows all about his characters, it may well be that facts are misleading things and of all these memorabilia, the letters of complaint, the crumbling log book, perhaps we are most fortunate in the surviving letters of the Mate of the *Whisper*, Handel Evans. His miseries and his eagerness to inform, caused him to put pen to paper more than at any other time in his life and, in a way, he is almost the co-author of this account. From the outset his dislikes are plain.

From the beginning of the voyage, he writes, *the Captain was very short with his officers, confining himself to his quarters in the daylight hours with hardly a courteous word for the passenger and charterer who was herself courtesy and consideration personified for all of us, especially in view of the cramped conditions and the very severe weather experienced later. You will remember that the Captain thought fit to prohibit a prayer at the outset, a decision we all had much cause to regret. From the beginning, there was a marked aversion to any form of religious worship and on the first Sunday at sea, thinking that the traditional service would naturally be taken by the Captain, I went to his cabin. He had hardly been seen in the daylight hours and from the beginning had taken all his meals alone. He required me to state my purpose through the cabin door! This was only after a week at sea.*

For Billy Bones, Flower Flohr, the speechless German, Jackie Breeze, the three-fingered sailor, fat little Willie Twomallow and the others, it was not such a bad voyage at all, and we can guess the secret was the food. Warty Scuse could cook, and while the food was good, they went to their work with a will. The man was no beauty, but his galley was his empire and he ruled it with a benevolent generosity. It made the voyage as far as the fo'c'sle crowd were concerned, and whatever Harry Grail's objections and dark mutterings, they had no sense of foreboding. The questioning of little Tommy Dance, the peggy boy, grew less lewd. They settled down for the run. But naturally the question of the *Avalon* came up eventually, although in its proper context of strange happenings at sea.

Willie Twomallow who was short and tubby with a thin mop of blond curls, a cheerful fellow always first to turn out when called, was the cock of the fo'c'sle when it came to yarn spinning. They sat off watch on their bunks, or around the plain deal table, a smoke-oh on, Billy Bones for the moment finished with his mouth organ, and Flower Flohr's huge hands busy darning a sock. Here it was in the peace of an evening's run with the wind set fair that the *Whisper*

60

proved herself a well found ship and in that comfortable fug, by time immemorial, it was the custom to yarn away the last hours of the light. There were other mysteries besides the *Avalon*. There was the *Caerleon*, a little Newport barque which had set out for that same nitrate coast loaded down with coal, only to find that beating around the Horn set them back time after time until finally the Captain declared himself to have been the subject of a visitation from the Almighty himself.

"God came to him, boys," said Willie Twomallow, his plump nodding face as round as a melon. 'Go back, Cap'n, put about,' says He."

"Says who?"

"The Almighty."

"Gerraway!"

"It's true, boys, up he come in his night shirt and stocking cap – the Cap'n, I mean, and says to the Mate who was standing the watch with two men lashed to the wheel and the wind howling and hardly a rag of canvas holding her – they just couldn't get a slant – and the skipper says, 'Rouse the hands, Mister, we're putting her about!' 'But Cap'n?' the mate says, 'It's bound to change!' 'Are you doubting the word of the Almighty God?' says the Cap'n. Danny Matthews it was, a man without a blemish on his character and as teetotal as a boot.

" 'The Almighty God?' says the Mate.

" 'Yes, Mister, I felt His presence,' says the skipper.

" 'What tack was He on?' says the Mate, a real hard Cardiff bastard by all accounts, but the skipper told him he'd see him in his cabin when the hands were roused. So around they come, and glad the crowd was, I can tell you, eight weeks they'd been trying to round Cape Stiff – and then they run before it for home."

"For home?"

"For home, boys. They give up. And when he got the Mate down to his cabin, he says that there's more things on heaven and earth than meet the eye. 'Laying on my bunk, I was, hoping to get a bit of shut eye with the lampwick trimmed when I felt the air move,' says the Cap'n. 'Yes, Mister, a perfect stillness came, in all that wind and noise and her timbers groaning, and in this stillness there was no shape nor sight nor sound, but inside me.'

" 'Inside yer?' says the Mate with a quick gander around for bottles and the like. But the only thing he saw was snuff.

61

" 'Yes, Mister, inside of me. I felt this perfect calm and it was my own voice talking to me then, talking to me but not belonging to me, like as if it was suddenly the property of another and it said to me, my own voice, it said, "Put her about, you'll not round the Horn this trip in peril of what awaits you." '

" 'And,' says he, and I heard this from a man that knew him all his life, 'And all the while I was waiting for some doubt to come, some question to be asked, some reminder of my responsibility to my owners for I knew full well what was writ large on my orders, the very bill of lading I had in front me.' Now is there any man here has seen one of them?" asked Willie Twomallow.

"Yes," said Harry Grail. "They finishes up: 'So God send thee good ship to thy desired port of safety.' "

"So they do. Well, old Cap'n Matthews was reminded of his responsibilities and sitting there, a great fine white head of hair on him like a halo there was, and with the Mate looking at him and sniffing him for drink, the Cap'n says, 'The voice that spoke was my own voice but the words it said was another's, but I knew in my heart I must obey.'

" 'They'll have your ticket,' says the Mate. 'It'll be an enquiry. Tapping you, they'll be as to the soundness of your mind. You'll never get another ship. Why don't you take a dose of Blaud's for the kidneys, or just leave it to me? The wind must shift, or we'll run for the Cape of Good Hope. Cargo's cargo,' says he. 'My God is aware of that,' says the skipper, and sitting there – he never looked healthier – not a wild man, nor a drunk man, not a raging man, nor a broody man . . ."

"Not like old carrot-head aft aboard of this un!" put in Jackie Breeze.

"No boys, a man in full possession of his senses sat there and looked at him, this real hard Cardiff bucko, and fetched out the log-book and his pen and ink and a pinch of salt for to dry the paper and said, 'I'll make the entry now, Mister, and you can state and mark your objections. Around the Horn this ship will not go.' And so, fair play to him, he wrote it up fair and square, giving the latitude and longitude of it while the Third Mate kept the deck, and then fetched him down and added his own signature, and home they come, putting back into Newport a hundred and ten days out and the hatches never moved since the day they left.

"Well, you can imagine the commotion. As soon as she was

spoke, the owners got word of her and down they came looking for damage, wondering whether she'd sprung a leak or whether there was fever or scurvy, but there was nothing – nothing save the calm on that man's face. Twenty years he'd sailed that ship, summer and winter, and more trips round the Horn than any man in the port. A 'Frisco man through and through he was, a real downeast johnny cake . . .

"So down the owners came in a rush, tall hats and whiskers and stiff collars and carriages. 'Did you have any trouble, Cap'n?' they asks. A good and reliable man they knew him to be. 'Is she overheating below? Wasn't she properly tommed? Did the cargo shift?'

" 'No, sir,' " says he, producing the log-book duly signed. 'I received a visitation from the Almighty God as is here recorded, together with the latitude and the longitude of it.'

"Well, you can imagine it. Same as the Mate thought, it's medical. It was all, send for the doctor, and looking for bottles, they was, but he sticks to his ground and calls his paper. Naturally, the crows forward was all cock-a-hoop. More days, more dollars, says they, but the owners was already calculating the cost of it. Two hundred and ten days out and back, and not a penny profit, and their charterers waiting at the other end of the world for a cargo that never came and ore standing idle that hadn't never been collected. 'But why, Cap'n?' they asks. 'Thirty years you bin with us, man and boy. Was it the seas? We heard terrible reports of ships lost?'

" 'It was the Almighty,' says the Cap'n. 'He came to me and spoke to me as here recorded under my own hand and duly witnessed!'

"Well, that was the last time he said it. Very sorry, they was, after all these years he'd been in their employ, and not a mark against his good name, but in the circumstances, they says, and if he'd take their advice, a spell ashore and the waters of some spa, maybe . . . A good dose of Llandrindod Wells might put him right, and purge the bad out of him.

" 'Be warned,' he said. 'The Almighty came to me and spoke to me, not with the tongues of angels, nor the clash of cymbals, but quiet and soft and inside me in my own voice but through me and it was a Divine Illumination.'

"Well they got the Mate up on deck and he says, 'Strain,' he says, 'nothing like raving or shouting, but plain strain.' As it happened he had a brother ashore with a Chief Mate's papers and give him the command, he'd shift her so fast there wouldn't be time for a cobweb to gather. And so, they give it to him, his command, and he turned around in a single tide and warped her off, the old *Caerleon*, Cap'n Matthews watching her go from the pier, his wife on his arm and not knowing where the next penny was coming from. He stood there until she was hull down and only the tip of her mast showing, the tears streaming down to his beard and knowing he'd never get another ship again. Oh, he was in his right mind all right, but they wouldn't listen to him."

"And what happened then?"

"This is it, boys. It took half a year for 'em to find out. The *Caerleon* was first spoke all but a mile from that there previous recorded position by a homeward bounder who reported her to Lloyd's, but never ever seen again."

"Lost?"

"All hands."

"Wreckage?"

"Not so much as a spar."

"Crew?"

"Shark meat."

"And the Captain, Cap'n Matthews?"

"Died in his bed with his grandchildren around him, eighty-four and still teetotal as a boot!"

"No more visitations?"

"None."

"Took up religion big?"

"Not him. Got a job on the blocks and tackles in a foundry ashore."

And they believed it, for it was true and Willie Twomallow had heard the story from his father who had also spoken of the *Avalon* and Joshua Hannah.

" 'Topside Joss', they called him. A good driver, mind, my father swore to that, but hard. He remembered him standing the deck night after night, a big man in a big soft hat which he tied down with a bit of binnacle wick, not speaking for days. Rain, sleet, hail, snow, squalls, nothing shifted him, nor worried him. If there was any fear they had, it was that he'd drive a ship under through not loosing sail."

"My brother sailed with him too," said Harry Grail, "and he thought different. Clump and clout was his motto, from the first time he ever got a command – and a swallow on him like a pelican's!"

64

Morgan Morgan, the most wide-eyed listener, had no information to give about his father.

"Never seen him, not for years. 'A wanderer you was born', my mother said, 'and a wanderer you will die'. And so he did."

"Murdered," said Harry Grail, "by that sailor-killer."

And then he told them the story of the Greek, and the apprentice's beating heart lying on the poop deck, and the mysterious letter which arrived too late for the trial.

LOG OF THE BARQUE WHISPER *OF SVEYNTON.*
Jack Hannah, Master.

Monday 14 December:
Lat. 21°.06. S, Long. 34.21. Breezes from E to NE.
Lat. 23°10S. Long. 35.39. Pleasant breezes from ESE to NE.

Tuesday 15 December:
6 p.m. Came up and spoke bk. Byzantiam *49 days from Cardiff to Montevideo. Men employed reeving new lanyards to fore rigging.*

We had been at sea for fifty-one days, wrote Evans, *when Senhora Salaverry bade me call her Felipa, and for a joke asked if I would leave her calling card with the Captain as she desired to make his acquaintance.*

Then, just as they were into the doldrums, that song broke out again.

> *"Sera . . . phina!*
> *Seraphina's got no shimmy.*
> *I bin down and yes, I seen her!*
> *Sera . . . phina!"*

Then there were light winds, and then no wind at all. They were in sweat corner, as Harry Grail described it. "And with that moistening quim ever ready, boys, winking at us all!" And Harry Grail described that too, for in a certain light it was actually visible.

Chapter Five

It was in sweat corner that Senhora Felipa came to the Captain's cabin wearing a kind of pantaloon. She also wore a turban, her bare feet with the straightest of toes were encased in leather sandals and her coolness in all that heat a miracle to all on board. In the centre of the turban, she wore a golden brooch in the shape of a butterfly which glittered in the brilliant light as Jack Hannah sat slumped in his chair, the sweat wet upon his forehead and soaking his entire body. As wind is the breath of life to a sailing vessel, so its absence is a kind of death. Up on deck the sails hung lifeless from the yards, banging and slapping against the masts, the sun a ball of fire, dazzling and scorching in the sky, softening the pitch on the seams of the deck which you could hear bubbling in the baking heat of the day.

Now and again, a faint breath of air was felt, a ripple of a catspaw breeze, and Evans would give an order, "Lee fore brace!" and the watch would scramble to man the braces and haul the yards around, but the breezes did not last and they scarcely made a mile. A fly in treacle, Harry Grail had said, and it was an apt description, living as they did for a capful of wind, and the capful soon expending itself. Five days they had drifted before the Senhora made her appearance. By now, the crew hung about the decks, seeking what shade they could as the *Whisper* rolled endlessly from side to side, a dead thing seeming no more than a hulk of straining timber on that burning ocean.

A knock on the cabin door, and Jack Hannah bade her enter. With the light behind her, her presence was somehow all the more eerie in that muslin garb. There was an air of oriental charade about it as if she had just boarded them, a spirit come to torment them further. As of habit, he stood up. As usual, he bumped his head. She seemed to glide into the little cabin, and there was the perfume again, that amused wet mouth, the understanding look.

"Senhora?"

"Doldrums," she said. "I have experienced them before. But surely, it is ridiculous that I have driven you out of your own saloon?"

66

"You don't drive me."

"Then I prevent you. Please. May I sit down?"

She did not wait for his reply, avoided his chair and placed herself delicately upon the rumpled sheets of his bunk. He could see the lithe brown contours of her figure, her strong smooth thighs, and above all, her amused almond eyes in the calmness of that passive face. The butterfly brooch glistened like a charm. Where was Ali Baba? he thought. He wouldn't have been surprised to see her chained to the mast of a slaver's dhow, and he blushed incredulously. Seraphina was too incongruous a nickname even. And she did not sweat at all.

It must have been in the early afternoon, the full heat of the day waning, but men lay asleep everywhere and a ghostly kind of silence hung over the ship, the only disturbance being metal ladles banging on the racks in the galley and the slats slapping the masts.

He was forced to sit down. He couldn't stand there bent like a crow. He turned his chair towards her.

"You have . . . er . . . everything you need?"

It was his first enquiry after her welfare in fifty days!

"Everybody is most kind . . . in the circumstances."

"Damned hot!"

She came to the point.

"You avoid me, Captain?"

"Yes," his reply was guttural, a choked affirmative. He could actually feel the sweat running down his calves.

"We avoid, usually, only what we are afraid of?"

He glowered.

"Damned hot!" he said again. His hair lank with sweat, was flattened upon his head. He hoped his stare made it plain he wanted no intimacy.

She smiled.

"Would it not be better to discuss things?"

"Nothing to discuss."

"You have questions, surely?"

"They'll be answered no doubt."

"Your father . . ."

He got up from a pool of sweat and closed the door.

"There are questions, yes. Naturally."

"Well, then . . ."

"Which I will put to him myself," he sat down again in the same pool of sweat.

"There are some blows which might be softened, Captain."

"I don't," he wanted to say, "believe you at all." But there she was, like a genie come out of a lamp.

But he spoke formally. He said, "There are facts unexplained. There is a good deal of doubt. It is all incredible, beyond belief. Even what is recorded and sworn to as evidence is not possible, hardly, but it happened."

"And you do not want to discuss it with me, or anyone else? Is that what I am to understand?"

He did not answer, but sat there glowering.

The heat was like a levelling illness, draining away at every part of the body, pressing away at the skull, clouding the mind, hammering at the eyeballs, pressure, pressure all the time. He found it hard to frame sentences.

"There will be matters to discuss when we reach our destination," he said wearily. For some reason, he thought of the gunny sacks they'd brought to off-load the cargo. Had they enough shovels? If the *Gazela* was aground, it meant shovelling the guano into sacks and then bringing it over in the boats. It was filthy stuff, the stench would be terrible. He'd better make sure the boats were caulked in readiness, but it was pointless in this heat. It was all the Mates could do to get the men to haul the yards around as it was. The caulking would have to wait. Somehow this routine was pleasurable to think of, however, better than addressing himself to this mystery in front of him. He scratched his head. His fingers came away bathed in sweat.

"You do me an injustice, Captain, if you think I cannot imagine what hurt you have suffered," she said in a low voice.

Her very lucidity offended him!

"Well, that's as it is, Senhora."

"Fatherless for most of the time, I was married at fourteen, you see?"

Good God! Would the woman not understand he wanted no intimacy? What was she telling him?

"Fourteen?" he said. *"Fourteen?"* And yet was he surprised? In every conversation amongst decent people, women were never spoken of except in hallowed tones of reverence as the weaker sex, but there was not a part in the United Kingdom where you could not buy a girl of thirteen for a few shillings and nothing said. Virgins, of course, were extra. That was the way of the world.

"Your father allowed that to happen?"

"He was a trader. He traded me."

"He must have been an outcast."

She seemed to look at him with all knowing eyes.

"With some men, excuses are their passport to survival, their very calling cards."

"Yes," he said.

"And their absence is far more desirable than their presence?"

"Yes," he said again. "But your husband?"

"He was forty-three. In the end, he owned my father. My father could not pay his debts, so there was a certain proposition. It was not the English half he sold, but the unfortunate colour of my skin, that half. That was normal. A trade with a dago, you understand? When rules are not quite so strict?"

He could see it, picture it, and his mind added to the details she had not supplied, a man down on his luck in some up-country trading post, a mining or logging camp perhaps, a little store, perhaps some half-worked silver mine or plantation. People went native easily enough and the rest followed. The world was not Beatrice Trevoake's world, nor did the crisp little homilies of Sveynton apply to most of it. It was not even the sea, nor the ports, the sailor towns, it was people swarming like flies, buzzing over dungheaps in places he had never seen. South America, he thought, more whores than priests, and pellagra and dysentery and consumption – he had seen enough of the ports, beggars and their sores, frail children lying like insects, even British sailors bitten to death as they lay drunk in the gutter by insects he could not name. You never had to pull down the eyelids over the corpses, the eyes had always gone. It was worse than India because somehow India was more foreign. There seemed to be so many more people in India, so more had to die. But South America with its mixture of races, its variety of noses and bone structures, was somehow closer to Europe, a Europe gone wrong in the melting pot, and once the blood was mixed, it somehow produced a frailty and often a terrible beauty that could never survive. Children were born old and died young. It was a fact of life. Perhaps they were never even children.

She continued to look at him intently, as if time were running short, as if she had waited long enough. She gave an apologetic smile.

"I would cry at night – at fourteen – fearing a hand under the blanket."

He sat bolt upright. What else was she telling him? And why? "And I knew that I would never escape unless I found some freedom. But freedom was owning things, and how could I ever own anything when all I owned was myself – and that not for long after my father had sold me? You were never sold, Captain, merely abandoned. But then of course, you were white. Where you lived, there were machines, and rules, and your little chapel sent pennies to heathens, while all we owned eventually was a burro, a cart, and some worthless bits of paper, our title to a silver mine full of shot ore."

"You . . ." he said. He was spluttering. "Your English is perfect, Senhora."

Her smile was frankly amused. If she had not pulled enough rabbits out of the hat, now she produced a horse!

"I am a British citizen. At least, I have a dual nationality."

"Your husband . . ."

"My second husband was also half-English."

He noticed the "was".

He cleared his throat. Enough of this!

"You have got your own life, Senhora."

"Come, Captain. There are questions you want to ask me about your father. I am trying to say that I understand your hurt, what this news meant to you. I do not know what was said in England about his disappearance, but I know what he experienced – or some of it – for he told me."

"I hope you did not discuss this with our owners?" he said hoarsely.

"Oh, they were only interested in profit. It was very clear to me what kind of men they were."

Disreputable, he wanted to say. That he'd included her with them, seemed to have slipped him by in these few seconds.

"You have your flies too!" she smiled.

That was uncanny, the way she seemed to read his thoughts. He would never forget that phrase. Someone had once said, the only gift of God in South America was flies. Perhaps she really had seen through Belasco? Then who was using whom? And there was another thing. She seemed to know so much about him. Everything she said about her own father could have applied to his, he sensed. That was uncanny too. Oh, it was a deep matter.

He shifted his immense bulk in his chair and looked away from

70

her. He remained on his guard. She was the kind of woman who sucked you dry, he thought. Baggage! Well, he wasn't having any of it. Coming in here in that heat . . . She was lucky to find him clothed.

But suddenly, like a shadow cast from the back of his memory, he felt the dryness of Beatrice Trevoake and again had an insight into where his future might have lain. Beatrice with her stiff unbending spinster's air, the very whiteness of her skin, her forbidding aura – even at twenty-three. Her whole attitude added up to a procession of dont's! Hers was a world of rules, all right, rules and obligations, formalities, cautions, and after three years with the ring on her finger she was as stiff as a board with him. And she made him feel so damned clumsy and awkward. Then there was the total blanket disapproval of her parents, he was sure. He knew well enough that her sisters laughed at him openly. She was the ungainly one, but put him beside her, she looked like a ballerina! They'd actually said that in his earshot. "If he is going to sit on a chair, you'd better insure it!" Her mother's interruptions in that drawing room were not so much for her daughter's virtue as for the well-being of the sofa. And her father – well on the way to being a civic dignitary – well, he was only an apron's length from the sawdusted floor, a groveller born. If his stringy daughter hadn't been so tall, they probably wouldn't have received him into the house at all! Why on earth had he never thought of that? And if she really had put herself out on his behalf with her employer, why in all the years since they'd known each other, did Henry Chauncey-Vernon have to wait so long to make any kind of offer at all? The fact was, he was sure, she'd hardly said a word to her employer and so there was no question of disloyalty now, despite the memory of that forlorn figure on the dock wall. So then . . . the doldrums . . . he'd at last read Beatrice's number, he thought, and seen through all of them. They must have thought him a prize idiot. One thing that had happened since he'd cleared the land was that he'd quit the Trevoakes for good and all. He was no longer bespoke. It was as if distance gave clarity to his thoughts on the land and land-bound problems.

But where did that get him on board? Careful . . .

The sweat seemed to be rolling out of his eyes. All right, baggage, perhaps I do owe you something. He looked at her again.

But her eyes were too soft for the harshness of his feelings. One thing he had learned and that directly concerned her. She was a different woman away from Belasco. Maybe a half of what she said was true. Whether it was, or not, it didn't matter provided they got a cargo home. As for his father, he would meet that when it came. He'd been a fool to brood. Why didn't he have some fun with her? By God, he'd remember that phrase all his life – a hand under the blanket. He could just see it, hairy and podgy and fingering. He'd like to have seen Beatrice Trevoake's reaction to the phrase itself – never mind the hand! Fourteen, she'd said she was, and a great big buck with his gut swelling over his belt reaching for her in the middle of the night. He was seeing it already and it made him sweat all the more. He'd guessed she was a whore – they were all whores – but when you got down to the nuts and bolts of it, it wasn't pleasant. Brazil, he thought. She'd got some money from somewhere, probably made it in silver – he'd heard there'd been fortunes made. The whole continent was going to be opened up. Railways even. And that meant coal, and ships, more and more ships, and more and more trade. A ship of his own and with a connection, he could set himself up. You only had to raise the capital and make the connection and you were in, and no doubt this was in the owner's minds. Well, if only he could get into it himself. How much better than listening to Beatrice's recitations of Miss Annie S. Swann's homilies from the *Ladies' Home Companion*!

So he gave her a smile, more of a grin really, perhaps the most human expression that had ever come to his face in his whole life. Suddenly he was out for gain, for profit, a fast coin. He felt he had joined the world!

"I have been discourteous, Senhora Felipa."

She shook her head impatiently. This was not what she had come for.

"Your father had moments when he treated me as a human being," she said. "A human being and not a back street whore. It saddens me that I cannot expect the same from his son. He was everything to me. And he was British. In Chile, there are certain licences that are only given to foreigners."

"You mean he was useful to you?"

"Yes, but more than that."

He suddenly did not want definition, not on that score. And she seemed glad he did not ask. Again, he felt a strange closeness to her. An unnatural closeness.

"Then why did he disappear? Why did he never come home?"

72

"He must tell you that himself. Perhaps because there were things he could not face."

"*Me?*" Jack Hannah said. "My mother . . . his responsibilities?"

"Perhaps. And then he had lost his ship remember, or he thought he had lost it."

"Thought? You either lose a ship, or you don't."

"No, Captain Hannah. You and your certainties! Things are not like that. But here we are . . . We are talking. We have achieved something. We are not entirely in the doldrums."

She rose noiselessly, as enigmatic as ever, but suddenly leaned forward and put her hand upon his shoulder and he could feel her coolness. It might have been a nun that touched him, and for no reason that he could discover, he felt ashamed of his boorishness. He looked up into her face as it smiled down upon him, his throat dry once more. It was such a motherly gesture, mother, whore, nun, what next? he thought. He felt his senses quicken. That low persuasive voice, those all-seeing eyes, her own separateness from any woman, or image of any woman he had ever met, forming in his mind and adding to her aloofness. And yet she was suddenly less remote now than previously. There was almost a religious quality to this aloofness as if his torments – and they had never ceased – were understood even before he explained them. It was disturbing to say the least, but what bothered him most was the sense she gave him of his own limitations. She made him feel an ignorant man, half aware of newly perceived mysteries which had never previously troubled him. That there was a gentleness, a quality of feminine experience outside his ken which he had long been aware of without quite being able to define it. What was his life but work and struggle? What did he know of pleasure? He had been brought up on one principle, and he had followed it like a longshoreman's donkey. You must work your fingers to the bone, he had been told, a washerwoman's maxim, but with them all in the family it had always meant showing up the next man, exposing his weakness, demonstrating that the bone was not meant to crack, so you concentrated, first on the next man to be bettered, then the man after that. You had always to prove yourself, always to be available, ready, steady, and first to the mast, first called, first started and last to finish. Otherwise, you were ordinary, one of the crowd, and the man who'd get on was always noticeable in the crowd. He was not therefore a relaxing man, never had been, and theirs was not a relaxing family. So work had been

73

their god, sewn into their blankets, and crocheted in the wall in improving homilies. It was the same on every ship, always the duty to prove himself as witness now, for there was not a job aboard he could not have done better than any man there. If it was strength, he had the strength for it. If it was the capacity to stay awake for days on end, the eyes to remain open in the most merciless of winds, staring unblinking and without fear in his heart at the most menacing of seas, then he had those eyes too. Then he was sober and reliable, careful and cautious, but all dash when the occasion called for it – as fearless as any God-fearing seaman could be. And no tallyman nor broker nor crimp would pull the wool over his eyes either.

So spoke the confidence of youth on the outward voyage. But there were other thoughts as well and he returned glowering to the deprivations of his life.

What did he know of pleasure? he asked himself again. Who touched him, who held him? Wasn't the truth that nothing in his adult memory had ever softened him – nothing? And who cared whether he lived or died? Work your fingers to the bone, he thought. It seemed to be imprinted in his mind, the story of all his past, eerily unearthed now by this strange presence on a windless ocean. Well, he had done that all his life and what pleasure had he had from it save a reluctant hand pressed upon his knee on the grocer's uncomfortable sofa? Fingers to the bone when this one's touch now was as relieving and caressing and as light as a soft breeze upon his immobile shoulder. More than anything his body knew if his mind would not admit it, and he suddenly felt the promise of things to come.

"Trust me," she said. It was the merest whisper.

There was a clattering of footsteps on the companionway outside.

"Captain, sir. If you please . . ."

He heard Evans's voice like a startled shepherd's. The crew had various names for him. They had recently invented another: Evans Bo Peep.

Evans entered, stopped when he saw the Senhora's arm still on his shoulder – perhaps she deliberately kept it there.

"Well?"

"I didn't mean to intrude, sir."

"You are not intruding." At last her arm fell away.

"I think you had better come up, sir. There's a cloud – a kind of haze – weather building up in my opinion. You can smell it and the horizon's darkening."

He rose. She stepped back. Evans looked from one to the other. You could see what he was thinking for his face was a barometer of indecision. What were they all waiting for but a change of weather?

"Very good."

"I thought I ought to warn you, sir."

The light was going already and now Evans was unctuousness personified. Behind them the Senhora smiled like an Indian in the gathering darkness. "Indian! Indian!" He would remember that.

On deck, the hands had noticed the cloud spreading across the sky. It was dense and black. The pig had been off its food all day, and now the fowls huddled up in the corner of their pen as if they were the first to know what was coming. As they looked, they observed a greenish tint to the sky but still that black cloud advanced slowly, obscuring the horizon, and a heavy downpour of rain seemed certain.

Jack Hannah called the two Mates together.

"Mr Waters, I want the square sail got up from the sail locker and rigged over the after hatch. We want to catch any fresh water that's going."

"Sir."

"Then, Mr Evans, I'll have extra gaskets put on the sails and everything moveable secured on deck. Pass the word to the carpenter. Then an extra lashing on the boats."

"Aye aye, sir."

"And you'd better send the lad down to the Senhora's cabin to make everything fast there. We don't know whether there'll be wind, but there'll be water all right. That cloud is full of it."

The Mates went away and the watches were set to work. They were glad of something to do and busied themselves, readily glancing all the while at the advancing pall. Normally, in the doldrums the men went about half naked, but the Senhora's presence had meant a certain restriction, and as Jack Hannah cast his eye over them, he began in the time honoured tradition to whistle for a wind and soon it became apparent that whatever was to happen, was now imminent. Gradually, imperceptibly, the sea began to whiten in colour as the dense black pall bore down upon them. Even the swell seemed to have lessened and Billy Bones who stood in readiness at the wheel had his hands upon the spokes ready to counteract any movement of

75

the rudder. The men, having spread the sail, stood by with the yards squared, ready to haul them on the back stays, but now the silence was eerie as they watched the sky lower itself as it advanced.

It was a frightening experience, this silence, the light lessening all the while, their own stationary position upon the sea evidence of their powerlessness, and all the time the atmosphere was so heavy that it seemed as if the sky itself was exerting a pressure upon the skull and the pressure continued, the darkness inching down upon them so that as each second went by it became more and more difficult to breathe. The heat remained oppressive but now it was clammy and Jack Hannah felt the sweat trickling freely down his body once more, his very muscles fluttering with anticipation. Weather could do this to you, even in this stillness announcing its presence by inducing physical changes in your body. It was at such times as these with the sky lowering that hallucinations were produced, he was sure. Reason seemed a trivial thing when the atmosphere became so oppressive, and no matter how many times you had experienced the doldrums, each such occasion produced the same effect. It was not only in violent weather that you realised that men were small, frail and insignificant, as were the ships they sailed in. Stillness reminded you just as much of all that vastness of water, and when you lost the wind, it was like breath disappearing, as if your reason for being was slipping away from you imperceptibly as you stared and stared into nothingness. You literally became a dead thing, without breath of life, or movement or any sound, save those induced by the lazy banging of inanimate objects as they drifted helplessly along. And when the change came as it would or God help them, there was all the pain of being reborn, manifested now by the anticipatory tautness of his stomach muscles, the twitchings of his calves, the watchful nervous silence of the men and the sudden scuttlings of the livestock who had remained inert for days.

Then suddenly it came, a rending flash of lightning immediately above them, parting the dense black cloud which now surrounded them, a flash without thunder, brilliantly illuminating the stark outline of the limp canvas hanging overhead, thrusting the masts and spars into sharp and stark relief as if a burning torch had been suddenly put behind them and was then immediately whisked away. There followed on this flash – as burning white and eye-damaging as a manganese flare – a rumble of thunder in the distance, out there beyond the immediate enveloping blackness, and then the peals came again and again and more searing flashes of lightning all around and above them so that there was total darkness, and then forks of white light as brilliant as some chemical explosion. These forks were so white and bright that they hurt the eyes and with then came cannonades of thunder skidding along the sky, reverberating and coming back at them as if they were now walled in, one peal following the next, a violent alternating pattern or light, blackness and whiteness, blackness and whiteness, of such an intensity that the peals of thunder added to the impression of both physical and psychological assault. Before, the pressure of the sky had seemed to bear down upon the skull but now it was the turn of the ears to be bombarded and the eyes to be forced open and the senses stunned, but there was still no breath of wind, not one solitary movement. It was as if they were being singled out and squeezed by the elements, boxed in by the darkness, blinded by the vivid flashes, and suddenly on the main yard arm above him, Jack Hannah saw a ball of static lightning form a bluish glow like a halo. It hung there and then rolled along the yard, seeming to cling to it for a moment before flickering and disappearing. These corposants, or St Elmo's fire, came one after the other like ghostly puffs forming on the mastheads, danced away in a frolic on the metal fabric as if they were some strange advance guard inspecting from on high, then disappeared as rapidly as they had come, the forks of lightning still raging and striking and splitting the intense darkness about them. Blacker and blacker it grew, and the flashes did not stop.

They were blue tinged, now lighting up the puffballs with a strange electrical hue, and then the father and mother of all flashes coincided with a loud peal of thunder and the cloud was torn apart and then the rain came, vertically in aimed gouts, compacted into a block of almost cubic dimensions which seemed to be coming at them deliberately with motive and vengeful intent, thousands of gallons falling as if a dam had broken, the slung catchment sail, the tubs and buckets placed about the deck, full to the brim within a minute. That rain hurt, blinded, seared. You felt you could choke in it – if you were not stunned by it – for where there had been little air, now there was none, and you could not see at all. It was not in any way possible to open your eyes to look for'ard and Jack Hannah heard a man cry out in pain, and perhaps then, as it was the severest vertical deluge he had ever experienced, he had one of those rare insights into the ferocity of the elements, an understanding of so

77

many of those unexplained and mysterious disappearances at sea. Had they not had scuppers or exit ports for the water falling on the deck to remove itself, they would have sunk in the same minutes that it took to fill those tubs. As it was, he was up to his knees in water for it went on and on, the barque scarcely moving as the sea remained flat, and now even the monotonous sideways rolling of the ship had stopped for the sea had flattened under the onslaught.

He just stood there, feet braced, head bent, soaked like them all to the skin, stung by the very force of the downpour, and then he heard a laugh beside him and turned, blushing and gaping as he saw the Senhora, her hair uncoiled and sleek as a water rat's against her face, that frail muslin costume now transparent as it clung to her exposed limbs, and she was actually laughing while he stared and stared at her, her body as good as naked before him, the contours of her breasts and nipples – they were raised – as clear as her glistening teeth as she laughed and laughed.

"Madam!' said he. Fortunately, the sailors were midships, but Billy Bones, his head under his arm and crouched over the wheel, was staring at her as at a nymph. "You'd better get below!"

"It is . . . such fun!" she laughed at him.

"Below!"

Like a huge grubby schoolboy, it was all he could do not to point to her crotch, that small black patch as visible as the whites of her eyes.

Then the wind came, first far above them and witnessed in the break in the clouds which seemed to be scudding in a different direction, clouds running like sheep for shelter at a different altitude in a separate world above the masthead and avoiding them altogether. But it did not avoid them for long, and soon a light and steady breeze came from the south-east. In the deluge, Jack Hannah had seen, then lost, the Senhora who had tripped gaily away from him, patting the gaping Billy Bones on the shoulder while he ordered the Mate to form a gang to hand the buckets of fresh water from the spread foresail into the water tanks. It was all go then, but soon came the rippling seas running before the distant wind and marking its progress and the long low swell that finally announced the trade winds. They were on the move at last.

"The trades!" somebody shouted and Flohr, the big speechless German, soaked through like them all, grinned and clapped his hands like a child and then the orders came thick and fast.

"Lee fore brace!"

"Keep the yards off the backstays there!"

"Set all jibs and stay sails."

"Fore and main sheets aft!"

"Sweat up the top sails sheets and halliards. With a will there, lads. Handsomely now . . ."

And so they gathered up way again, hull down for the roaring forties, a bone in the *Whisper*'s teeth once more and the heat gone, the days for flying fish sailors, as they said, the breeze never lessening.

While Evans wrote copiously in his never-ending letter:

After the doldrums, the Captain rejoined us in the saloon.

Chapter Six

It was Tommy Dance, the ship's boy, who first noticed the change in the Captain. About three hundred miles south of the Equator, the ship had come to life again, never lessening her progress forward, maintaining a steady six knots, fair winds and fair weather, cloudless skies meeting them day after day. This was before they changed the fair weather canvas for the storm suit and before Evans started imagining things about the heat of the coal (and before they found out he was right). For Tommy, the entire voyage was an adventure. It was all new to him. The ship was new, the crew were new, the Senhora was new and so was the Captain. And although it was hard – harder than he'd ever imagined – even though he had three brothers at sea and had served his time as a boy on the pilot packets – it was what he wanted. They had a saying in the village, you can't sail home unless you sail away. By it they meant that you must forage for your joys, that comparisons were necessary, that the pleasures of the homecoming must be won by the pains of the leave-taking and the distance run. Well, he was prepared for all that. But there was a further maxim of his father's which he also carried with him and this was simple too. Make yourself glad to be where you are, and not where you wish to be. It was wise advice for trying times and he remembered it. He was anxious to learn, to acquit himself well, to savour the eventual pleasure of walking into the village with a bag over his shoulder a year hence, when they would ask him where he had been and he would reply "all over" in the words of the real blue water men. He had seen the sea in the eyes of his brothers all his life, in their tales and table manners as his mother said. And he had gone to sea with a kind of inevitability to find out for himself. It was the only cure, his father said. (Yes, and a dog will always return to its vomit, his mother added bitterly. She saw the future.)

The Senhora apart – she was an extra! – Tommy's duties had been clearly prescribed by the cook from the outset. He was peggy boy, general dogsbody, the servant of all. In port, he had to scrub out the saloon, clean the cabins and companionway and do as he was bid in the galley, but at sea he had also to turn out with the men as required. As far as the Captain was concerned, he had seemed to require little looking after once the Senhora was aboard, and as far as he understood it, some words had been exchanged between Evans and the cook which meant that the Senhora was an extra priority on his list. He was thus her boy as well as the cook's and so his duties had virtually doubled.

How he had scrubbed that cabin of hers until it shone and shone and then he had helped with the unpacking, lining the drawers of the chest with clean newspaper, no easy task in the coal laden air of the port, and once they had sailed, he it was who regularly served her coffee, her glasses of lime juice, and finally was even allowed to do her washing. This was the lady's maid part of his duties, and to tell the truth, it gave him certain privileges, and if ever the cook was chasing him, he always had her cabin to busy himself with. Of course, there were the chores of the galley, potatoes to be peeled when there were potatoes, salt horsemeat to be hammered into digestibility, the pots and pans to be scoured, the stove kept alight and the endless brewing of the thick coffee which was in demand day and night. But if he wanted a spell-ho, he could always go and find a job to do in the Senhora's cabin.

He was allowed in when she was not there, and when she was, she welcomed his company and encouraged him to talk. What did he know of the Captain, of the two Mates, the carpenter, the sailmaker? Which of the men was the strongest, who amongst them was considered the best seaman? At times, it had seemed as if he were the focus of all information in the ship and he'd at first been embarrassed by the lewd enquiries of the seamen, but they'd worn off once the novelty of her presence had been accepted. The talk of the fo'c'sle was sailor talk anyhow and when he lay there at night, it was the yarn spinning which interested him most, the gossip about the Captain's father, the general revulsion for Evans and all the stories of strange happenings at sea, beginning with Willie Twomallow's account of Captain Matthews's refusal to round the Horn. That was one to savour, that was, and he could actually hear himself recounting it at home. Then there was Harry Grail's account of a mysterious Greek hanging for a crime he did not commit, with lurid details of the execution, and the most bloodthirsty tale of all, a human heart lying pulsating on a poop deck. But of them all on board, Tommy disliked Harry Grail most, more even than Evans who fussed and cavilled and

81

punched his Bible at all of them, given half the chance. Harry Grail's glittering black eyes were embittered and mean. There were no complaints about the man's ability as a seaman – he it was who'd counselled Tommy on the first climb up to the royal yards – 'Don't let go of one rope until you've hold of another!' – and also made sure he'd shinned aloft to windward, but there was, despite his skills, a brooding quality of resentment to the man, a sourness that gave a rough edge to his tongue. He cursed frequently and was a man of two faces, one for the officers and one for the crew, always a dangerous resentful presence whose spirit smouldered like a strange inflammable cargo kept within him.

All these perceptions, Tommy kept to himself. He had got over his seasickness, got over the novelty of the *Whisper*'s motion – she rolled much more than the pilot boat he'd been used to – and once they left the doldrums, he'd felt the sun on his back and he'd seen a change come over the whole ship's company.

First of all, the Captain allowed him a crack at the wheel. It was his first relief from all the domestic tasks of the ship. He'd been set to work scraping the pitch from the deck when the Captain called him over. So far he'd hardly addressed a word to him and Tommy had kept warily out of his way. That ginger beard and immense bulk spelled temper. But now the Captain was all smiles.

"Tommy, come here."

He'd got up from his knees. The deck seemed to have more splinters than timber and his back was aching. The Senhora was there too, seated on a little folding chair before an easel. She was painting and he'd fetched the box of paints and the canvas up for her. He did not know what she was painting but whatever it was, it put her in a good mood. She, too, was all smiles. Billy Bones was at the wheel again. It was warm and breezy. They were just into the trade winds. A perfect day.

"Let the lad get the feel of her," the Captain said. "Keep your eye on the course, son. Just take the strain. Watch she doesn't back."

Bones stood behind him, checking the spokes.

Gingerly, he felt the rounded timbers of the spokes. You could feel the sea and the wind through the wheel. The *Whisper* throbbed like a live thing. Above him the canvas bellowed.

"Don't let her fall off," Bones said. "Brace your feet, son. Get the weight of her."

He knew enough not to put her through the wind, made sure he was relaxed and began to stand his trick with mounting excitement.

Then the Captain told Bones he could have a spell.

Bones looked dubious.

"The lad'll be fine, I'll keep my eye on him."

And so Billy Bones went forward and the ship was his.

It was a tiny moment, but he had such a thrill of pleasure. This was the life. And in the course of an hour the Captain addressed not one word of correction to him. Then it was he noticed that the Captain had eyes only for the Senhora. First he had his back to her, then he leaned against the rail eyeing her. Then when the easel wanted adjusting, he was there in a stride, swinging the large canvas upwards with one hand. You did not need any special eye to know that he was demonstrating his strength all the while they chatted just out of Tommy's earshot. For weeks, they hadn't had a social word out of him, but now he chatted. It was the beginning of a brief time of relaxation it seemed, and when his trick ended and it was time to lay the table in the saloon, he noted that there was an additional duty for him as the Captain called for extra water to wash in. Of course they were not short of water since the deluge, but it soon became obvious that the Captain was taking pains with his appearance. He now wore a suit of white tropical ducks with a coloured neckerchief which made him seem much more youthful. And after the meal was over, he and the Senhora lingered on while Tommy cleared away. This went on for three or four days, the painting sessions, the men put to work for'ard out of earshot, Evans kept busy on the night watches and socialising in the saloon, banter and laughter and even a glass of port one night, and everybody in the ship knew about it. Then the cook used a strange expression which Tommy was to remember all his life.

"You mark my words," the cook said. "He'll be shieking her before we're round the Horn."

But in the general hilarity and good spirits, old Slushy Scuse the cook was the solitary exception. He had not eaten for days and was even off his own delectable cooking; there was a yellowness to his eyes that gave him an even more evil appearance and his muttering increased day by day.

They were about three hundred miles off the coast of South America, to the south of Rio de Janeiro, when they saw the body of an Indian in the water. They did not alter course or make any special commotion, but the current brought this strange brown figure towards them, one arm limply extended amongst a mass of foliage which they had been sighting at intervals for days, always a sign that land was near. The cloudless skies of the southern hemisphere had been constant and the Senhora's painting had continued as had her poop deck chats with the Captain. Now he had begun to look forward to each day. He whistled in the mornings. He paced the deck with a jaunty spring in his step, the weight of the past and the threat of the future temporarily put aside. What the hell, he said to himself, what the hell? His distrust seemed to have melted from the time of sighting what he called her tropic face. When the sun shone, it was different. There are some faces, as he admitted to himself earlier, which grow upon you, in which you read a timelessness, some evidence of a kindred spirit. Whenever he looked at her, she was calm and accepting. He had ceased to think of anything she might have to hide and as the days went by and she was constantly there, he felt that he could not maintain his own distrust. He could not say quite why or how, but her calmness, her very serenity seemed to act like a mirror which had the distressing effect of revealing his own turmoil. He looked into that face and saw his own aggressive plank jaw and aggrieved eyes and chided himself. What had he to complain of? He had his command. Then that reflective face with its daily calm caused him to look back on his own life with a more philosophic examination of his own sense of hurt, the very sparseness of his feelings and the grey landscape of his childhood seeming to slip by in a haze of images which left him with a dulled sensation of being without, a parade of affections missed, all of which had led to the main thread of his life, his total single-minded devotion to work. If he was not exhausted, he was not happy. But now, he had begun to see it in a most un-Victorian way. There was so little pleasure in it. Fingers to the bone was the right phrase, but now he realised that all his efforts were for other people, companies, ships, profits. He was a slave to principle and it had produced its own kind of grubbiness of the spirit, he thought one day. A dangerous thought for a man who had only just been taught to laugh.

And in this reflective frame of mind the Indian appeared, a piece of flotsam upon the sea. The Senhora was painting a little cameo of Billy Bones at the wheel and he lolled beside her at the ship's rail watching her idly, the ship sailing itself as it had done for days, and

84

he was reminded of his father's phrase, "Pigs can sail 'em!" Well, he wouldn't agree with that but he'd been idling like a pig as had the men, for he was allowing them to catch up on their sleep before the Horn. And Bones, now a mandatory figure at the wheel for he was the subject of her composition, had few complaints since she shared her lime juice with him and made constant enquiries as to his welfare. He enjoyed being the centre of attention. "Cap'n in a good mood, and M'lady putting his arms where she wanted them to be!" He was sitting royal in sunshine weather!

But what was it about, Bones? Jack Hannah asked himself. He didn't look like a picture book helmsman. He was small and wiry, but untidy in a flowing shirt three sizes too large for him with spiky hair and a narrowness of feature with sharp darting eyes that reminded you of a benevolent rat, a rat who was quite willing but couldn't quite manage to keep up with the pack. If he looked like anything at all, it was an unsuccessful pedlar.

"He is harum scarum," she said, laughing at him with her eyes once more. As if to say – everything you are not! She'd actually managed quite a good likeness. "He is not a hero to himself, you see."

"And me?"

"You, I think, must always be a hero."

She'd remarked the other day upon his presentation gold watch. "A hero's watch?"

"A watch," he'd said. No more. Well, it worked. You could raise money on it if ever you were strapped!

But she was teasing him. Heroes had roles to play that never left them. And life, in her eyes, was too complicated to have to be continued in one constrained role at the time. You always had to be the same. There was always a limitation on your expectations. How boring to be a hero!

He didn't understand. If she was referring to him – he'd seen a man in the water and gone over the side to get him. It was as simple as that. That there'd been a hell of sea running was immaterial. If something hadn't gone wrong, the man wouldn't have been in the water. And he'd been lucky. Well, he was strong and fit. That he might have been drowned, hadn't occurred to him.

She said, "It is three parts opportunity."

"What is?"

"Heroism."

He didn't think of heroism at all. It was a word which other people applied. His gold watch was for a physical act. It might have been a swimming cup. He shrugged his shoulders and she did not pursue the matter. If she wanted to paint Billy Bones at the wheel in his rags and tatters with his bunion visible and his hair standing up like wire, well, let her. She'd made a mistake with the number of spokes in the wheel, and he'd pointed that out. She was grateful for that.

"Thank you, sir!"

"Get it right."

"And d'you always get everything right?"

"I try to."

"And if you fail?"

"I haven't failed yet."

"When you do, you'll begin to learn."

"For that I'll need a teacher."

Fast talk! How he would have liked Beatrice Trevoake to witness that exchange.

Then the brushwood began to appear on the sea, slicks of driftwood, branches with berries upon them and he watched them with interest. He could just imagine how relieved the old navigators must have been when they saw such signs, especially if they had baked for days on end in the doldrums. Then it was that the sight of the dead Indian, a limp shoulder rising and falling on the water as the body turned, caused another change. He'd seen it first about a hundred yards ahead of them as the patches of brushwood drifted past. He'd been about to give an order when the body rolled and his eye just made out the man's head with a trailing fuzz of long black hair. Seeing his attention caught, she'd joined him at the rail and the body turned, the nose and teeth in the opened mouth discernible despite the work the birds had done on the corpse. It seemed to thread its way past them in the water and he felt her shiver beside him, and he had a sense of her past once more, the mystery of it and the still unexplained things. You did not often see bodies this far out at sea. Perhaps it was in some way entangled with the driftwood and brush so that the fish had not been able to get at it. Perhaps the Indian had been carried out on some raft. They would never know except that the body had been curiously preserved and he was only conscious of her shiver and the fact that she suddenly decided to stop painting. She muttered something in Spanish and turned away.

Normally, he sent for the boy to carry the easel, but now he decided to help her himself. That was the first thing. He'd had to check himself from doing the physical jobs he'd done as a Mate. Evans was not quite up to the work as far as strength went and when they'd changed sails, bending on the Number One suit, a full day's strenuous labour with both watches employed, manhandling every stitch of canvas, it had given him the opportunity to lead by example again. Each new sail was sweated aloft and stretched out above the yard to be ready for instant bending and setting as soon as the old sail was lowered. He'd enjoyed that, racing up the rigging, testing himself, doing the seamen's work much to Evans's disapproval, but he'd felt that old cock of the walk feeling again. Let them see what he could do!

Only Grail had matched him, even earned his compliments, but Grail, avoiding the challenge, merely nodded and went his way. They'd completed all that and continued on their southing, and he'd enjoyed himself. One thing he'd found he did not have as Captain was the temperament to stand aloof. If a thing wanted doing, it was a challenge immediately. That was another thing he'd have to learn, to stand back and assess. But not yet, and when she decided to pack up her easel, it was the most natural thing in the world for him to sweep it all up, canvas, easel, paints and accompany her to her cabin. Evans was asleep as were half the crowd, the rest taking it easy at their caulking under the eyes of Waters who kept the deck. So he went below, following her, and when they reached the silence of the companionway, he could see she was strangely upset. And when they got into the cabin she was crying. He was absolutely mystified.

"What is it?"

She shook her head dumbly, defenceless suddenly and that was a new experience for him, for previously he had always felt himself threatened by her, his own mind moved to a relentless desire to question her, to get at the root of his pain, all the multitudinous questions as to his father's destiny which so obsessed him. Then, this partially abated fear withstood, he had sought to avoid her. She was such a creature of evasions. Even her politeness offended. He was unused to it. Nor had he experience of feminine wiles. And in this querulous, defenceless mood, she made him even more helpless.

The oval of her face was less of a mask than he had ever seen it. She looked older, more worn. She had troubles too, he realised for the first time, for it was a genuine anguish – as to that he would swear. Just the sight of that body turning over in a batch of brushwood on the water, seemed to have added years to her face. And her eyes, normally inscrutable, were haunted now, narrowed like an animal's in pain. He stood there, the great awkward lumbering bulk of him, like a schoolboy clinging to school books. Impulsively, he dropped the easel and caught her arm.

"Felipa?" They had been on first names for a matter of days. "What is it? Tell me?"

His concern was genuine but at the same time, he felt a new power which had daily been growing upon him. He could afford to relax and need not worry so much about her, nor the ship. They were swinging along and her articulateness had ceased to be a threat. His hand remained on her elbow. She did not answer, but turned her face away from him looking stubbornly at the deck, her breasts heaving. Then the sea helped as the cabin door swung shut behind them. He was closer to her than he had ever been and in the confined space, he was concious of her neck persistently bent away from him, her face hidden. Whatever perfume she wore, she must carry in bulk, for he could smell it so strongly that, save for the gentle lift and fall of the deck, you would not think they were in a ship at all. Now he felt his excitement quicken. Her shoulders hunched but he drew her forcibly to face him, while the deck gave a slight lift and her body came against his in a gentle movement that had the most violent results for suddenly, to his amazement, he felt his arms slip around her and she leant against him, first accidentally, then by design and he could feel her softness, a sudden total yielding and lack of spirit, indeed a collapse of whatever defences there had been. She was almost limp and rested her head against his chest so that he could feel her coiled hair slipping under his chin. It was like oiled grass. Still she did not speak, but the effect was electric. He could truthfully say that he had entertained no desire for her at all. She knew too much, dominated too much. She was a damned nuisance, but there she was, another burden to be borne. But he reckoned without flesh, and now there occurred to him a cool thought in the heat of the cabin. What was the matter with him? She was there to be taken.

It was as if in that sudden moment of silence, as unexpected as a squall, the most normal of reactions had come to this haunted man as unexpectedly as an act of charity might occur to a miser. She made him feel dull and boorish. He would not trust her out of his sight. True, they had recently been conversing and that kind of chat was a rare thing for him, but what she had appeared to be, was nothing to do with what she was now. Available, in one word. Defenceless, in another. And for all his puritanism – he was steeped in it – he felt his lust rise. He had drawn her to him. She had not moved away. Why hadn't he seen it before? Again and again, it occurred to him. Her flesh was there to be taken, those thighs to be parted. He was disturbed himself by now – in a second's contact – and he ran his free hand down the small of her back until reaching its extremity, he cupped it clumsily around her buttock. It was as good as an announcement of his intention. There were so many things that bothered him, but of one thing he was suddenly sure. He was not going to leave that cabin a virgin.

His hand had announced his intention. No signals came to counteract it. It was no comradely gesture and now there followed a series of shameful thoughts which would also haunt him later. The body of the unknown Indian had also affected him, and for once he had no scruple, no inhibition, and without quite knowing how or why, there came to him – perhaps with a full consciousness of the occasion as it was for him the first time – the thought that he must not hurry – that she was not going to be rewarded so easily, that he was not going to reveal his innocence, and also that his sense of superiority was not just male, he was also white, no damned Indian, and this very fact gave him a kind of cruel repose. It might belie the gentleness of his behaviour in the last week; it might do him no credit as a God-fearing Christian, but it was very much present in his mind. He was going to master once and for all. She was, after all, only a dago.

And once begun, there was no stopping. There could not be. Feeling the pins in her hair sharp against his jaw, he began to remove them with trembling fingers, dropping them one by one on to the cabin floor until her hair began to uncoil, layer after layer until it fell thickly to her waist, the oil she used sticking to his fingers. She maintained her silence and made no resistance although her breathing, like his, grew heavier. This done, his hands slipping in that hair, he began to remove her blouse, but here the oil on his fingers and the intrusion of some tiny catch defeated him, so he tore away at the offending strap, moving his huge hands down along the soft flesh padding her hips towards the pantaloons and proceeding further. She gave an imperceptible moan, lifted her face in the half darkness, and suddenly his mouth was down against hers, his tongue probing and it was not so much a kiss as a slow continuing blow. She was still

89

half dressed but she came up to him completely, her bare foot completing what his clumsy fingers had failed to do. Now, in the rush of blood to his very scalp, he felt her fingers knot at the hairs on his chest while the other hand sought his neck and further provoked, he seized her suddenly and lifted her bodily, dumping her on the bunk so that she was crouched and staring at him while he simply moved his hand and unbuttoned himself. Not a word was spoken, and, determined now, he suddenly drove her thighs apart with his knee, grunting as he did so, slightly amazed at her assistance, entering her, his hand greedily reaching for her buttocks as he felt himself begin what he thought of as an attack. In that frenzy of movement, her mouth, first imprisoned, slipped away from his, but only for her teeth to bite at his shoulder as she sobbed and panted, her acquiescence total. He could feel her hair in his mouth, the pressure of her thighs, her lifted, scissoring legs, and then the release came wetly with such an upsurge of emotion that he was moaning himself and he lay full upon her until, victor in the end, receiving a darting series of kisses as she held him by the hair, showing a softness and delight on her part which he simply did not understand. He had not removed his belt, the buckle had bruised her. Yet she made no complaint and smiled at him mysteriously in the darkness, one hand smoothly and playfully caressing his ear as if she could not have enough of him.

Shieked at last, he thought. It was a sailor's phrase for a sailor-made occasion. The only thing he needed now, was the latitude and longitude of it! By God, he'd half a mind to put it in the log!

He was still conscious of her flesh and the lack of embarrassment as she lay open-legged, her head back against the bulkhead, smiling at him in the darkness. There were so many surprises, the hair on her body, the blood-drawing bite, the moist wetness of the woman, her hand eager to help, the all embracing quim. He had still not lost the eagerness to explore and cupped his hand proprietorially at her full breast, noting the whiteness of her teeth in the darkness. Her nipples had come up like little stalks but whatever had disturbed her had gone, drifted by like the body of that nameless Indian. Well, here was another he thought, doing up his fly. He felt light-headed, but bursting with confidence. He would have imagined guilt, remorse, pangs of conscience, an awareness perhaps that he might have done something which would compromise his authority as Captain. You could do nothing on a ship without someone finding out. Ships were worse than streets, full of prying neighbours. Every dropped hairpin told a story. But not a bit of it, he did not bother himself. He chuckled. Plans formed. Next time he would shiek her standing up. He liked the warm feel of those strong thighs. And there was more room in his cabin. And the devil take the consequences! From now on, he could not leave her alone.

Look at her! That coconut oil. She was never English. There wasn't a word said. Not a tear in sight, not a morsel of regret on her face. Ships were the place for shicking all right. The gear was stronger. You could take a purchase with your feet. Even the sea helped, rolling you on. And she liked it coming at her hard, that was a good thing. And didn't make him beg. She knew, in short, who was boss. He had never felt better in his life. Hi ho, Rolly!

"Well, then," he said. "Well, then . . ."

No answer.

"Tonight," he said. "When the watches have changed. In my cabin. And leave that oil off. Can't get a purchase!"

She smiled. "Master", he half expected her to say, or "Mastel" as the Chinese girls did, calling after you in the streets. You heard them once, you never forgot those gleaming eyes in the dark. "Mastel, Mastel, you want short time! Me got sharp teeth."

But she said nothing, smiled wet mouthed and wet eyes. Well and truly shieked, he thought again. He felt not the slightest alarm and did not want to leave, amazed at the suddenness of the event. The no-talking bit was the best thing, no politics, no God-stuff, this was one you could shiek without any sense of responsibility, and fast too, a pier head jump wasn't in it. Perhaps it was her colour that led to everything. The tarbrush was all bonus. He did not realise they were so hairy. And it was the first time he'd seen her sweat. His, he thought, his for the taking. His sweat and her sweat: fusion.

He nodded, and left and did not see her stretch herself luxuriously as the door closed. No one, not anyone on board had any idea as to the true nature of her thoughts.

"Full and by," he said on deck. Shieking, he thought. Yes, siree! You would think he had invented it!

Mr Waters noticed the heat of the deck beside the forward hatch first. It was greater than you would expect even in the tropics. He began to pad about bare-footed, testing it gingerly with the soles of his feet. Evans noticed him and joined him.

91

"Overheating," Evans said. "Some of that coal was damp when we loaded it. It couldn't be avoided."

He feared the dangers of spontaneous combustion. In an iron ship, a cargo on fire could be battened down for weeks and ships had been known to make port with their sides red hot, plating buckled and paint blistered, but a wooden ship was different. Once the fire really got a hold, there was no stopping it and immediately their main concern was to test for smoke and take the temperature of the coal. Usually, the main centre of heat was confined to a relatively small area and if they were lucky, the coal could be taken out and cooled. They could also pour water in, but then it had to be pumped out. There was a choice. Either they could close all ventilation with the aim of smothering the fire and then making a nearby port, or open the hatches, dig the coal out and cool it along the decks.

"If we take the hatch off, the air could fire it at once." Evans said.

"There's no smoke," Waters said. "It's just hot."

"A matter for the Captain," Evans said. He shook his head gravely.

But the Captain was entertaining and his closed door was like a blow in the face to Evans.

"Captain, sir? If you please . . ."

"Who's there?"

"It's your Chief Officer."

"Oh, what is it, Evans?"

Evans could hear laughter, a smothered giggle. He flushed. His lantern jaw dropped, a heavy brooding sulkiness coming over him. This came into the category of goings-on. And what else could you expect of Jack Hannah's son? He'll have to be watched very closely, the owners had said. 'He is not a man we would normally employ.' Then the laugh came again, a rich fruity laugh and he knew it was the Senhora's. She'd hardly spoken to him for days. He'd changed his opinion now. In the saloon, she had eyes only for the Captain. He'd noticed how she could not stop touching his chair and on the poop deck she hung around him like a nurse. Now Evans hardly bothered to shut the crew up when they broke into their Sally Brown's or Seraphinas. And the Captain scarcely had two words for anyone. The doldrums had done it. And those rounded limbs. You should never take a woman on a ship. Sure enough, once the fine weather had set in, slackness followed it like fog. And now they were laughing at him behind the door. He put his mouth down to the keyhole: the indignity of it! (That night his letter would progress into a volume!)

"The safety of the ship, sir," said Evans primly.

"Has the wind shifted?"

"The deck is hot, sir. By Number One hatch."

"Is there smoke?"

"No, sir, but . . ."

"Stand on it until you see smoke."

"But, sir?"

"Smoke you understand? Then tell me."

Evans went away.

"Well?" Waters said.

"The Captain is entertaining," Evans said again.

Waters grinned.

"Well, there's no smoke."

"Most improper," Evans said.

Harry Grail had noticed their concern. You can keep nothing secret in a ship. He hovered about them, his immense arms crossed, eyes watching every movement. He'd been in ships which had caught on fire before, but he said nothing, merely studied their faces, then went away, shoulders hunched, a small ball of animosity. He had eyes for the other too, had lost no opportunity to cross-examine Bones. He even knew how little she wore underneath those gypsy's pantaloons, and he'd also seen the body of the Indian. Nothing escaped Harry Grail.

In the fo'c'sle, he said, "Carrot-top's getting his oats."

"Seraphina's getting hers more like. I bet you could drive a horse and cart up hers."

Harry Grail felt the bulkhead.

"What are you doing that for?"

"It's hot."

"Course, it's hot."

"We'll be shovelling tomorrow. You wait!"

"Not me," said Billy Bones. "It'll spoil my appearance for the painting!"

And they laughed at that. Nothing wrong with this voyage.

"You mark my words," Harry Grail said. "This'll be another one like the *Avalon*."

"Gerraway! They aint no Greeks on board. Go on, show *us* your bleeding heart!"

Lying beside her – it was the third day now since the tumultuous event in her cabin – Jack Hannah listened to Evans's voice as if it had arrived in a dream. He was gone on her, potty on her, couldn't get enough of her. Her face seemed to swim before him like a face from some dimly remembered religious picture. When he was with her, he could not take his eyes off her and when she was not there, he began to catalogue her features, bone by bone. Perhaps he liked those high cheek-bones best, or the laziness of those dark eyes beneath their heavy lids. Perhaps it was the very heaviness of those breasts, the feel of her, those cupped buttocks straining beneath him. Her eagerness had come as a total shock. Everything he'd heard had led him to believe they did not like it, that it was dirty, an act of revenge, but she merely smiled at him, approved his desire, silently urged him on. And she seemed to have lost the capacity for speech. There were no more questions for the moment, just the wonder of discovery. She was the only person he had ever met who did not make him feel clumsy. She had a way of holding his shoulders when they embraced, balancing on her toes, gently moving her body so that it could drive him into a frenzy. And afterwards, she was all softness. He knew what yielding flesh meant for the first time in his life and although he had probably spoken more to her than any woman, he was very conscious of his inarticulateness.

He wanted to show her that he was capable of great tenderness – he had discovered that. But now he was struck dumb by another thought. Within three days, he knew he never wanted her to leave. He could hardly believe it, but it was true. Down in her cabin, it had been the joy of conquest, a battle won. But in his cabin, he had discovered there was no battle. And she made him feel ashamed of his selfishness. She was so womanly. Experienced, of course – he remembered the two husbands – but somehow it didn't matter. It didn't make any difference to his wanting to touch her all the time, and that he could not stop doing, but there was more yet again and it was in his own mind, a pressure building up that seemed to shame him because he could give no expression to it. Perhaps the real shock had come with her acquiescence, her very willingness to be taken as take her he did, eight, nine, ten times. But it was not enough suddenly and the pleasure of it wore off. He wanted then to find new words, some way to explain this new feeling. He did not even say thank you. He said nothing. He beckoned. She came. From being a forbidding woman of my story with an ever present shiftiness and whose every sentence seemed to have been rehearsed, all part of a vast but undisclosed confidence trick, she had become mute, and that he did not understand. It was as if she was three persons, the baggage wearing a hat and looking down upon him, laughing at him, a creature of witticisms and politeness, and then there was the dancing mistress, talking about his father, the madame who said he avoided her – that was the doldrums lady with her startling admissions, the husband whose podgy hand reached for her under the blanket. But then again, there was this new silent woman, the Indian whose hands were gentle, swift and sure, and totally knowledgeable – they knew exactly where to move along his body – and it was this woman who said not a word, the one who left him with a sense of his own deficiences which he'd never had before in his life. And that was the mystery.

He also despaired of what was happening to him for he could not describe it, nor control it, and his very inarticulateness now seemed shameful. He was a lesser man already – in the space of three days. Propriety had gone, innocence had gone, his guard was down, and yet he still retained a sense of foolishness when he was not with her for then he felt the great ginger oaf again. First, she made him feel so sure of himself, and then left him empty and drained, worrying about an inadequacy that had never previously occurred to him. It was perhaps a first dawning of the fact that he was incapable of love. He was the robber, the confidence trickster, not her. And that struck him dumb too, a sad thought which finally drove him from his cabin, leaving her still mute and smiling on his bunk, turning her back to him finally as if she herself had discovered another world in the silence between mutual desire, creating an even more secretive world whose mysteries added to all the other things he did not know about her.

They'd had three days, he thought. Perhaps it was too much, too intense, too sudden. It did not occur to him as possible that it was all they would have.

He said: "I'll go and see what Evans is worrying about. You'd better confine yourself to your cabin for a while."

But even a brief leave-taking was not simple. He must stay away from her and he wanted to see her with her guard up again – perhaps in order to break it down, he did not know. Suddenly, from being a straightforward, single-minded young man with a clear view of everything that affected himself, he was full of complexities. With all the satisfactions of the predatory male, he'd thought he'd conquered

95

but within hours he knew it was nothing, that was the incredible thing. It made him blink with embarrassment. And now the world outside that cabin was making its dingy presence felt. He'd have to lie to Evans. Tell him he was having his portrait painted. But perhaps he wouldn't bother.

"There," Evans said, pointing to the deck. "It's hot at night. That's what drew my attention to it. Other parts cool when the sun goes down."

"No smoke?"

"No, sir. I've been watching it very carefully."

"Hm . . ." He remembered Evans's parrot answers to his questions on the stowage of combustible cargoes. Still, Evans couldn't help the rain. Some of the cargo had eventually been loaded wet and had overheated. He came to a decision.

"Rouse the watches."

"Now sir?" The light was fading.

"If there's any glow, we'll see it in the dark. We'll need lamps, baskets and shovels. We'll get at the centre of it and heave it up in baskets."

Evans winced.

"You could fan a flame, sir."

"I could, Mr Evans, but that's a risk we'll have to take. Another's that the weather won't hold. I want every lump out of the centre washed down and cooled. You can rig a gyn over the hatch and we'll split up into parties, eight men down to shovel and six up here to souse it. But first we'll get the hatch off."

"All hands then?"

"Yes. I'll go down myself with the first party. It'll keep their tongues quiet."

They removed the canvas tarpaulin and took the hatch covers off one by one. He could feel the heat at once, but there was no tell-tale glow, nor any explosion. Once the hands were roused, he led the digging himself, making a platform for the others, and this was the real surprise of the voyage to the men, to see the Captain grafting, coal-heaving with the crowd. They had never heard of it before and the sight of that immense back – he soon stripped off – bending and heaving as they filled the baskets and brought the coal up on deck with the cargo gyn rigged to the mainstay, was so unusual that they worked without complaining. They worked in pairs, all stripped to the waist, each basket being hooked to a gantline when full while another gang of men on deck ran along with the hauling line until the baskets were lifted up and then emptied along the decks into piles of coal which were then doused with water by the Mate. Then the gangs changed round, each party taking a turn in the steaming fume-ridden hold where the air was soon thick with coal dust. They were fortunate that there was no real fire, just over-heating, and for safety they poured hundreds of buckets of water down the hold, and then pumped it out again. They washed all night and half the next day and all the time the Captain led them, doing the work of two, his jaw clicking and grunting with effort as he shovelled and shovelled, saying little, barely recognisable save for his bulk. At the last, it was his own immense stamina that drew complaints.

"Because 'e is a horse of a man, he expects me to do as 'e do do," said Morgan Morgan.

But for the most part, they admired him and fell to work with a will. This was a man you could follow, not like old Green Pole Evans, farting about with the water buckets like a milkmaid.

"Looking like a collier, he was, boys. I never seen a captain work like that before."

And there was general approval. This time they were lucky, Harry Grail said, lucky they'd caught it in time. While Evans confessed his private thoughts to paper:

My own view was that he was punishing his body for the evil there was in it. He worked until the early hours down the hold and Purgatory itself could not be better recreated with the fumes and the swearing and the very heat that I had myself noticed earlier. I asked him several times to take a spell and while I perceived the dangers to the ship if the wind changed or weather got up, there was no reason in his so exhausting himself. It was not simply a matter of setting an example. A ship's officer is not a coal heaver, but in mixing so freely with the men in these conditions, he was further separating himself from the time honoured traditions of the sea which require the Captain to stand aloof. It also weakened my own position, seamen being what they are, and remarks were addressed to Mr Waters and myself that verged on the familiar since we were not ourselves blackened. However, watching him, I formed the opinion I have stated, that he had done something disgusting to his own body and wanted in some way to castigate it. At any rate, he worked himself into a state of exhaustion and Mr Waters and myself kept the deck for two days and nights following.

As to his behaviour off Cape Horn, there are entries in the log-book which speak for themselves . . .

Chapter Seven

LOG OF THE BARQUE WHISPER OF SVEYNTON.
Jack Hannah, Master.
Sunday 12 January:
56°37'. 67°28'. Heavy squalls. SW with heavy sea. 10 p.m. Wind
drew round to S. Wore ship. 10.30 p.m. Very heavy squalls from
SW. Ship plunging heavily into WSW sea.
Monday 13 January:
56°14'. 67°47'. 9 a.m. Cape Horn N by E. Diego Ramurez visible
in the WSW from aloft. Variable winds from NE to ESE.
Strong and dirty with heavy seas. Bar falling rapidly. Cannot carry
canvas against SW sea. The force of the wind so great that the ocean
smoked. A violent squall passed over the ship at 7.30 p.m., when a
meteor about the size of a man's head burst at the masthead like a large
rocket, came down mainmast and passed off to leeward.
Galley swamped 8.30 p.m. No fire possible. Hove to. Later relit fire.
Treated Samuel Scuse, cook, for constipation as per medical guide.

His eyes now red-rimmed with exhaustion, Jack Hannah gave his
mind to the problem of the cook only after fifteen days of the most
violent weather imaginable. He had been round the Horn six times
previously but never had the winds been more from the north of
west than the south of it. This meant that he'd put the *Whisper* under
short canvas hoping for a slant to set her on her course. But she kept
on making leeway and day after day went by without making
progress. Daily, hourly, he'd scanned the sky for a shift of wind, the
slightest clearing or movement of rising cloud, ever ready to wear
ship the moment it would pay, ready to get sail off in time and to put
it back on again, but the slant never came and try as he might to sail
into the teeth of the wind, he could never keep sufficient sail on to
keep the *Whisper* moving. Far to the south, there were dangers
enough, but the oceanic weight of waters between the two oceans of
the Pacific and the Atlantic whipped by winds into waves up to sixty
feet high meant that it was impossible to meet them head on, and on

either tack the roll of the ship was alarming. Now the spreading hills of water loomed up in mountainous walls, jerking the ship into the troughs while the wind whimpered, then howled, then raged, so that they could not face it and when the squalls broke the surface of the water in the distance was churned up into an appalling whiteness as the sea seethed in a madness of spume.

Time and again Jack Hannah had called to the helmsman, "Hard up! Lee forebrace!" as the seamen moved at the run to the braces to haul the yards around and there they were hanging on by their eyebrows, the lee rail well under, up to their waists in a flood of water as it poured over the rail. In the eerie half-light, he could often see mountains of water surging towards the ship, their crests foaming white and smoking, matching the height of the masts as they rolled, squall following squall in rapid succession, and they were shaken from stem to stern, rolling all the while, rolling rolling in a never ending hubbub of motion. The Senhora had disappeared to her cabin with the first violence, and Tommy Dance was kept below to attend to her, both lost from sight and mind as the weather increased in fury. Jack Hannah persisted in trying to sail to westward, although the ship became almost unmanageable, drifting idly, then carried to leeward by the current when the rolling got worse and worse, and when he saw an albatross swooping down upon them and, after a disdainful inspection, swoop away effortlessly on their desired course, he felt the ship's impotence more keenly. Day after day they kept at it, rounding Cape Horn twice, but going forwards and backwards, and still they tried again but the drift to leeward continued. But still he kept looking for a slant and although their exhaustion was increasing hourly, he was far from spent. The only way to beat the Horn was to keep attacking, to punch the wind, and although they lay for days virtually hove to, he never stopped looking for the slant that he knew must come. It was an act of faith. Already, the fo'c'sle was awash with water and had remained so for days. With every sea that broke on board more water entered until there was not a dry shirt or guernsey in the ship. Pillows, blankets, mattresses were soaked, the bogey stove went out, men slept in their sodden clothes in damp blankets, their wrists sore with the chafing of their oilskins, not a man without a salt water boil where their oilskin cuffs rubbed, and although they kept the galley stove going at first and there remained a daily hot meal, the cold, the weariness, the sullen, never-ending lurching of the ship began to dampen spirits and Evans was already advising a change of course, stating that they should put back for shelter to Port Stanley. But Jack Hannah kept on. The slant must come.

After the sight of the meteor and with the galley washed out, Evans drew his attention to the cook who had been picked out of the scuppers in a semi-conscious condition, and between them they brought him to the Captain's cabin. It too was a mass of debris as lashings had carried away, but there was some respite from the wind and once they got the cook laid upon the bunk it was apparent that the man's condition was serious. He was an unlovely fellow at the best of times for thick clusters of warts hung from his neck and chin, but his figure now seemed frail and the unnatural yellowness of his eyes and general sallow complexion indicated some long-standing internal complaint. They'd got Tommy Dance to help undress him, and Evans and the boy stood back as the Captain began to remove the soaking trousers and the coarse Welsh flannel shirt. Scuse moaned with his eyes closed and it soon became obvious that he was no lover of fresh water for the body stench came off him pungently. More disturbing still, however, was the distended belly. Beside it, his limbs were thin and emaciated and, suspecting appendicitis, Jack Hannah felt gingerly in the SSW corner of the abdomen, bracing his feet all the while against the constant rolling of the ship.

Little Tommy Dance watched, his eyes bright with apprehension while Evans stood there swaying, his face grave and nostrils wrinkling at the smell. The stomach was as hard as rock.

"How long has he been like this?"

"I only recently noticed his skin," Evans said.

"The man's emaciated."

"He never eats much, sir," Tommy said, "and when he drinks, he can't keep it down."

The Captain pressed gently around the stomach. Scuse groaned.

"He's clogged, sir," Tommy blurted out.

"There's a spirit stove there. Get a kettle and boil some water. Then we'll want some soap," Jack Hannah said.

Part of being a ship's master was being doctor and housewife, and Jack Hannah had the rough and ready knowledge of practical experience. Men were never medically examined before signing on. By tradition, all unwell sailors were dead men as illness was a luxury no ship could afford. However, he'd watched his past captains set many a fracture with improvised splints and had once assisted at an amputation, a knife and poker job which marked the ship-board limits of surgery. But for constipation of this extremity, he had no experience. There was a bottle of castor oil in the chest but the man could keep nothing down. Very well, they must pump warm soapy water into him. There was nothing else for it.

Evans was again hesitant.

"The intestines are not to be lightly interfered with, sir."

That was Evans. Life itself was not to be lightly interfered with! A touch of the Beatrice Trevoakes in that answer!

"The man is dying."

"Perhaps it is the will of God."

No, he was not going to take that let-out.

"Bring me the paraffin tube and turn him over."

They got their slant before the operation was finished, however. Scuse began by vomiting and groaning in abject misery, and the Captain, hearing Waters cry from deck, hurried to don his oilskins, leaving the casualty to Evans. A disturbing rumbling of sound came from the cook's stomach and he had Evans keep him warm and dry and told him to stay with him. The cook's deathly yellow colour had not changed, but short of surgery, there was nothing he could do, and now the progress of the ship took priority and he went hopefully up on deck, glad to be rid of the fetid air of the cabin. Waters met him with the news that the wind had shifted to the north-east. It was necessary to wear ship. At last, they could stab in the right direction, but putting about meant raising a repaired lower topsail, and the task of bending the repaired sail marked the first casualty of the voyage. All hands were summoned and carried the sail along the main deck to the lee side, and they then hoisted it aloft. But when the sail was spread out along the yard and the sail made fast to the jackstay, Jackie Breeze, the three fingered sailor was caught looking elsewhere as the ship crawled into a sudden trough and suddenly lost his footing. Slowly, imperceptibly, with an amazed look of incredulity upon his thick browed face, he was detached from the mast with hand out-stretched and then fell silently and without a cry, his body as graceful and composed as a diver's as he was pitched by the motion of the ship directly into the sea. Jack Hannah did not see him go, but Mr Waters gave a choked cry, high-pitched and childish, hardly like a seaman's cry at all.

"Man over, sir. Starboard!"

Harry Grail started as he stood beside Jack Hannah, and darted to

101

the weather rail, but even in the brief change of wind, the seas had not abated and the rollers astern towered above the stern rail like the assembling faces of a rapid succession of cliffs, each one raising up and presenting itself at an implacable height, becalming the mizzen sail for a few seconds while the stern dropped into the trough of the sea. Out of the corner of his eye as he followed Waters's outstretched hand, Jack Hannah saw Breeze surface momentarily as the wave caught him and swept him up to its crest, his deformed hand rising for a second in a mocking and half ironic gesture as he mounted the crest, then to disappear for ever as the *Whisper* maintained her course, even her reduced canvas taking her away, upwards and downwards before the continuing and ever-following seas. The momentary glimpse of that raised hand was all they would see again of their shipmate. There was nothing that could be done, and all aboard knew it for no movement of the sails, nor the lowering of a boat was possible in time for any successful rescue. Even had they a boat suitable, by the time they had gone about and lowered it, the search would have been hopeless since their visibility was by courtesy of the sea and dependent on the unlikely circumstance of both searchers and rescued rising to the thirty foot crests at precisely the same time. And a boat could scarcely have lived in that sea, even had they the men to handle it. Jack Hannah would not order it, nor would he have gone himself. This was Cape Horn, and when he had advised a hand for yourself and a hand for the ship, it was not a joke. Poor Breeze had failed in one or the other, but the irony was that they had come this far, and experienced much more violent seas and winds without mishap, and so his death, sudden and without warning, was one of those incidents of a ship in passage that had neither rhyme nor reason, a single soul slipping away from them by some unknown act of carelessness with no blame attaching to anyone save poor Breeze himself, and Jack Hannah took his eyes away from the soon vanished figure without a single exclamation. There was nothing meaningful that could be said.

"Standby the weather fore braces!" he called, his mind healthily busy at once as he scanned the seas for a break, a smooth interval when he could wear the ship. He was looking for a wave of abnormal size, one which towered above the others and made its approach visible from a distance when a valley amidst the seas would be followed by a plain of smooth water which he hoped would last long enough for him to change course. When it came, his voice was unnaturally harsh. One man lost was not uncommon, but it was still a death.

"Hard up the helm! Haul away weather fore brace! Lively now! With a will there, lads!"

Now with topsail set, the ship paid off before the wind and began to make progress. The danger was that the ship would be struck as she was brought before the wind when they would all fall back into the trough of the next wave and lie before it helpless. Then the sea would take charge as it ever threatened to do, but the moment of danger passed, and at last they came smartly up to their desired course, and after all those days of endless beating, it was as if the loss of poor Breeze was a token offering accepted by the sea, a gift which was repaid by their instant progress on the new course. The sea never gave without taking. Having taken, it relented.

But the faces of the men acknowledged no such homage. They were those reflective stares which, together with their silence, were proof of their concern, an unspoken bond with the dead man whose death was the first reminder of the uncertainty of every life. They were good seamen and were not yet critical, there was no blame that could be attached to anyone. In silence he had fallen and in silence they mourned him, each man's thoughts in that moment, private and unknown.

"A good lad, Breeze," Mr Waters said. "Cheerful as they come."

It was his sole epitaph. Jack Hannah grunted wearily. Had the man's grip failed? Was he himself in some way to blame for signing a partially crippled man? He did not think so. The man had been eager to come. Ashore, goodness knows what awaited him, unemployment, poverty and disease most likely. Three fingers or no, the sea was his trade until his last breath and now the sea had claimed him. He hoped he had been wise enough not to try to swim and that the struggle for life was soon exhausted. Perhaps that hand raised in ironic salute said all things to all men, a last courageous act in an unknown life which had known little but toil or squalor. Perhaps it said everything. Or nothing.

"Three fingers," Jack Hannah said. It was the three-fingered hand which was raised, he was sure. You offered the sea a weakness, the sea took advantage. "I'll need you to witness the entry in the log."

"Aye, sir. There was nothing you could do."

"I didn't mean that. I know that."

Mr Waters moved away.

Down below in the cabin, Evans had a sorrier tale to tell. The cook had suffered what seemed like a stroke.

"A spasm took him. Just as we went about."

Scuse's eyes were closed, a dribble of green bile colouring the corner of his mouth. His breathing was faint and his skin even yellower. The injection of soapy water had not worked.

"Jaundiced," said the Captain. Well, there was nothing further to be done. "Put him in the Senhora's cabin."

"The Senhora?" Evans's face was a mask of disapproval.

"She can move in here. Keep him warm and lash him to the bunk. There's nothing further we can do."

"Some stimulants, perhaps?"

"You said it yourself, Mr Evans. He can't keep anything down."

Jack Hannah just wanted the man out of the way. Better to die as Breeze had died, suddenly and violently, than to degenerate into this corpse-like state.

"Get a man to help you carry him, and sew him in his blankets."

"He's not dead yet, sir."

"He soon will be."

Grail came into the cabin, arms akimbo, eyes glittering, and picked up the thin emaciated body as if it were a child's. The cook's eyes opened once, then closed.

"We've done everything we can."

Grail made no answer, and went out, Evans following, with Tommy Dance whose eyes were tearful, overflowing as he left. The cook was the kindest man on the ship. Then the Senhora came, proposed hot poultices, some relief of pain. The Captain shrugged his shoulders.

"Thank you," he said.

But the cook died within a day, never opening his eyes, nor speaking again, and then they passed the Horn.

"You can bury him, Mr Evans," Jack Hannah felt sickened suddenly.

"But, sir?"

"I've no appetite for it."

And so it was that as the weather cleared and the rockbound lee shore of Tierra del Fuego slipped further behind them and they ran into oily swells once more with albatrosses and mollymawks soaring above them, that Evans's words about the sure and certain hope of

104

resurrection remained in Jack Hannah's mind. Two men dead and gone, but at last the *Whisper* made her northing and soon they were in the Pacific Ocean at last while Jack Hannah began to brood once more. Turn and turn about, he thought. Already, the voyage was beginning to daunt him. Two men dead, but it was none of his doing. And as for the Senhora, she'd stayed in his cabin after the cook died and they continued to cohabit as if they had assumed a married state. He knew the men were talking openly and his allowing Evans to read the burial service was a further slip. Something had changed in him, he knew, a weariness had set in, casting its own Cape Horn blight upon the man of ambition and purpose who had left Sveynton all those months before. It was as if the voyage, like life itself, had followed a course through time, and now, here he was, suddenly dropped into a doldrums of the spirit with neither energy nor will to shift himself. Why was he brooding? On what was he brooding? And what had caused the change?

He sought to define his predicament. Worst of all, it was as if he had suddenly aged himself, moved into a darkness of black depression which would not leave him. For the first time in his life and for no single reason he felt himself a mortal man and was uniquely conscious of alternatives to every decision. There were evasions now, even in his own thinking, and with the sailing of the ship made easier he began to brood again, beginning on a course of behaviour which Evans noted with a spark of recognition. Evans had sailed these waters before long ago as a young apprentice and encountered precisely similar moods in Joshua Hannah, Captain of the *Coquimbo*.

Evans addressed himself to paper. He believed in paper. On paper, he could let himself go and his words survive to this day:

He does not speak in the day and is already handing over certain of the Captain's responsibilities to others. He left the reading of the burial service to me, and also the matter of choosing a new cook. I recommended Bones, the able seaman, who is a cheerful enough man, a wise choice, I thought, since his constant companion and friend is the German Flohr who is big enough to silence any criticism. The poultry is used up and the livestock washed over and we are now on half rations and the excellence of the fare on the voyage out was at a price – the price of using up stores at an alarming rate. However when I suggested Bones as cook, the Captain stated that the Senhora needed him as a model for her art work – this in a seagoing ship! He would not agree to my suggestion, nor listen to it, so I rated Morgan with misgivings

since I am sorry to say that he is not very clean in his personal habits.
However, as far as the Captain is concerned, as soon as we left the doldrums
it seemed to me that he was a haunted man and I was reminded of the
behaviour of his father who began on the voyage of the Coquimbo *as if he*
were the crack Master on the list, and ended it gibbering into a bottle. After
Cape Horn a strain of melancholia came upon the Captain which even the
highly immoral presence of the Senhora in his cabin failed to lessen. She
remarked once in jest that she was his nurse, and my own view even then was
that she was nearer to the truth than she realised.

So Evans wrote. Nightly, he pondered upon the relationship,
keeping his distance, a brisk and efficient and different man himself
in warmer latitudes, and now he assumed a new cheerfulness. Oh! he
had seen it all, captains without a blemish on their characters who
suddenly cracked and went into themselves. Some would, by their
behaviour in one voyage, give the lie to years of impeccable conduct,
years of passing examinations, satisfying their owners, piling up lists
of fast passages behind them with sterling deeds done, handsome
praise following them wherever they went – then one voyage, one
part of a voyage, one promotion, one significant command, one
incident even, would break them suddenly and no immediate explanation could be offered and Evans hoarded such stories to himself
and dwelt upon them. The behaviour of such human beings was
explicable only if you believed they each had a predestined course to
run, as Evans did, and so he bided his time, watching and waiting.
Successes born of the confidence that came with brute strength and
ignorance could vanish overnight. Men said their luck went, and
with it, everything else. But Evans did not believe that. The future is
but the past seen from another slant, he thought, a view from
another door. And that past fought against the future often, he was
sure. Perhaps it was a very wise thing indeed to have shipped with
Joshua Hannah's son. Parson Evans, they called him in the fo'c'sle.
But recently, since the funeral service, their attitude had very
definitely changed towards him. Well that could continue. They
would see, he said to himself. They would see. He had a premonition
that he himself would come into his own.

While all this time Jack Hannah's face wore a permanent frown.

Perhaps it was the deaths which had upset him, he would think
later. They were unexpected and meaningless, a pointlessness to
them that somehow made them irritating, more irritating than if
they were occasioned by some act of folly, or negligence, or were

106

simply further evidence of the great power of the sea. Had they been struck by the father and mother of all waves which boarded them and swept half a dozen men over, it might be taken as some awful warning, further evidence of the perilous nature of their calling. But the weather was easing when the wretched man fell. And as for the cook – for a cook to die of constipation! – that was another act of unreason in Jack Hannah's eyes. He felt death itself was trivialised by such deaths. And in the same way the unexpected bad weather in a Cape Horn summer was bad, but not as bad as he'd experienced previously. As for their progress, well, they'd waited for their slant, and eventually, they'd got it. But what troubled him more, was that the very rounding of the Horn brought him less satisfaction than he'd expected. This had led to his recalcitrance. It was his business to take the funeral service and he'd shirked it. True, he'd stood the deck, but Evans, got up in his best uniform, had read the lesson and the men had noticed it and were strangely grateful whereas he'd only been given time to study the pinched face and tearful eyes of the peggy boy, reflecting that here was the beginning of a sea life and feeling strange doubts as to its end, another ominous train of thought. In a seaman's life, what was the point in time when you started looking back and began to think that the best was slipping behind you? Dangerous thoughts.

Then the Senhora had moved into his cabin with her gear. She had not moved back when the cook was buried.

"Would you prefer me to return?" she asked, studying him carefully all the while now, those lovely eyes grave and expressive, ever anxious to please.

He'd shrugged his shoulders. What was the matter with him? He did not even know himself.

She was so careful not to take offence that her very tact was offensive! That was women for you! Then there were a series of minute happenings within the confines of her cabin which somehow got him down even more. By this time, they were on hard tack, salt junk and dried peas with a stiffening of ship's biscuit and no variety in the fare, day by day. Perhaps his melancholy could be explained by the food? But he'd eaten hard tack before. He'd begun to brood in his cabin chair and had brought out the *Avalon* cuttings again, sitting there staring at them and not saying anything while she, like a demure and dusky housemaid in a dust cap, had begun to darn his socks and repair his shirts, ever busy with her needle and yarn. One

day young Waters had come in to report something and had burst
out laughing.

"What's the matter with you?"

"Nothing, sir."

"Then why d'you grin like a jackass?"

"To see you so contented, sir."

"Contented?"

"All that's missing is a coal fire and a dog at your feet!"

"You'd better watch your tongue or you'll feel my fist!"

He had brooded on that too. So had Waters who told Evans but he
dared Evans to say anything. But the slur remained. So she thought
she had him cornered, did she? How he'd changed! Cape Horn had
left other marks, caused another death in the heart. Now he dwelt on
trivialities and they began to obsess him. First, there was the matter
of her undressing. He lived in a jumble of clothes. They seemed to be
everywhere, clothes, pins, shifts, shimmies, cottons. He'd come
into his cabin and it was like coming into a milliner's, but he only had
to growl or shout at the slightest obstruction, and she would be on
her hands and knees grovelling to pick up her things, her heavy
breasts swinging all over the place. He thought she ought to take a
purchase on them when they were not wanted (by him!). If the
voyage seemed like a journey through life with his own doldrums
marking the halfway stage, their brief weeks in the cabin seemed like
a whole marriage. He was all over her, then she couldn't keep out of
his way enough, then he'd had enough of her, and the aura of her
capable big breasted domesticity. Then his desire left him. There
were two bunks in the cabin, one he normally used as a sofa, but in
the Senhora's residency he lost the use of it and within a day and
night of her moving in he realised his mistake. There was no room
for two in there, he said to himself, but what he really meant was that
he felt himself to be suffering from the infernal, cloying suffocating
regime of women. There was now no feeling of delight or conquest
on his part: he merely felt himself to be inconvenienced. The sheer
volume and weight of her clothes were enough and once, when she
came to embrace him from behind, he stiffened, but in the wrong
way. She was getting him down now, he thought, sucking him in,
enveloping him totally. Like a squaw, he thought, a squaw who had
placed a mark of ownership upon him.

And she wanted to talk.

"You are worrying over these men?"

"Not me," he said. "Seamen come and go. And when they are gone, they are gone for ever."

"It was not your fault."

"I do not think of it."

"But you are not yourself?"

He did not even want to talk about himself.

"My darling . . ." she said, her eyes filling.

His churlishness now reached a high point. Shieking talk, he thought. He was back now to his old boorishness. He grunted and turned away. She seemed to sense his resistance and seated herself away from him. He'd just noticed her habit of lying about half-dressed: her brothel habits! God, how could anyone stay married!

He said: "Before we get to Chile, perhaps it would be best if you took Evans's cabin."

She gave a little start, there was a flash of pain in her eyes, but no sooner had it come than it was gone. She stood up, inscrutable suddenly, her lips coming together firmly, standing quite still, her hands clasped together, a muscle twitching in her rounded cheek, then falling still. The Indian looked at him again, he thought. All she lacked was a coloured blanket and a bead necklace. He'd meant to say that he didn't want agents, officials or people like that coming on board and finding her in his cabin looking like a washerwoman's parlour. But he didn't. He'd just as good as kicked her out, he was to think later. At any rate, he said no more while she just looked at him for a moment, her cheekbones glistening and her face deadly still, and he had another strong reminder of her difference from them all. Felipa was gone, the Senhora was back on board.

She said: "I will not inconvenience you further."

"I just meant . . ."

"Have the boy come for my things."

And then she left. But she didn't carry her moods for long and minutes later, he heard her laughing with the helmsman on the deck.

"He run out of juice," they said in the fo'c'sle. They too could smell the land and dreamt of *pisco* and girls themselves. "Them big ginger ones maybe just can't stand the pace of this here continental shiekin'. Short fallin' all the while," the knowing ones reckoned.

And then the song broke out again, with a subtle difference.

109

"Sera . . . phina!
Seraphina's got no shimmy!
We all bin down and yes, we seen her.
Sera . . . phina!"

The Captain's loss was Mr Waters's gain, I am sorry to record, wrote Evans.

While the Captain now gave his mind to their landfall, and once more the image he had of his father returned to haunt him, and he grew leaner and paler and stalked the deck at night. What did she think he was, a squaw man? Well, let her suffer on her own, as he had suffered.

Chapter Eight

Dry decks, a billowing surge of canvas aloft and a froth of laundry about the lower yards marked the little *Whisper*'s progress up the Pacific seaboard. Clothes so stiff with salt that they would stand unaided were thoroughly washed and basted, but in all this fine weather with land near, the Captain, we can presume, kept himself to himself, reverting to the pattern of behaviour which had marked the start of the voyage. Their coal was to be discharged at Talcahuano and hereafter they would proceed to the still unnamed islands of their destination in ballast. Facts about their daily progress are plentiful but in none of these terse log-book entries nor even in Evans's wordy account is there any real indication of what went on in Jack Hannah's mind in this flat period of the voyage. Finger-posts of impending disaster are the dramatist's privilege, perhaps even his duty to his audience, but none can be easily detected in the pages of the documentary evidence that survives. Did Captain Bligh, I wonder, have any idea of the fate that awaited him in the dog days of the *Bounty*'s voyage, or of the certainty of an eventual landfall in that incredible four thousand mile journey in the *Bounty*'s longboat? And if he did, what novelist of broad canvas would dare to compose a time-encompassing work which included both Bligh and the MGM public relations officer who described the dour son of a customs official as "a seagoing disaster with hair like rope ends and teeth like marlin spikes"? Then again, Fletcher Christian's reply when asked by the indignant Bligh to give an account of his disloyalty – "I am in hell, Captain" – might have had a very private meaning.

For my own part, knowing the fate of all on board, this uneventful part of the voyage, devoid of any incident of interest, seems to have been a time of withdrawal on the part of the Captain, and since the story I am telling is only partly one of the imagination, my guess is that Jack Hannah was victim of his own doubts for the first time in the voyage. I say he kept himself to himself as a captain should, but of course it was too late for that since every man aboard knew that he had dismissed the Senhora from his cabin. In one sense, he was thus a

111

revealed man, and it is my guess that he began to brood upon his life and conduct, daily going over the multitude of happenings which had brought him to that moment in time. We are not only what we seem to be, but what we have always been, and I am ascribing to him all the dangerous aggressions and the sense of hurt that characterises a fatherless child. And perhaps he also felt that very Victorian belief of the dominant male that the woman had softened him, that he had become a lesser man as a result of his indulgence. Evans wrote at this time, *The Captain is going in on himself*, but what did he mean? Again, we can only guess. Perhaps Jack Hannah had divined that he was not quite the man he thought he was and it may be that he also had an inkling, a whisper from the fates, that this, his first voyage, might be his last, that he was in fact not of the real stuff of which captains are made. You may say that he could not possibly have divined that, any more than Evans would dream of his own eventual success. But we do not know, and perhaps it is safer to do no more than state that the *Whisper* arrived off the rocky capes of Chile, the bays and beaches becoming visible through the first grey smudge of land until finally they saw the red foothills of the Andes sliding down to the sea.

"La-a-and ho!" would be the cry. Then the crew would be chattering like children, we can safely presume, the anchors and chain cable ranged upon the decks in readiness, and within a week or two, the harbour at Talcahuano would encompass them. It requires no stretch of the imagination to see the agent put out, spruce in panama and in tropic whites, a box of cheroots under his arm as a gift. He would, of course, speak the same tongue as the Senhora who would be as anxious as any to complete the business arrangements. If the Captain had "gone into himself", it would cause comment. He might even have omitted the traditional courtesy of a glass of whisky.

"*El Capitán – el está enfermo? El no dice nada. No me ha ofrecido muchos vasos de whisky cuando comprado una caja de cigarros?*"

And the Senhora's terse reply: "*El Capitán es un gringo.*"

"*El es un fuerte hombre?*" – a fine figure of a man?

"*El esta vacio por dentro. No paesta atención a el.*"

The crew would not have understood this, but for Evans, the Senhora reserved a precise question, we can be sure.

"How many days to unload?"

"We should average fifty tons a day. We'll be clear in a week if the

112

surf keeps off – another week should see us empty. Then it depends on the return cargo."

Evans, still ignorant of the nature of this return cargo, would explain that nitrates would have to be bagged and stowed in the hold by hand, a bag at a time, a slow business. But first, they had to unload and this inevitably meant a pall of coal dust hanging over the ship. The coal dust would be everywhere, and so the Senhora went ashore and stayed there. Mr Waters went ashore too, as soon as the bottom of the hold was showing, and it was the first time in his life that he had gone ashore without a shipmate.

One night he sat alone in the foyer of the only respectable hotel with his hair washed and brushed tight against his skull, done up to the nines in white duck trousers and a pressed reefer jacket. He had certain expectations. Like Evans, he hadn't had a civil word from the Captain since they'd sighted land, and like Evans, he wondered what had got into the man. He'd come ashore with the agent who had gone his own way, and then made his way alone through the twisting streets, passing the adobe and mortar shacks, avoiding the fandango houses and brothels of the universal sailor's Shit Street where the sailor harpies and whores looked out from the shadowy windows calling in their shrill voices for custom. He had other things on his mind, and seated in the foyer of the shabby hotel, a glass of *limonada* before him, he looked out at a little square watching the evening parade of the town's few dignitaries, the haughty hidalgos, their clerks and servants, for the most part of mixed Indian and Spanish blood, the mixture of races, the mestizos, Negritos and pure Indians, the drab horses and dogcarts all providing a colourful spectacle, a background to his thoughts. The voyage had been endless but it was not without its windfalls and it was not for nothing that he was a philosophical young man. Nor had he indulged himself ashore, despite a mouth as dry as a parrot's cage, as he put it. So he sipped his *limonada* purposefully, one thought in his mind. The name of the hotel was not difficult to forget – the Hotel de la Inglaterra. And *she* had said she might come – this once only – Felipa, an apple that fell off the tree, that one.

The Senhora was in Evans's mind too. He had remained on board to wash his smalls, having seen his own watch go ashore, released at a last minute whim of the Captain's. There was evil enough in the men's hearts he was sure, but then they were like children. He'd given the little boy his advice, and left it at that. Now he rubbed at

113

the heel of a sock by the galley door while the Captain continued to pore over his charts in the cabin. Evans had a feeling something was up, since he'd just been told ballast was to be put on board, and they weren't loading ore after all. That was a surprise, but he'd taken particular pleasure in not asking the cargo. He'd have to be told in good time. Well, let that time come. What occupied him most was the behaviour of the Senhora.

"Oh, daughter of the Chaldeans lie down!" he said to the heel of the sock. "Thou shalt no more be called the lady of our kingdom."

And then, as he rinsed his long underpants: "Lord, who shall abide in thy tabernacle? Who shall dwell on thy holy hill?"

"I will," he answered himself. When the shadow of the Captain fell upon him, he did not stir. The man was civil enough – now. But the rot had spread as far as Evans was concerned. He'd seen young Waters go ashore and before that, he'd seen Waters coming out of the Senhora's cabin – his cabin, by rights. "Plenty of greens on this ship," Waters said. There was no doubt of his meaning.

"Have you ever loaded guano, Mr Evans?" the Captain said.

"I am bound by ship's articles the same as every man," he replied stiffly. "My duty is to load whatever is here for us and I am sure you will not find me lacking."

After what had happened, did the Captain think he was in the mood for friendly chats? The Cape Horn blight only struck those who laid themselves open to it. Now Evans was beginning to show his disapproval openly.

In the shoreboat, the port watch of the *Whisper* were coming ashore for the first time in four months. At last, they'd got the coal off their bodies, from under their nails, from their hair, and were at last properly sluiced down with thirsts that would soon be slated. Behind them, there rose the masts of moored ships, ahead of them palm trees and patios ringed with gardens, and close by the sailmaker's lofts, the chandlers, the stores and waterfront cantinos, the Calle Marina, Shit Street itself.

There was only one delectable topic of conversation and perhaps it was the presence of the Senhora on board which had sharpened their appetites. Billy Bones sat in the bow thwarts – he would be first ashore, his feet the first to test the ground reeling up at him. His small scamp's face was crowned with an ancient bowler hat which he had purloined from old Sam Scuse's kit. It was three sizes too large for him, but he wore it flat-a-back, and with it a waistcoat and wing

114

collar, further unexplained accoutrements, his German pal beside him in the cleanest of white shirts with sleeves rolled to the elbow so that his huge hams of arms bulged out of them, his impassive face grinning happily as he smoked a cigar bought from the Chilean boatman. Morgan Morgan, fat little Willie Twomallow and Harry Grail wore crumpled cotton trousers and shirts, with decorative red bandannas, and young Tommy Dance sat beside them, straining his eyes at the contours of the approaching palm trees, others ranged along the boat with the Chilean boatman, bare-footed and swarthy at the oars.

"Eat first," Harry Grail said. "Get it down you. Vittles first."

Morgan Morgan wasn't so sure. He had a mission.

"You know good place, plenty jig-jig, Johnny?" he said to the boatman.

The boatman grinned, white teeth flashing in the half light.

"You go Madame Gashee's plenty jig-jig."

"D'you know what I'm going to do?" Harry Grail said, putting on the bowler. "I'm going to have one for the cook, then I'm going to have one for Jackie Breeze."

"And then?"

"I might try a little fizzer for myself!" A Grail joke in a temporary paradise! Well, paradise is where you find it!

Morgan Morgan, a kind man, had brought some disinfectant soap for the boy.

"Well, you don't want to go home nasty, sunshine, do you?"

Tommy Dance did not know. He wore a large cloth cap pulled down over his head and appeared buried in it as he stared at the beach, while the boatman strained at the oars. He felt very nervous. There was no one he could confide in, only Morgan Morgan had taken any interest in him.

They struck up the song again.

> "Sera . . . phina!
> Seraphina's got no shimmy!
> I been down and yes, I seen her!
> Sera . . . phina!"

"I give you card," the boatman said. "You no like Madame Gashee's, you go Cantina, 'Live and let live'."

Willie Twomallow took the card gratefully. "They got two anyhow. Gives you a bit of a choice."

The journey to the beach seemed never ending.

While Mr Waters waited and waited. She had not actually said she'd meet him, but she'd given him the name of the place. He'd eaten by now, his eye on the bead curtain leading to the interior, brushing away the flies with each forkful, his tongue burning at the hot chillies. Perhaps he was expecting too much. It had only happened once. She'd been in her cabin crying. He'd gone in – in his dungarees to see that her trunks were lashed down, but it didn't take him long to see which way the wind blew. The lips, the eyes, the flare of the nostrils, told him everything. The Skipper had given her the boot. Well, he was healthy and there he was. But he couldn't get any rhythm going. And then he'd seen the looks the agent was giving her. Perhaps she collected men wherever she went?

She'd been out of the ship since they'd docked. Somehow he had no doubt what she was up to. And now she hadn't come. Well, he was chancing his arm anyhow. Probably he'd only caught her on the rebound from Jack Hannah. And he'd become a rum one, a real Jack-me-Hearty as mate, but give him a ship of his own, he was like all the rest, a mask, and broody with it. They got the weight then, a cloud, on top of them and it wasn't only canvas, but a special strain. Ah, well, easy come, easy go. And it looked as if his appointment was not going to be kept.

Mr Waters rose finally and put a few pesos on the dingy tablecloth. No one had spoken a word to him save the waiter. He went through the foyer towards the doorway and the street. There was a large nondescript potted fern just to one side of the door and as he approached it, he was just in time to see a carriage draw up. Instinctively, he stood behind the large fronds of the plant as he saw the Senhora descend. She kept her back to him but he could just see the other occupant lean forward to the door. It was the face of an old man who looked down at her, evidently a seaman in a crumpled reefer, but then he gaped for there was no mistaking the face, the nose, the piercing hawk eyes which although rheumy were of a definite stamp. The old fellow was obviously up to his ears in drink but under a soiled panama, the Hannah features looked down at the Senhora, a shaking hand extending to clasp hers. And then the cab was gone and he had a profile of that beaky nose, the sagging rolls of flesh about the scraggy chin hiding nothing. It must be – it couldn't be – but it was – old Josh Hannah. He remembered seeing his picture once. And the way they clasped hands spelt a

116

certain kind of business he'd no doubt. He was obviously in a hurry too, for the carriage sped towards the docks. And then the Senhora did not enter the hotel, but went off at a rate in the opposite direction without even so much as a look inside to see if he was there. What a tartar she was!

Mr Waters stared blankly from behind the palm, distrusting his eyes. Sense returned. It couldn't be Josh Hannah. Josh Hannah was long dead.

Eventually, he shrugged his shoulders, waited a moment before he went into the street, then threw a centavo to a beggar. It was too good to be true, he thought, her coming there especially to meet him. And she'd obviously forgotten him altogether. He'd had his ration for the voyage and the only thing he could do now was keep his mouth shut. The full enormity of the occasion did not dawn upon him. It was one personal taste which had whetted his appetite, but he did not fancy Shit Street, knowing that the crowd would be there. He hoped the crew were looking after little Tommy.

It was the behaviour of his shipmates which daunted Tommy, however. They went along in a shuffling group through the side streets of the old port, then across a rickety bridge on to a dirt road full of holes and presently the street opened out before them, saloons and bungalows ranged side by side and back to back with large illuminated windows in them, candles and oil lamps emphasising the shapes and faces of the girls who sat and posed there. Some of the girls, dusky and sharp-featured, screamed like parrots, others posed seductively, some wore tattered lace mantillas with flowers in their hair, some had very little on and as they screamed or chattered, here a soft twanging guitar was heard, there from the patios at the rear, a sharp savage burst of guttural sound in a flamenco chorus, the Spanish influence omnipresent. It was a warm and sultry night and the street smells were mingled with the odours of a stew of cooking from the rear of some of the establishments. The crew's idea was to have "a look-see" first and Billy Bones and Morgan Morgan had bought bottles of *pisco*, the fierce native spirit, which they passed around and drank as they mooched along, a still eager and anxious party. Tommy did not like the burning taste of the drink, and although they had given their money to Billy Bones to act as treasurer, he had declined his share after the first unpleasant mouthful. The sometimes savage shouts of the girls disturbed him. They had a way of hawking their wares from the backs of their throats like

117

fishwives, and often the frank obscenities, the suggestive movements of their hips, were off-putting because of their aggression.
There was a desperation in it that offended.

"You got sub, Johnny? You got pay note?"

"Me do, you watch, John!"

"*Rompa* the cooler-allnight de jiggi-jig, *dos pesos* long time in!"

"You want exhibish, Johnny? Me got donkey."

He surveyed them all as if they were greedy wives turning over
sole at the fish market in Sveynton. Competing cockle women
shouted like that.

Then the crew began to quarrel as crews will. Harry Grail wanted
an exhibition, Morgan Morgan "a bit of music with it", Tommy,
feeling the ground come to meet him still after months of pitching
decks, merely wanted to sit down. When they finally entered a
cantina where a bevy of girls seemed to come out the walls at them, it
was only because one of the girls had leaned out of the window and
stolen Billy Bones's bowler. Then, bristling forth on an expedition
of recovery, they were trapped, surrounded by girls, pushed into
seats and encouraged to drink. Soon the girls of the house were lined
up, a mixture of all ages from fifteen to fifty, and, if anything,
Tommy felt sorry for them. He sat on the edge of a bench with the
poke of his cloth cap pulled down over his eyes, looking apprehensively about him as if he expected the Vicar of Ennal's Point to come
striding in, wearing his tweeds, carrying his walking stick and a
collie dog snapping at his heels. The glamour of the attractions was
not as advertised for there was a savagery in the air, a threat of
violence which he could not quite define and his every instinct was to
run. Everything was too noisy, too certain, although Willie
Twomallow had started undressing the first woman he saw.

A *señorita* came up to Tommy, all hair and flashing smile with the
liquid eyes and brown skin of the Senhora. But she was thin and
tubercular, little more than a frightened child herself.

"Me gooda girl, shorta-time fifty centaros?"

"Just your dap, Tommy," Morgan Morgan said happily, seated
himself with a buxom mestiza.

But Tommy only smiled wanly. The speech of the men was
becoming slurred already.

"Now my good ladies, we got all night but we're looking for
something a bit special," Billy Bones said impatiently. "Let's have
the titties bared if you please, and who's got a guitar then? Music

118

with it! We're all taffies on this watch, you know. And chapel boys have got the biggest!"

But they were getting drunker every minute and presently began to quarrel. Who did Bones think he was? Harry Grail could organise his own jump, and said so. Only the big German kept them apart. The youngest girl still hovered about Tommy interestedly.

"Go on Tommy!" Morgan Morgan urged. "It's on the kitty!"

An older woman spoke sharply to her in Spanish and she took his hand urgently, clearly under some pressure to solicit his custom, bending forward to whisper in his ear. She had heard his name.

"Nice for you, Tommy. Many times you like?"

But he could smell the terror of the Madame and took her hand as much to help her out as anything else. She pulled him to his feet and the sailors cheered. Then she drew him through the bead curtain to a narrow corridor and paused outside the open doorway of her room. A candle was already lit, revealing a single bed and a crucifix upon the wall, the only decoration, which he looked at gravely. That was Catholics for you! She stood inertly beside him studying him, but his eyes had already sought out another exit at the end of the corridor. She caught his arm and protested and he knew she was fearful of the Madame's reaction still. Then she attempted to kiss him, to open his mouth with her tongue, but it was the action of an unwashed drudge and he drew away. Now he did not want to offend her and fumbled in his pocket for something to give her, but all he could find was a lucky rabbit's foot. This he took and pressed into her hand. To his surprise, she began to cry.

"You no fuckee?" she sobbed. "Please you fuckee. No fuckee—no money!"

He swallowed awkwardly. He did not know what to do. Affecting surprise, he pulled up the poke of his cap, took her hand and led her to the rear doorway near the street, but she continued to cry. Manfully, he pointed to his person.

"Poxed up to the eyeballs," he said in a shrill voice. "No good, kid." (That would make a story in Ennal's Point when the century turned.)

But then he bolted for the warm embrace of the night air and ran all the way to the beach where he had the good fortune to run into Mr Waters who grunted, then fell silent with his own preoccupations. But he had made a purchase of melons in a string bag and shared them on the journey back to the ship.

119

"Thank God there are two Christian souls aboard," Evans said when they boarded. He was watching anxiously for them like a verger on the rail.

The Captain did not appear but they saw a light in his cabin. "Poring over his charts," Evans said. "He says to me, 'Have you ever loaded guano?' and I told him, 'I am here to do my duty'."

"Guano?" Mr Waters said.

"Yes, and a long haul too. Juan Fernandez Islands, he condescended to tell me tonight."

"That's not a guano port?"

"We're off-loading from another vessel."

"What vessel?"

"A Chilean vessel."

"Rum," Mr Waters said. But then he remembered what he had seen. Perhaps it was a family business after all, father and son in the guano trade. Shit for sale and money for it!

"At any rate, you two are not the worse for wear." Evans said. "There won't be a man without a sore head on my watch in the morning."

Out of the corner of his eye, Mr Waters saw the stern of a little schooner hull down on the horizon, evidently having only just left the port an hour or so before. Somehow he knew the schooner had a passenger. Connections, he thought woozily. Everything was connected if only he could see it. He'd bet old man Hannah was on board.

"You didn't see the Senhora?" Evans said.

"Yes, in church," Mr Waters grinned and jerked his head towards the Captain's cabin. "Praying for a smile to come on old Black Jack's face there!"

But Evans did not smile either, although he said a most perceptive thing.

"He has forfeited his right to smile."

"Forfeited?"

"That is what he feels, I am sure. I'm sure his character is disintegrating. This man is a haunted man, can't you feel that? He has abandoned his God. There is nothing left for him now."

Evans's bony face was sepulchral in the moonlight. He nodded gravely. When you looked at him, you inevitably thought the worst of him. Everything about him was sombre. He had a graveyard look. His face seemed to be polished, with that dome of a forehead,

120

those undertaker's lips, the outline of the skull visible behind the flesh. You could hear his voice, deep and melancholy from afar, the perfect man to read the burial service. "Man that is born of woman has but a short time to live . . .", the words might have been invented by him. They were said, not with relish, but with the total certainty of deep conviction and Evans was the perfect reminder of the inevitability of death. You might joke as the sailors did, inventing nicknames for him, and call him "Happy Harry", but now Mr Waters felt a clamminess of his own spirit and a new perception came to him. If ever there was a Jonah, Evans was. And if ever there was a ship to quit, this was it. He knew it now at this very moment. He felt doubts more than at any time in his life, more than a general uneasiness, an awareness of other factors besides the sea pressing down upon them in exactly the same way as that doldrums sky had seemed to lower itself, as if it were reducing the volume of the earth's span allotted to them. There was somehow less room to move then, just as there seemed to be less time in front of them now. The voyage, the *Whisper*, the Captain, the Chief Officer, the Senhora, were too much for him, too much to comprehend or to cope with. There was so much he did not know and it was just as well, he thought as he went below. It was probably safer.

But Evans, after questioning Tommy, gave him an apple, virtue's special reward.

"Thank you, sir," Tommy said.

"I am not as bad as they point me out," Evans said. "You didn't, did you? Indulge?"

"No, sir," Tommy said.

"I am very pleased," Evans said. "But the dangerous time will come when you hear the others boasting. Then, you'll need more than an apple."

A Grail joke, an Evans joke, it was the sunshine part of the voyage.

Chapter Nine

LOG OF THE BARQUE WHISPER OF SVEYNTON.
Jack Hannah, Master.

Tuesday 21 February:
At Talcahuano, Completed discharging. Ballast taken in only after
14 days delay.

Wednesday 22 February:
2.30 p.m. Sailed for Juan Fernandez Islands. Fresh N Winds.
Stunsails set.

A variety of excuses was given for the delay in ballasting the ship at
Talcahuano, Evans wrote, *but the fact that Senhora Salaverry did not live*
aboard for three whole weeks may be regarded as significant. At first, the port
authorities offered shingle dredged from the bay as ballast, but as it was in a
liquid state and could not be properly stowed without being liable to shift in
passage, I pointed out the dangers to the Captain. I was well aware that
ships had been lost in passage from one South American port to another and
that runny shingle was the probable cause. I said every bucket that came on
board would have to be inspected and weighed before being paid for, and that
in the event of our not getting a full cargo at our destination, it was imperative
that we be properly ballasted for the voyage home.

This quite reasonable safeguard caused the Captain to fly into a temper
and on one occasion he siezed me roughly by the shirt in front of the men and
began using the vile language which was so characteristic of his father. He
accused me of being an old woman and a Jonah (to which Mr Waters nodded)
and vowed he would put me ashore in Juan Fernandez, marooning me there
like others before. I said if you mean Alexander Selkirk who was the
inspiration of Daniel Defoe's admirable Robinson Crusoe, *I would accept*
quite happily but the tale I would have to tell would not reflect very
favourably upon him. All the weeks we were in port (when the Senhora was
accommodated ashore) his behaviour became lamentable and I began to fear
for his own sanity. Although fresh vegetables and meat were in plentiful
supply (I made the ship's purchases in the early morning street market – at

very reasonable cost) he confined himself to one meal a day for by this time he had brought bonded stores on board and at night we could hear him dropping empty bottles out of his cabin scuttle. There were quite a number of them floating on the tide and we became the laughing stock of other ships.

He only went ashore on ship's business, returning as soon as he possibly could, and although we were invited several times to church services on other ships, he could not even decline in a civil way and the other captains ignored him thereafter. We just lay to our moorings, further delays being occasioned by his rudeness to the agent. The port authorities came up with hard ballast only after I had explained the delays to Senhora Salaverry. The crew all this time were set to routine tasks aboard the ship, going ashore in alternate watches, but on the last week, the presence of American vessels caused us to curtail shore leave for fear of losing our men.

There was an insurrection at this time further north in Chile and although we heard rifle shots from the interior, no further evidences were occasioned in the port. Some of the men were placed in irons after attempting to go ashore and it was a time of much unpleasantness which was not helped by the Captain's indifference. There were three cases of seamen's pox amongst the crew and I was obliged to forcibly enter the Captain's cabin to take permanganate of potash crystals from the medical chest, but he had by this time drunk himself insensible and did not know whether it was day or night. Consequently, I informed Senhora Salaverry and within a day of her return to the ship ballast was delivered. Then, from the moment we left Talcahuano, and until we sighted Mas a Fuera, the nearest of the Juan Fernandez Islands where lay our cargo, an atmosphere of distrust and suspicion was present on board. The men went about their work unwillingly, softened and polluted by their contact with the harpies ashore, and the Captain continued to eat his meals alone in the cabin. During all this time we experienced strong, northerly breezes, a head sea and later thick fog, but the Captain did not appear in the daylight. No further information about our return cargo was given to me and it was only when we made our landfall and put into the furthermost point of the island when the Captain appeared, demanding to know if I had put a leadsman in the chains. I had, and at a depth of twenty-four fathoms we were getting black sand within two cables, and when we anchored at dusk, the wreck of a vessel was sighted upon the reef. It was clear to me that the vessel had been thrown at least fifty yards upon a rocky promontory from the water's edge and that lying as she did on a lee shore with tidal waves not uncommon in these parts, the greatest of caution was required.

However, the Captain now called me a washerwoman to my face and informed me again that we were to off-load guano from this vessel ashore. He gave no explanation of his behaviour and although the light was fast going, he called for the German seaman, Flohr, to assist him take the jolly boat into the shore immediately we had anchored. I pointed out to him that we had no reliable charts, that not one of us knew the coast, but he told me curtly that if one vessel could be wrecked there, so could we. It is my belief that he chose Flohr as companion because the poor fellow could not speak at all, although at this time it is only fair to say that we all thought we were merely scavenging a free cargo from a wreck. The jolly boat was brought alongside and at the last minute Senhora Salaverry jumped into it, nearly swamping it even alongside the ship, and this was one more example of slackness and the way things were now run on board when left to the Captain.

At this time, of course, we had no idea of the conditions ashore but throughout the voyage we had a feeling that things could get no worse, or that one act of folly was of itself but part of a procession of follies, each new one in some way a relative of the last.

For myself, I watched the jolly boat put off from the ship with an apprehension that was felt by all on board. What now? we thought. What next? And why had the Senhora pushed herself into the boat at the last minute, clearly against the Captain's wishes when she had not addressed a sentence to him for weeks? It was over five hundred yards to the top of the promontory and although a mast was stepped with a small lug sail, there was surf visible all along the shore, quite a bobble on the water, the slightest mistake enough to swamp a little boat so heavily laden. The Senhora's presence as ever, I thought, was unwanted, a danger now to lives as she had been to souls before.

"Sit on the gunnel!" Jack Hannah said. "When she heels, lean out backwards. D'you understand? We'll have to trim her."

He stood with his knees bent, the tiller in his hand, crouching in the stern. He was aware of Evans's warnings, but one thing he really understood was small boats. Of course, it would have been more sensible to wait until morning but nothing could stop him boarding the grounded vessel at the earliest possible moment. And they soon found themselves moving at such a lick, that he felt all the exhilaration of having a small boat under him. The responsiveness of the tiller gave him the feeling of being master of himself once more and after the turmoil of self examination he felt the need for action and to take command of himself anew. He had already seen enough of the outline of the grounded ship to know that no ordinary wave had put her there, but soon, as they made the first of a series of tacks, he began to recognise certain distinctive lines. There was no mistaking her squat bulk. She was a copper ore man like themselves. At first fooled by her changed masts and rigging, he now perceived the length of her hanging bowsprit, and recognised her. It was the *Avalon*. She had neither sunk, nor been burnt as reported.

"The *Gazela*?" he said sarcastically. He could see the Senhora's face staring mutely at him under a headscarf. Now it was her turn to look apprehensive. "It's the *Avalon*, my father's ship."

But her coldness remained.

"Had you asked me, you would have been told."

"How much damage?"

"The *Gazela* has broken her back."

He could see a narrow bay well past the tip of the promontory and abutting the saddle of rock on which the vessel lay, a cleft in the rocks opening below the bow whose damaged bowsprit tilted downwards in an ungainly angle like a broken beak. A tangle of rigging lay alongside it and the surf broke a few feet away so that it was likely that there was water enough for them to nose the jolly boat in there. What had obviously happened was that the vessel had been picked up bodily by a huge wave and been dumped high and dry on to the platform of rocks. But the dumping had a curious symmetry to it for she was placed at right angles, parallel to the cliff face. He could understand the difficulty of getting her off. Unless the same sea conditions prevailed which had put her there, it would be like removing a building. He wondered how much water was in the nearest bay, his eye appraising the neat line of the surf as they moved first towards it, then away as they tacked, the halliards of the jolly boat straining, the thwarts creaking and the repeated lapping of the water indicating the speed of their movement. They kept on the same tack, angling the bow just wide of their destination, his eyes scouring the water for any hint of obstruction. Flohr had his eyes on the water for'ard, frowning with concentration, but the Senhora never looked towards the shore once, her eyes remaining pointedly on the Captain's face.

The *Avalon* still in existence, he thought. The change of name was one more thing to be hurled up against him in Sveynton.

They reached a halfway mark, and he began to tack, savagely snapping a command that made the Senhora jump.

"Stand by to go about!"

They braced themselves. He released the sheet and put the tiller

125

hard over, the sail spilling the wind then tightening as he now headed straight for the distant bows of the *Gazela*. The Senhora moved clumsily during the manoeuvre, cracking her elbow and wincing, but he ignored her. Put him in a boat and he was master again.

Now he could see the approach clearly, noting an ominous swirl of water marking a tide race in front of the little cove ahead. He would do best to back in under oars for the final run in. Out of the corner of his eye he saw the low outline of a building on top of the cliff above the promontory, a flag staff just visible at the centre of it.

"What's that?"

"It is a fort."

"Fort?"

"Where they keep prisoners. There will be no shortage of labour."

Labour be damned, he thought, but every ton of guano shifted would have to be got off in the ship's boats for he could not risk the *Whisper* and he wasn't going to have her over-run with jailbirds. It would be a pulley-hauley job all right, first to load the wretched stuff in sacks, then to bring the sacks out of the *Gazela*, load them into the boats, get through that surf, and then repeat the whole laborious process alongside the *Whisper*. Perhaps he'd be glad of the prisoners.

He was moving in too quickly and decided to tack again.

"Ready about!"

This time the Senhora moved with more dexterity and when they tacked, Flohr gave a strange animal grunt pointing across the bay to where the dim shape of a corpse appeared, carried by the current in a jack-knifed position, the buttocks raised and head trailing. They tacked once more and drew nearer, getting a second view of the bloated face of a Chinese woman of indeterminate age.

"A slave," the Senhora said.

He knew it was a woman by the way the body floated.

He wondered if she had come from the *Gazela*. The body drifted off silently in the tide race, the hair trailing like weed.

They were beginning to lose ground against the tide themselves and he decided that they would row the remaining distance. Now they could hear the rumble of the surf breaking.

"Can we get right into the cove?"

"You can aim for the bowsprit. Just to the right there is a gully."

"Thank you!" It was the most useful information she had given him to date.

She looked after the vanishing body thoughtfully.

He released the main sheet and brought the sail down in a sudden movement of billowing canvas, calling to Flohr to take the oars. They needed his immense shoulders and arms now for the tide rip had to be fought and soon they came under the lee of a large rock and into the cove beyond as they backed in over the surface, the jolly boat rising and falling but the oars holding them steady until presently there was the crunch of shingle and they grounded stem first. He sprang out of the boat, knee deep in water to steady her. A quick shove and she was almost dry and above them the *Gazela*'s bowsprit towered in the darkness, evidence of splintered timber everywhere. It must have been an immense wave to have taken the ship so far over the rocks but the presence of deep water in the cove meant there was still a chance of refloating her. At the back of his mind, he saw himself returning with the two ships in company and he could just imagine the shout that would go up along Sveynton dock, "The *Avalon*'s back!"

The Senhora stepped gingerly out on the shingle and looked up at the tangled mass of rigging. Now they could not escape the smell. Mingled with the stench of iron and barnacles, the usual odour of maritime decay, there was a sicklier more pungent smell which seemed to come from the fo'c'sle above them, a latrine smell of guano and human filth. Rags of sails remained on the yards, a boat's falls dangled over the rocks, and even in the darkness, they could judge the force with which the vessel had been plunged on to the rocks. This was a wreck, mystery ship or no, and the life had gone out of her. Beach rats scuttled into the shelter of the rocks, and further away an immense ghost crab the size of a football flitted along a stretch of sand before the cove.

The Senhora approached, caught his arm apprehensively.

"There's a ladder under the cliff – on the other side."

No light was visible, but Jack Hannah had the unmistakable feeling that he was being watched. He could not see the decks of the ship for she towered above them, canted at a slight angle towards the cliff. He picked his way over the rocks, the Senhora still holding his arm, and he felt strangely comforted by her nervousness. It was better than the totem he imagined in the boat.

"What happened to the ship's boats?"

"He must have sold them."

"You were partners then?"

"As I told you – yes."

"And that fort on the hill up there. The government – are they friendly?"

"Very friendly. Your father makes himself useful to the authorities."

"By doing what?"

"Prisoners have to be delivered, and supply trips to the mainland."

"The ship is stolen," he said. "And people must know her. There are copper ore men up and down this coast who might recognise her."

"Only if they were looking for her."

"Does he say he owns her?"

"He will tell you himself."

"Yes," he said grimly. And a good deal else besides, he thought.

They made their way up rough steps to the cliff, leaving Flohr to guard the jolly boat. Halfway up, a ladder extended to the deck. When they reached it, they could see the full extent of the damage along the splintered decks and now the ammonia-like smell of the cargo was omnipresent. All the deck houses were tilted, stanchions bent, the masts raked sideways at a crazy angle. It was as if a house had been dropped from the sky, landed with a sickening crunch and remained lopsidedly exactly where it had fallen. The stench was so dreadful that no one could live aboard for long, and as they walked they could hear rats again as they left the holes in the ship under them.

"You'd better wait here," he said to the Senhora.

"No, I want to see it again."

"It?"

"The ship."

Perhaps she had an attachment to the vessel? He did not know. He put his foot on the ladder, felt it give slightly under his weight, then went rapidly across it, and jumped heavily on to the deck, feeling timber crunching underneath him. He knew that sound. She was beginning to rot. Wishing he had brought a light, he called to the Senhora, the sound of his voice echoing against the cliff, and there were a series of movements within the vessel, a curse and a sudden scuttling as if he had roused more rats. He went forward cautiously and stopped as a light appeared, a head preceding it in the darkness of the companionway. A tallow lamp flickered, giving the slant eyes of a Chinaman who next appeared a ghostly hue. The face at once

128

began to grin, nodding several times as if recognising him. It was
thin, emaciated, yellow, lips curling over broken teeth.

"Who are you?"

"Me John Tiger, boss. Me belong Captain Hannah. Long time
Captain's tiger."

He stared as the man raised the lamp and began to examine him,
nodding to himself appreciatively.

"Where's the Captain?"

"Him below."

"*Below?*"

"Him come down wait for you from fort."

The Chinaman chuckled, nodded, then bowed as the Senhora
dropped down on the deck.

"Captain say you come by and by. You and missee same time."

"Is he well?" the Senhora said nervously.

The Chinaman made a silent cupping motion with his free hand,
then pointed down the companionway towards the saloon. He wore
a cotton smock with a thick leather belt outside. On the belt was a
chamois leather bag which he clutched protectively. Evidently it
contained some objects of value. There were sounds of movement
below, a slamming of drawers, and then Jack Hannah heard the
unmistakable roar of his father's voice.

"You tell um come plenty chop-chop and bring whisky!"

He started at the sound but if he felt anything, it was total relief.
Like father, like son, people had always said and the voyage might
have been an act of destiny designed by some ironical wit in order to
make him understand the facts of his father's life which certainly did
not begin and end in the prim front room of that little waterfront
cottage in Ennal's Point. Well, now he was the man for him, he was
sure and ready for the meeting. His nervousness had gone completely. Only the Senhora remained strangely silent, a mute figure
beside him. Now there could be no more secrets.

He clambered down the steps manfully, ducking his head as he
strode along the uneven deck, then entered the saloon where his
father sat, his huge bulk hunched in the Captain's chair, a filthy shirt
flowing over his belly, looking older and more frail than he'd
expected. This man was a shadow of the father he remembered, a
victim, a casualty, as derelict as the ship. Lank strands of white hair
straddled his bald pate, but the eyes were the same, sharp and
menacing, so was the pitted nose, and so too was the mouth

129

ironically twisted into a sardonic grin. The shoulders and arms were thin, pitiably so. He showed no sign of emotion, the rheumy eyes appraising the son like a meat trader searching for a flaw in a beast. His hands had a marked tremor, but he disguised that by scratching himself absently, a scarecrow movement that gave away his age. But his voice had retained its strength, displaying the character of old.

"The Mammy's boy," he said unfairly. "Bit of a shock, I suppose?"

"More than that," Jack Hannah said, prim suddenly.

"I'm sure you never missed me?"

"I wasn't allowed to forget you either."

"Forget me?" the old man was immediately suspicious.

"Your reputation."

"Oh, that. Mister Chauncey-Vernon and Co. They didn't want you as Master then?"

"Not at first."

"And then they changed their minds?"

"Yes."

"Of course, I knew they would. That's why I sent her back there."

He had not addressed a word as to the Senhora's whereabouts.

"Why?" Jack Hannah said.

"To do a bit of trading. Where's that boy? Johnny!" he called, then cackled. "Sit down, you'll get used to the stench."

The Senhora entered with the Chinaman. Her eyes were cast down. She seemed contrite and girlish, yet another mood appearing on display, deliberately sitting next to Jack Hannah as if for protection. The old man hardly gave her a glance.

"Bring whisky," he said to the Chinaman.

The Chinaman looked delightedly at them both, then went out again.

Then the old man laughed at their silence, stuck a grimy finger into his ear, scooped at the wax.

"Well, what did you expect?" he said impatiently, as if anxious for an opinion. "Tell me . . . Born in pig shit, I'll die in bird shit – is that it?"

Uncannily, Jack Hannah felt closer to the Senhora than to his father. Years separated them, years, oceans, continents. The man who had gone hurtling himself out of that little cottage was a different man altogether from this ill-kempt stranger. He knew at

130

once that the man had never had a moment's remorse in his life. He was incapable of feeling, a jocose, paunchy, shifty-eyed ruin. But he was not incapable of evil. Seventy-odd years of deception, wildness, drunkenness, bad temper, and violence had been fined down to the cynical amusement of age. The scarecrow could still hurt, however, nodding away there like an irascible and disgraced headmaster.

"Well, well, well!" he exclaimed. "And not a word to say between you? A good job I wasn't murdered!"

"There are plenty of questions," Jack Hannah said.

"What d'you mean? They hanged the Greek, didn't they? And Yates was dying. Oh, I know what you're thinking. Well, let me tell you, there may be questions but there'll be no answers."

"You planned to lose the ship for the salvage money?"

"Not at all! I didn't get the salvage, the owners did."

"Chauncey-Vernon?"

"Right!" the old man said. "I was under orders but I couldn't get a crew I could trust to do it till I put in for one."

"And the Sveynton men?"

"Jibbed it. No gumption. Jacks the lot! So I got the Greeks to do it, to set her on fire and put me over with the Sveynton men in one boat, while they took the other. It was to be all above board, a real fire, everything and everybody thinking it to be genuine. Only the Greeks got ideas above themselves. They murdered the lot, set her on fire and put me over all right – but without the boat. Very greedy, they were, they wanted it all. I didn't have a chance, didn't see the ship for days, bleeding like a pig, I was, hanging on to a spar in the water, then we both drifted up together in a calm, me and the ship. The Chink was still on board, hiding all the time. He'd put the fire out, but he was too weak to pick me out of the water. I floated alongside for a day and a night before he got a rope to me and then we had to rig a jury mast, and sailed her together."

"The two of you?"

"The two of us, yes. By that time, after a month of it, I reckoned she was mine."

"Where were you heading?"

"Ah, that's another story, that is," he gave a shifty grin, "but there was a mutiny like they said, only it was a mutiny against the mutineers, you might say. By the time we made a landfall, the ship was hardly recognisable 'cos of the fire, and we'd painted the name out. 'Course, I was lucky I knew where to go – I was heading there

131

anyway. I could have made it in the cutter, only I didn't have the cutter, I had the ship."

"You had somebody waiting for you?"

"Of course I had! What d'you expect?"

The old man's voice was sharp and sarcastic. The details were no longer important to him. What was important was that he had triumphed, and more disturbing still in Jack Hannah's eyes was the complicity of Henry Chauncey-Vernon from the start. He did not doubt the inference and this news was like a light cast upon a dark place. No wonder he did not want to employ a man who was the son of a fellow conspirator. And as for his father's difficulties, and his survival after being thrown in the water, they were less important than his original plan. He had somebody waiting for him in some remote Brazilian hideaway, some unknown river port, no doubt. But who?

Jack Hannah remained silent. The printed pages of testimony at the trial of the mutineers were probably worthless, as many lies as there were facts. The fact that his father had recruited a gang of cut-throats who proved too much for him was not surprising, but if the crime had been planned, there were others involved in Brazil. He looked sideways at the Senhora who had remained silent with eyes downcast as if waiting for the further revelations which she knew must come. At last there would be no secrets and the *Avalon* mutiny, whatever the truth of it, had suddenly regained its proper place in the past. These questions mattered still, but not as much as the present, and now Jack Hannah determined to have it all out. He was not going to leave that cabin with a single doubt.

"There are more things," he said curtly. "Many more."

The old man laughed. "I daresay. But before you start accusing me," he winked lewdly, "I can see you've been at her."

"Please . . ." the Senhora's voice implored in a sudden scalded plea.

But the old man's frank stare was scornful. He jerked his head, chuckled malevolently.

"You know what she is, don't you? Didn't she tell you? Can't you tell by her?"

"Don't!" the Senhora said again, a single sob.

"Obvious, I should've thought. That's why I sent her. Send a whore about a whore's business."

Jack Hannah stared across the filthy table. The rheumy eyes were

knowing and frankly amused, a cruelty in them that was obvious –
with that look did men inflict the most terrible tortures. The stench
rose from the bowels of the ship, from the decks, the companionway, the broken scuttle, permeating everything, but it was nothing
to his father's iniquities which seemed to extend from the past into
the future and were seemingly never ending. He remembered
Felipa's phrase, "My father was a trader, he traded me", then his own
tortured feelings finally, for no reason that he could think of, the
lonely body of that solitary Indian turning over and over in the
brushwood upon the water, and the thought came to him that all
men who had any decency at all would turn against a man like his
father, and with that thought came another, and he had a deep feeling
of remorse at what he felt to be the offence he had committed against
Felipa. He did not know what to believe as to the veracity of his
father's statement – he doubted it – it was said to wound, a twist of
the knife in the long-formed scab – but no matter, he felt then, in the
face of this vileness, a sense of compassion for her that was unique.
They'd both been used vilely and were both victims. So much for his
father's slight, his so-called revelation. It was the final separation. He
had never felt more separate from one human being, nor closer to
another in his whole life.

But Felipa began to sob openly beside him and impulsively he
caught her hand, a movement that caused the old man's grin to
widen and Jack Hannah to look away. From the old man's great
flushed face, however, you could quite clearly see that his messenger
had done exactly as she was bid, and they had not finished yet. He
cleared his throat. She nodded. He was a survivor, and so was she.

"Right!" the old man said cheerfully. "Let's get down to brass
tacks. You'll have to off-load into the cutter, but I don't want a man
of yours to set foot on shore. This is a dago country. There's a war
on. Very touchy, they are, and come the first light there's plenty of
things they'd rather not have you see. We don't want no *lenguas
largas*, nor pryin' eyes, if you get my meaning? Well, have you got
that? Myself, I never thought you had much nous."

"You can trust him," Felipa said. "We have done everything I
promised."

Far below them in the depths of the ship, they could hear the rats,
disturbed by the sudden footfalls, now scurrying aboard the ship
once more to continue their pickings. The beach, the cliff, the ship,
were all alive with them.

Chapter Ten

For three days the *Whisper* and her crew lay at anchor, stewing in their own sweat, finding no respite from the heat, the stink of the guano growing worse every day. It was already bagged in the holds of the *Gazela*, but the bags were rotten and a fresh supply was taken ashore to protect and strengthen the rotten bags. In the morning, they could see the fort on the cliff top quite clearly and by midday chain gangs were at work under overseers who carried rawhide whips as they bullied the files of half starved men who were visible from the ship as they lumped the bags down to the little cove. From here, the ship's boats plied at irregular intervals. It was an endless chain of activity and there was indeed no shortage of labour as three files of men crawled like ants up and down the gangways which had been erected alongside the stranded vessel. The prisoners were mostly Chileans and their emaciated bodies showed that they had been in captivity for some time. The more feeble of them suffered the curses of the overseers and one poor wretch who kept falling was freed and whipped, his weak cries floating over the water. From dawn to dusk the gangs worked, at a pace which they could hardly match on the ship, for the boats had to work through the surf and the pile of bags on shore grew and grew and since each bag brought on board had to be properly stowed under Evans's eyes, the shipboard work was slow.

Jack Hannah allowed Flohr to remain in charge of the jolly boat which shuttled to and from the cutter and they could see his bent figure gesticulating to the overseers as the bags were dumped on board, then hauled off to the kedged cutter and the whole laborious process repeated.

It went on and on hourly and daily, and although at first there were mutterings amongst the men at the speed with which they were required to work, and dark glances cast at the happenings ashore, the Captain told them that without the prisoners they'd have a double job to do. The brotherhood of man did not extend to the loading of cargo. The prisoners bore the brunt of the labour without respite and the cruelties of the shore were no concern of the sailors. As it was, he was in haste to complete the loading and be off. His father had gone back up to the fort and once he saw a uniformed party standing on the cliff looking down, but they made no contact. His father had kept out of the way since the dawn which followed their arrival and the seamen were given no chance of a sight of him, the telescope being prudently locked up. He was principally concerned that nothing should happen to delay the loading, but with some of the Sveynton men casting suspicious looks at the *Gazela's* lines, he did not want the bother of explanations. The heat, the stink of the guano and the ominous chink of the prisoners' fetters ashore oppressed them all, and he was concerned to work as fast as possible in case the glass fell and a sea got up, in which case further loading through the surf would be impossible.

Evans complained and complained. There was wrongdoing in the very air. Evil lay all around them. Why were the authorities so conspicuously absent? Then the men were exposed to the sun all day, hardly more sheltered than the wretched gangs ashore whose cries continued, as did the overseers' whips.

"It's inhuman," Evans said. "Inhuman and ungodly."

"If I complain about their cries, they'll beat them all the more," Jack Hannah said.

"Then there's the vessel."

"What vessel?"

"It's very obvious to me, sir, that vessel is a copper ore man."

"Well, Mr Evans?"

"And a well-known copper ore man."

"What are you saying, Mr Evans?"

"With blood on her decks."

"*And?*"

"There's more to this, sir, than we've been told."

"Yes, Mr Evans. There is."

"The men are talking quite openly. It's the *Avalon*, they are sure. And another thing, if I may presume, sir – there are a number of bodies visible in the tide race every day. The men can't help seeing them, and they're not from the chain gangs. Poor sickly creatures, they are, many of them females, and if you ask me, sir, all gone with fever. This is a putrid place and the Lord alone knows what is happening up there beyond that fort. Have you ever put into an island and no one comes to look at you? Very odd, sir,

135

nothing ashore there for a Christian soul to speculate upon, I'm sure."

"Which is why no one is allowed ashore, Mr Evans."

Jack Hannah was glad that the Senhora had returned on board. It was undoubtedly the healthiest place, although the stink of guano was everywhere. Whereas before the coal dust hung in the air, now the heat added to the stench and made the ship an even unhealthier place and while he was naturally anxious to be off, there was ample time to consider that garbled story of his father's. Standing about the decks, he had gone over and over it without coming to any positive conclusion. There was no doubt about his father's influence ashore and from what he could gather, the Governor of the penitentiary had been instructed to give them every assistance since his father had performed some service for the Chilean authorities. There were many English seamen who had made themselves useful in both Chile and Peru, manning the navies, taking sides in the innumerable insurrections, and English or Irish names were common enough in the state service, but for Jack Hannah it was enough that he had his cargo. The rest, lies or not, was like a dank mist rising above the cesspit. Whatever was the truth of it, no one emerged with the slightest credit, least of all his father.

There were immediate difficulties in keeping the men at their filthy task and the lack of supervision ashore caused the *Gazela* to tilt upon her rocky platform. One night she seemed to be a permanent monument to folly, the next she had slipped forward at an angle, her masts canting forward to the sea. The shift had no doubt been occasioned by the removal of the cargo unevenly from the holds, and the weight of tramping men across her rotten decks had done the rest, causing her to look more like her old self with her bow dipped as if to meet an expected on-coming wave. With all her tragic history, she might have been slipping towards the sea anxious to remove herself entirely. They had three-quarters of her holds emptied and stowed aboard the *Whisper* after three days and the exhausted men had turned in when Jack Hannah found himself joined by the Senhora one night, both of them looking reflectively at the shore. The evening breeze had dropped, but there were bright stars dogging the moon and a sea swell remained on the water. Close in shore the surf kept up and above the cliff the dim lights of the fort could be seen. Further away, the big spring tide was making against a large rock which had been perforated by erosion with the result that the wind whirled through it at intervals making a low moaning sound, an eerie protest in the face of all the cruelties that surrounded it. This occasional whine, together with the constant rumbling of surf upon the shingle, added to the impression of unease which had been constant since they'd arrived. Perhaps it was the presence of those wretched prisoners herded together behind the walls of the penitentiary, perhaps the strange noises of the rocks, or merely the knowledge that the barometer had started to fall which caused Jack Hannah, free of one burden, now to feel another. He was sure there was a weather change imminent, and this instinctive feeling led him to another – a desire to have an end to this distance between himself and Felipa. He would have the voyage home to dwell upon his father's tale. Whatever the truth of it, he was finished with his father, and the past. Neither held terrors for him now, and when he thought about him in the future, it would be of a seedy old man, shifty and boastful, no different finally from all the beachcombers and casualties who haunted the distant parts of the world. Whatever they had been, their decline was total, men without honour or pride, sunk into degeneracy, and passing beyond even the hope of pity. As for this father's relationship with Felipa. Jack Hannah was less sure. Perhaps it was true, but if it was true, what did it matter? If the voyage had led him to nothing else, it had reminded him of the wanton cruelties of life as daily witnessed by the behaviour of the prison guards ashore. Life for most people – for three-quarters of the globe – was like nature itself, red in tooth and claw and only the single-minded and strong survived. It was a commonplace to say that life was cheap, but pain was cheaper and Jack Hannah wanted no more of it.

Perhaps he should try to convey some of his thoughts? His guard was down finally, and his new feeling for Felipa was simply one of affection and compassion. Whatever their true relationship – and he could hardly credit the old man's revelation they had still been through so much together. But his feelings, ironically enough, were brotherly. Besides, she did not look quite so brown in the darkness! But what to say? How he wished he were a more expansive person. Typically, he began with the weather. Now there were puff-balls of clouds scudding along and obscuring the stars. He sniffed. Oh, for the niceness of a vicarage garden, a sense of order, croquet balls and church bells! But he kept to the weather. Here he was again under a star-dogged moon.

137

"Wind," he said. "I can feel it."

"I warned you," she was composed and thoughtful, smiling ruefully in the darkness. They might have been standing together on the cliff at Ennal's Point!

"Warned me?"

"The *terremoto*. It did for us here."

Us, he thought. She could still couple herself with his father. But he worried about those clouds more.

"If there is any increase in the swell, we will have to be satisfied with what cargo we have." Typically, he had ordered the hatch covers and tarpaulins replaced over the holds each night so that they were instantly ready for sea.

"You are Captain," said she.

"Yes, and even three-quarters full, we have enough to make a substantial profit."

"Oh profit!" she said. As if it did not matter!

"And then a fast passage."

"I'll pray for that. What will you say to Mr Chauncey-Vernon?"

"Which Mr Chauncey-Vernon?"

"The respectable one," she laughed. "The owner of the *Avalon*."

She was curious and teasing, again really fitting his mood.

He hadn't decided. If what his father said was true and Henry Chauncey-Vernon had conspired to lose the vessel, it was a piece of information which might prove useful. But thinking that made him sound like his father, like all of them ashore. Nothing was done without hope of gain, no scrap of information wasted in case it could be used to some competitor's detriment. And if he thought like these odious manipulative people, he would get like them. But he was through with accusations too, he thought. It had all exhausted him. He who plays the dragon, eventually becomes one. How his guard had dropped!

"I have only had one concern really, in all my life," he said simply, "and that was to be a shipmaster."

"That is not an answer."

"Well," he hesitated. Perhaps he might say something to the *Avalon*'s owner. But he certainly would not use the information to obtain a command. On the other hand, others might use it for him.

"A shipmaster," she said. "The wind blows free, does it not?"

"The freedom of your own ship is a freedom, but I've no head for the politics of it," he said ruefully.

138

"You need a wife with a trader's instincts."

"Yes, I thought I would get one once."

"But you did not?"

"No," he looked down at her serious face which continued to examine him closely. It seemed an age since he had thought of Beatrice Trevoake, and a phrase of Miss Trevoake's god, the indefatigable adviser from the *Ladies' Home Companion*, returned to him. In a bizarre way its very Englishness seemed as refreshing as the thought of Sunday mint sauce or afternoon tea on some village green. *If I were asked what I considered to be the greatest drawback to married happiness, I should unhesitatingly answer, bad temper.* And remembering it, he chuckled and repeated it, explaining its context. It was incredible how Felipa's presence could create a backdrop of normality the moment she had divined the direction of his thoughts.

Her eyes remained soft and concerned, her voice husky and as far away from croquet-playing ladies on green lawns as could be imagined, but she succeeded.

"You do not seem to mind very much?"

"Well, that's as maybe," he said flatly. "For years you set your mind on one thing – you are going to marry so-and-so. It becomes implanted in your mind like a seed. And the seed grows."

"Watered, no doubt?"

"Yes, watered. The weeks, the years go by and suddenly a part of your future is assured because you have taken something – someone – for granted."

"And did you do that?"

"I did," he said quietly, and then he explained about Miss Trevoake and the understanding they had. He did not say that Felipa's own arrival had been the cause of Miss Trevoake's discomfiture, for by now he did not believe it entirely. Another change was at work in him. Things did not seem quite so clear; he had been critical of others. Now he was critical of himself. He was not conscious of being drawn out, nor of the help he was receiving; and he had no idea that Miss Annie S. Swann of the *Ladies' Home Companion* would have thoroughly approved of their delicate conversation.

Felipa listened and came finally to a conclusion.

"She is a shopkeeper's daughter?" she said with a smile.

"She would not thank you for saying so. She is a governess, but they are in trade, yes."

139

"And she will have a little capital eventually?"

"I hadn't thought of that."

"It would be the first thing I would think of!"

"Then you are more mercenary than I!"

"Is she attractive?"

"She cuts an imposing figure."

"Tall, like an English lady?"

"Yes."

"Severe?"

"Perhaps."

"There is an expression – 'well-disposed'?"

"No, but she has had much to put up with."

"In your behaviour?"

"And the sea, my profession, my absences."

"But that is a seaman's life."

"Yes, but she does not see it."

"And she has no ambition for you?"

"I thought so, once."

"But you were wrong?"

"Yes, I expect. I have been wrong about many things."

Now they took a turn about the deck, and for the first time, he began to unload his burden totally, finding a new precision, as he revealed his hopes and dreams, she drawing him out, but still with the same lack of information about herself. It was as if her real self came and went in flashes – like the silken underside of a cape revealed now and then by a mischievous wind. He remembered her sobbing in that filthy cabin on the stranded ship opposite them. The Senhora was entirely absent then and instead of the haughty madam, or the gentle creature now, there was a wounded soul pleading for some dignity. Could she really be a victim like himself? Why could he not accept Felipa as she now appeared so calm and accepting herself in this velvety night? Could he have had any more thoughtful, more sisterly companion? Besides, they had their cargo, or most of it. Why on earth could he not leave it at that? It was pleasant enough to have this gentle sympathiser. It took the dust and the heat of the tropics away from him, and he felt free of guilt at last, relaxed, another new experience. To think that after all his fears, she could be so disarming, such a friend. She even had good advice for him.

"I think Miss Trevoake will learn her mistake," she said when they returned to the ship's side.

"Miss Trevoake makes no mistakes," he grinned. "But she has an unerring capacity for pointing out mine."

"Then she must learn."

"No, it is over between us." He remembered that solitary garnet ring on the mantelpiece. "And she will not wait. The family will see to that. They'll put her into some business. Perhaps she would make a better parson's wife." It was incredible how he could joke about it, how the sense of dull hurt had left him altogether. Poor Beatrice, he thought. And yet, she had come down to the pier on that blustery day so long ago now. They had seemed to spend their courtship in farewells.

"We shall see," Felipa said.

"You mean, you will be staying in Sveynton when we return?"

"Oh, you must leave me to my business interests."

"And what are they? After this voyage, not ships and the sea?"

"Whatever leads to profit," she said. "Now then, could you have a more honest answer than that?"

He certainly could not, he realised, and he looked forward to the voyage home with a sudden youthful bout of optimism. Nothing she did was without effect. With any luck, he thought, they would make a smart passage home if the Horn proved kind, flying fish days once more and perhaps a time to relax. Why should all of life be such a joyless strain? He had his command, he had his cargo, and whatever he decided eventually, certain information which might or might not prove useful to him. It wouldn't be a hindrance if he could find out where they had found the deposit of guano originally either. That would be a bonus as it were.

He grinned. Miss Annie S. Swan and the *Ladies' Home Companion* were perhaps not so wrong after all!

"You must give me lessons for my temper," he said.

It was the longest, most civilised and most normal conversation which they'd had. And not a hint of impropriety, he noted. If only Evans could have witnessed it! He did not remember that she had once bitten him in her passion, or more importantly, the slight pitching of the bow which marked the onset of a longer swell from the sea below them. He did not notice either that the wind had risen and that the stars were barely visible. It was suddenly sultry, hot and threatening, but her new achievement was to create within him a kind of peace in which he felt pleasurably relaxed. Perhaps he could have done with a sister, or a kindly aunt, or Miss Annie S. Swann

141

herself for that matter. At any rate, he went below with a contented smile, the Senhora remaining a moment longer, her own eyes inscrutable and just the suggestion of a smile on her face. She might have been an actress, who having given an average performance, has been absurdly over congratulated, and then paused to remind herself of the gullibility of human beings.

The Captain's presence on deck kept Harry Grail below for the early part of the evening. He had much to think about and with his face to the bulkhead he lay half-curled in his bunk, the noises of the sleeping men around him evidence of the hard days' labour. The knotted and twisted wood of the bunk's panelling was as ravelled as his thoughts and although he had said little for days now, a pressure was building up inside him which would soon determine the fate of the *Gazela*. He was waiting for the Captain and his judy to go below, and also to make sure that the poor fools in the fo'c'sle were well down in slumber, and while he waited, he gave his mind to the events of their recent landfall, his black brows frowning, nose twitching, lying there like a muscular ferret, his body seemingly inert but every part of him on the *qui vive*. The ferret was only in its lair for the moment and what nobody aboard knew was that he'd caught a glimpse of the Chinaman aboard the wreck and noted from the way he was dressed – the seaman's smock and belt – that he was no ordinary Chinaman, but one who sat around where and when he pleased, paying no attention to the guards, and even had the galley stove going, munching his chow in all that filth like an evil bird whose nest had been fouled by others. The Chinaman was the *Gazela*'s Chinaman and Harry Grail would bet a pound to a penny that before that he'd been the *Avalon*'s Chinaman, and was no Johnny-come-lately but went with the ship.

He'd tried to wangle his way ashore without success. Young Mr Waters was in charge of the cutter and he'd approached him, touching his forelock, properly respectful.

"Old Flower Flohr there, sir? He's been in the sun all day. Might as well give him a spell?"

"No, Captain's orders."

"All for the best, I'm sure, sir, and I don't want to get anywhere nearer the perishin' place than I have to, sir, but he can't tell you when he's dead beat, old Flower. A willing horse he is, but you can push him too far. If you had a word with the Mate, or the Captain?"

"Captain's given his orders," Mr Waters said, stony-faced. He had other problems and was a little afraid of Grail. He could not be specific, but Grail was the sort of man you'd see grinning as you fell past him from aloft on a wild night.

Grail next tried Evans on the poop deck, always keeping the picture of the Chinaman at the forefront of his mind like a target in a fairground.

"Beg pardon, sir, the old German don't look too good to me. Looks as if he's going to keel over in this heat."

"It is very hot indeed."

"We'll have to watch for sunstroke, sir."

"And a lot else besides, I've no doubt."

"I was wondering if I'd give him a spell, sir. Baking hot, it is, on them pebbles, I daresay. Poor old Dutchie, he's been stuck there three days now."

"We're nearly loaded now, Grail. Done very well."

"I just thought, sir, that . . ."

"We're winning though. Don't want to change a winning team," Evans gave a weak smile, shifted his feet, busied himself with a halliard.

That was Evans. Wouldn't say straight out, but the inference was clear. The Captain had put the block on it, on any man going ashore.

In the fo'c'sle, the men hadn't shown much interest either.

"What d'you want to parley with a Chinaman for?" Willie Twomallow said. He was feeling the heat, his fat little cheeks drooping, clothes soaked with sweat.

"He looks like a johnny-long-time to me."

"What does that mean?"

"Long time Avalon."

"Oh, it's not the Avalon."

"It's the Avalon all right."

"Why don't you tell the Captain then?" Morgan Morgan said. "He's got his smile back this morning."

"No good asking him."

"Why not?"

"He wouldn't tell me."

"Why won't he tell you?"

The ferret eyes glowered.

"He don't like Harry's eyes," Willie Twomallow said. They had all had enough of the labour ashore and the sight of the fettered prisoners was no advertisement. There were no grog shops, the only women they had seen were the corpses of coolies. Mas a Fuera was a place to be quit of and the sooner the better.

So Harry Grail had turned his face to the bulkhead once more, his grievance remaining and festering within. The truth was, he was a man who had lived under a pall of deprivation for as long as he could remember.

First, it was his brother Walter lost upon the *Avalon* and, although they had not been especially close, Walter had actually brought presents home for the children and was a genial older brother. But there was more than Walter's loss and shortly before the *Whisper* sailed, Harry had suffered a particular blow to his self esteem when he had been rejected by his fellows in the village during a ballot to elect a new coxswain for the new pulling lifeboat. No one could question his seamanship, but some feared to give him authority. For his own part, Harry put his failure down to one of those bizarre strokes of ill luck which seemed to haunt the family. In the week before the ballot, when his chances seemed good, a long disappeared half-sister, Louisa, whom none of them had seen for years, suddenly created a sensation by attracting the interest of the national press. She appeared before the Liverpool magistrates where she was described as "a fine girl of twenty-seven years who for five years had followed the life of a sailor dressed in male attire". She had applied to the parochial authorities in order to obtain means and clothing to undertake a situation more in accordance with her sex. She was in the workhouse, in short, and an erstwhile penny-a-line reporter had seen his opportunity of making the national papers, obtaining the extraordinary information that she had never removed her clothes in all these five years before the mast! It was to be a lucrative paragraph but to Harry Grail, on his best behaviour to impress his fellows and his betters, it was like a thunderbolt, this reappearance of a moustachioed half-sister. Indeed he was quite sure that the ridicule which followed it had put paid to his chances of the only prestigious shore job he was ever likely to have. He'd had words with the successful candidate and shipped out in a hurry, and even now, all these miles away, the fires of memory were joined by his present concern to question the Chinaman ashore.

Finally, satisfied that all were asleep in the fo'c'sle, he turned stealthily in his bunk, slipped his hand into his sea bag and removed a long bladed fish-gutting knife which he did not keep on general display, then padded out of the fo'c'sle to the deserted deck. With his shoes strung around his neck – rocks hurt the feet – he slipped down the anchor cable hand over hand, noticing the increase in movement since the swell had crept up. He took pleasure in hanging for a moment by his strong arms then, crossing his legs, he descended further and entered the water like a mole going to ground, then swam gently with the tide helping him towards the distant *Gazela*. It was a long swim but he was a powerful swimmer, and his hands made the slightest movement in the water in an effortless side stroke. Like Jack Hannah, he had smelt a change in the weather. It might be the last time he could get ashore. If the weather was changing, they might keep a deck watch at night.

Now as he rose with the swell, his thick black hair matted and pressed to his skull, the bones of his face stood out, the moonlight shining upon them. It was an ugly face, the low forehead and thick eyebrows seeming to press down upon the thin, stubborn jaw. All his strength was in his arms and shoulders, and the face, brutal and insensitive, was curiously limited in its range of expressions. So much had happened to it, it might have been an over-used mask that did not continue to register. He was glad of the comfort of the knife in his belt, glad of the assistance of the tide, glad there was a light still flickering midships aboard the *Gazela*, glad he had given himself a chance to think, to go over the tangled web of happenings relating to all of them. He was pretty sure the Hannahs were in some kind of league with Henry Chauncey-Vernon, the owner of the *Avalon* (and the patron of the lifeboat committee), and he had never really believed the mutiny story. He had recited the tale of the apprentice's removed heart beating upon the poop deck, but at the same time no one as expert at gutting as he could be unmindful of the difficulties of removing a heart from a human body. There was a rib cage to begin with. You'd have to be pretty dexterous. It wasn't just a quick scoop like gutting a cod. Bones were liable to obstruct the sharpest knife. Yet it wasn't entirely impossible, and Greeks were generally thought of as bad blood, it was true, especially when they were shipped in a hurry on foreign ships. What did stick in his craw was that the *Avalon* had sailed from Sveynton with a local crew, and old Josh Hannah must have gone-a-looking for his mutineers. Buenos Ayres was a long way out of his run, unless he was also trading on the side. And why had the survivors put into that remote Brazilian island so far

145

north, when the vessel was supposed to be bound round the Horn? And although the bleeding heart story had been verified at the trial, it smacked of extravagance. You didn't have to disembowel a man to kill him, but then, they'd said somebody'd drunk the blood of the heart – that was all over the pages of the *Cork Examiner*, Harry knew, he'd had it read out to him. No, it did not make sense. It was like Louisa's reappearance, newsy stuff, unless of course, it was all true but was only done to put the fear of God into any half-hearted jacks there might have been aboard? That was a new thought. Old Josh Hannah might have put into Buenos Ayres to look for a real butcher, one man who would scare the daylights out of the rest. A bit of elbow work with a knife was a good persuader and with a Greek whose palm had been crossed . . . it made a kind of sense. Men in a state of terror at blood letting of a violent kind, would get hurriedly into any old boat. They could be hazed by such an abnormal occurrence. It wasn't the bleeding heart that was important, it was the purpose of it. At last, he felt he was nearer the truth, a truth that was made all the more exciting since he was sure there'd been a Chink on board the *Avalon* ever since she was commissioned. It was a good way to frighten a Chink too, he thought to himself.

The swim ashore was long but it did not tire him unduly and he was proud of that. All the voyage out, he had stolen food to build himself up. He would have eaten the decayed body of old Scuse the cook if he'd had to. He was no stranger to hard tack. As it was, he'd merely robbed his kit. And he'd kept low as far as the officers were concerned, and done his work well. He was the only one in the watch except the peggy boy who hadn't got the sailor pox. Well, he hadn't taken any chances in the normal way. There were other ways of killing the cat.

When he got ashore, he was careful to avoid the overhanging rigging about the bowsprit. He slipped his shoes on and made his way up the gangways on the cliff face. There was not a soul about, ashore, or on the land above. Finally, he removed his shoes again, stashed them away, and went up a side plank, swinging himself on board as noiselessly as a rat. Then he crouched down, looked cautiously about him, before proceeding below where the light still shone. The stench of guano and rot was everywhere and since the ship had shifted she seemed to be opening up, the sun had burned into her. He went down the ladder into the companionway, then saw the light coming from the half opened door of the saloon. To one side and nearer to him there was a cabin with the door hanging off its hinges and he darted into it, but the furnishings were roughened and splintered and as he felt around, it was clear there was nothing worth taking. With his foot he touched a bucket full of half burnt papers, but there were neither clothes nor any objects of value. Now he could hear the Chinaman's breathing and strange muttered sounds as if he were talking to himself. Half daft by the sound of it. The wind was getting up too – he could hear it whining in the rigging, and there was another sound coming from the saloon, the noise of metal objects falling on the saloon table like dice. Rum, he thought.

He took his knife from his belt and tested the honed blade against his thumb. It could split a whisker. He grinned, then padded out into the companionway. The Chinaman was sitting sideways shaking the small metal objects in a chamois leather bag and letting them fall upon the table. They glinted in the lamplight. Harry moved forward holding his breath and then saw that they were gold rings and the Chinaman, crooning to himself, was playing a game with them. Another step and he saw they were signet rings, evidently a prized possession.

Harry smiled, extended the knife along his palm, raised his arm and sprang into the saloon, knife outstretched so that the point of the knife was pricking the Chinaman's adam's apple as he turned at the sound, freezing as he did so, one of the rings falling on the deck at the same time. A cat could hardly have moved quicker, and like a cat pleased with itself at the suddenness of the attack, Harry smiled, drawling in a soft voice.

"What you got there, John-John?"

The Chinaman did not reply because he could not open his lips and the point of his knife had actually pricked the skin. He rolled his eyes with fright.

"Whose are they?"

Harry released the point of the knife a fraction of an inch, smiling evilly. "Whose?"

"They belong sailormen," the Chinaman said.

"Dead sailormen?"

The Chinaman nodded. Harry flicked his eyes over the leather bag. He knew the lingo.

"Dead sailormen – long time gone *Avalon*?"

The Chinaman tried to shake his head, but the point of the knife

147

would not let him. A trickle of blood came from the first cut in his scrawny old neck. When he spoke, his voice seemed to come from his stomach. The whisker of blood widened.

"Me no take from live sailormen, only dead mans. Lings belong dead men, all gone, long time gone."

"Sailormen belong *Avalon*?"

"Yes, boss. Captain let me keep lings."

"Captain Hannah?"

"Yes, boss. Captain Hannah belong them ship. Him know me sailor's fiend. He come back by and by."

"*Come back?*" Harry felt his stomach muscles tighten.

"Yes, boss. He leside fort with soldier boss. Too much guano stink. He come back look-see by and by, see Johnny Tiger. He no mind lings. Johnny Tiger long time Captain's tiger. Me fiend, boss. Me go away schooner Captain Josh. Plenty more guano birds. You fiend Captain Josh's son?"

In the silence, Harry Grail felt his heartbeats, the blood coursing through his veins, actually felt his sodden clothes drying on him. Alive, he thought, Big Josh was alive. He might have guessed it. The Hannahs got away with everything. He had taken the knife point to a sociable distance of an inch from Johnny Tiger's throat, and now he kept it there, smiling slowly.

"Johnny Tiger," he said thoughtfully. "You long time *Avalon*?"

"Yes, boss. Me velly long time."

"You very long time *Avalon*?"

The Chinaman nodded, puzzled, studying the knife point and the ferret-like face in front of him, as if trying to find out what gave it pleasure.

"Yes, boss. Me velly long time."

"Then you knew Walter Grail?"

The Chinaman wanted to shake his head but again the knife moved and would not let him. The answer was in his eyes, however, a quick flash of recognition and fear. Now the knife point rested against his lips, nicked it with a thoughtful testing movement. There was a dripping sound but Harry did not move his eyes. He did not need to be told the Chinaman was wetting himself.

"Him dead mans," the Chinaman said, but at the same time, his eyes went to one of the rings and following the glance, Harry Grail chose a ring, a plain gold signet ring and picked it up. He was quite sure his brother had never possessed such a valuable object in all his

148

life, so no sentimental thought arose in him, and yet, considering it, a further fact of Grail existence occurred to him. He was not so sure that Wally had never owned a ring. What he really meant was that his brother would not have brought such a valuable possession home with him in case the old lady saw it. You could feed a family for a month on what you could get for a ring like that. He picked it up and slipped it on his finger.

The Chinaman sweated. This was not a friend. This was very bad man. This man was so bad he thought everybody very bad. This man had a knife to speak for him.

"Bad trouble on the *Avalon*?" Harry said.

"Very bad mans. Gleek mans."

"And the Captain?"

The Chinaman made a stand then, a brave stand, ignoring the knife for the first time.

"Me Johnny Tiger," the Chinaman said. "Me mouth-shut boy."

Harry Grail was excited but even when he was excited he thought slowly and now there was a physical pleasure in keeping the Chinaman on edge. It was like the fight of a fish, he thought, the last fight, the very last hopeless fight. First there was the helplessness as you got it into a boat, the hook firmly embedded, and then with the weight of the hook and the total bewilderment of being caught would come the quivering of the haunches, perhaps a desperate flick of the tail, the very brightness of the eyes telling you everything. He had seen it so many times and admired it, the courage of it and the hopelessness. And the Chinaman was the same, weak on the hook, then cracking, cracking by trying to please, then finally making a last despairing stand, that "Johnny Tiger, mouth-shut boy". He could just imagine old Josh Hannah instructing him on that. Well done, he thought. But the end had to come.

With pale, unexcited eyes, Harry gave no announcement of his intention and suddenly thrust the long thin blade of the knife into the Chinaman's heart with no more difficulty than if he had been gutting a fish, grunting as he did so, feeling the Chinaman come on to the knife, slumping forward to meet his death. He had a momentary concern for the thinness of the blade – then eyeball to eyeball, he watched the light go out of the Chinaman's eyes. As he turned and withdrew the knife, Johnny Tiger slumped to one side with a gasp like a deflated bladder, knocking over a chair as he fell. Exactly like a fish, Harry thought.

149

He wiped the knife carefully on the side of the table and, straightening, he scooped the rings on the table into the thin chamois leather bag, folded the bag over and pressed it into his trouser pocket.

"Chink," he said. "That's one for our Wally."

He set the chair up on its legs and cocked an ear as the wind whirled in the rigging. He could hear the masts moving now and it was clear that up above them there was a pronounced increase in the force of the wind but he continued to stand there thoughtfully. He wasn't quite clear what the Chinaman had meant about the whereabouts of old Captain Hannah. If he was up in the fort that was too risky and he didn't see how he could winkle him out, certainly not without everybody on the *Whisper* knowing. But the rings and the bubbling mouth of the dead Chinaman were poor satisfaction. One bizarre thought occurred to him, an indication of the way his mind was running, and that referred again to those bloodthirsty depositions which had occupied so much of his time. It would be only fitting if Big Josh Hannah came blundering in there in the morning to see the Chinaman's heart on the saloon table. Well, he'd very probably ordered such a cutting himself. Spare no mercy on him.

But it was too much work, and too risky with such a thin-bladed knife. Harry had already pondered over the anatomical details and they puzzled him, so finally the Chinaman's body lay unmutilated. He had not got the real satisfaction he'd come for and with a lowering brow, he wiped the knife once more, moodily aware of another pleasure missed.

And then the weather helped him. The wind was stronger up on the cliff top than it was in the lee, blowing as it did across the island at a slant. It was worse up there even than in the bay and the fort felt the full sudden pressure of it. He was just about to leave, moodily aware that there was nothing much for him to steal, when he heard heavy footsteps on the cliff steps, then the creak of the gang plank as some booted intruder came clumsily down. The vessel was an echoing drum of noise suddenly, and he heard the old man call "Johnny . . . Johnny" in an irritated warble. It was old man Hannah come to survey the remnants of his bird shit.

Harry stiffened, then went hot-footed into the adjacent cabin just in time to see the flicker of the old man's lantern precede the booted feet and press himself against the bulkhead in the shadows as the drink sodden old figure passed him. Then, in the space of a second, he heard him grunt and swear, lifting the lantern higher to peer down at the Chinaman's body, but Harry suddenly scuttled forward like a rat, and went after him with the knife outstretched, striking on the instant and plunging it expertly in the right of the old man's shoulder blade without warning so that he never saw who or what had killed him, merely lifting himself upwards with the force of the blow, stiffening and going down over the corner of the table, the lantern still in his hand, his balding egg of a head rising once, then lolling forward, the face remaining hidden as it fell forward and the body finally slumping lopsidedly, drawn down by the weight of the head and shoulders, the legs and booted feet lifting off the deck, the final posture ludicrous; and the end of the Captain and the vessel actually began then with the force of the blow, for a dribble of oil flickered from the fallen lamp, a flame following it, and the Chinaman's smock began to burn. It happened so quickly that Harry's first thought was chiding. It could so easily have been the wrong man! But it was not, he knew, and he had not even seen the face of his assailant. It was as if the body had come to the knife knowing its destiny.

The flame spread up the Chinaman's smock which was as bone dry as the timber of the deck, but Harry did not wait to see. He was out into the companionway, darting along the deck, pausing once to steady himself when a rat came out of the darkness and bit him on the ankle, a sneaking stealthy pounce which sent his bare foot flying in a savage kick, but the bite was no more than a pin prick and he dropped down to the rocks and his stashed shoes and was in the water before the fire left the Chinaman's body. The spilt paraffin would do the rest, and on the swim back his only thoughts were of the swell which had got up considerably. He was swimming against the flood now and it tired him but he kept going doggedly, hearing the wind and the clank of lifting chain over the *Whisper*'s bows like a homing beacon. All done, he thought, all avenged. Very neat, it had turned out. He could imagine the old bastard hiding all these years, grubbing a living with bird shit in this pestilential hole. It was worse than trying to trade with seaweed, and that was what he'd come to, bleeding heart or no. He felt suddenly virtuous and cleansed by the killing. One Grail at least had been avenged.

They were all asleep when he got back on board. Tommy Dance moaned fitfully in his sleep but did not stir. Harry turned in wearing his wet clothes, the bag of rings hard in his crotch. Something to show for it. When he got the chance, he'd dig them into the space between the deck boards and caulk them over. Find a little spot, he thought. Easy. One of the rings was on his own finger and he felt it now with a pleasurable satisfaction. A knife, the rings, vengeance complete. He allowed himself a smile, a man of substance and property, a victorious Grail.

I pause here, in case you have any doubts. Of course, you may say I am making all this up. We know there was a *Gazela*, that she was very probably the *Avalon*, that Jack Hannah was never the same man again when he returned to Sveynton, and we also know that the *Gazela* was finally destroyed by fire and that the *Whisper* sailed with only three-quarters of her cargo loaded. Most of this is beyond reasonable doubt but the most important event of all I have described to date was none of these obvious things. I have deliberately left it casually stated and not drawn attention to it. When Harry Grail returned on board, I am presuming that he was unnoticed and that both the Senhora and the Captain were fast asleep. That there was no deck watch, I think we can safely assume. The men were tired, the ship was at anchor, the Captain should have been in a good mood and it only takes a good mood to make an arrangement with oneself to cat-nap. Nothing was likely to happen. Evans and Waters would be as tired as the rest. Perhaps Evans thought there should have been a watch kept, but he does not refer to it when he mentions almost every other defect in the Captain's conduct in his record. No mention was made of the weather at the island in the log, at least not until the *Whisper* was under way, so here again we can assume one of those quiet periods aboard when nothing really happened. Of course, a Board of Trade Enquiry would at once establish that a proper deck watch was not set, but this is of no importance and although I dare say you have guessed that we are in for bad weather again, my guess is that it is the sight of the blazing *Gazela* perched on her pinnacle of rock which is of the utmost importance to the rest of our story now.

Let us imagine them all asleep on board while the fire ashore in the grounded ship began to spread. She was already canted on her perch, her bow already pointed in the direction she would take on her last journey, her Captain and his servant well and truly cremated, the decks beginning to buckle as the flames crept up the tinder dry bulkhead. The fire would probably be noticed ashore first so it is not difficult to imagine that shouts from shore aroused them on board. But whom first? My guess is that it was Senhora Felipa, and even she did not hear them at once. She dreamed a good deal and at the back of her mind there were images, memories of sights and sounds that few could understand and certainly none of those present on board. Her mother, let me say it again, was Indian and believed in devils which haunted the water and ate the lips of liars, noiseless spirits who existed to plague those who came from the sea. Felipa, I have said, believed what she wanted to believe for most of the time. If I have made her seem like a tart, then she was a tart. I have made her speak with propriety, but then she could also behave with propriety. I have made her a business woman which she undoubtedly was, and an actress – as what successful tart is not? But more than this again, there was an inscrutability which disguised her real feelings, a mask which she had always had from the time she sat dressed all in white by the Sisters of Mercy waiting for the Corpus Christi parade. "Think a thing, you show it" was her instruction to herself and consequently there were always thoughts kept at the back of her mind which lay there half revealed. This was the Indian in her, the blood that was different. There were so many questions she might have asked. Didn't anybody realise that she'd had half-sisters who ate manioc raw and swam naked in the river, and then sat cross-legged around a painted headman telling them stories of birds who could remember and fish that came when you called them?

Once or twice she had escaped to her mother's village by the head waters of a river she had long forgotten and there she remained for a day or two, dressing as her half sisters did, feeling the warm earth under her buttocks, the sun on her back as they taught her to oil and plait her hair and also to worship the light of the dawn coming over the forest and never – as the children told her – never never to tell secrets to the breeze because the breeze had ears. And there was also a headman there who had made great journeys and it was he who had first murmured the name of the *Caleuche*, the ghost ship that belonged to a greater expanse of water than they could ever imagine. It was not a gringo story, and therefore not manageable nor dismissible nor something that could lightly be put aside like the fabrications you made up to slip through the traps which the Sisters of Mercy set for you. It was a story that somehow went with the wind, the same wind that had ears and told of the spirits that ate at the lips of liars. It was a story for a dark night, this tale of a ghost ship which prefaced, then accompanied disaster, but it was also a part of Felipa's consciousness and perhaps too, on this particular night, there was also something in the air, something in the sounds of the wind and the sea which entered her mind through that open porthole.

"Mosquitoes, more'n like," I can imagine the sceptical grunting. Never mind the stories of the black *mucans* in the hammock by the silver mine, tell us more about Senhora Felipa. What about her relatives, the whole procession of priests, traders, missionaries who taught her, or the first husband coughing quietly into a bandana in shaded corners, the hand that reached under the blanket finally weakening as tuberculosis stiffened it? And what about the Red Man as old Josh Hannah was always called on his infrequent and always unexpected visits to this tribe of half-caste gypsies always on the move? Where did the old Captain fit in with this shabby family of ne'er-do-wells always on the verge of gringo respectability, now at the edge of the harbour trade, now up in the mountains, first in one country, then another? The answer is very simple. The old Captain was Senhor Connections in everybody's eyes. For Felipa, the move to Chile had come with the second husband who had gone on from there to Peru when the Chincha Islands were opened up, rich deposits of guano then fetching a high price as a fertiliser and literally changing the country's economy. For a golden period, there was almost no need to work and anyone who could command a vessel was a rich man by their standards. And old Josh had come first to her mother, then to another of her husband's sisters, spilling his seed indiscriminately, then disappearing for years, finally reappearing with a Brazilian partner and a vessel that needed a cargo.

He was a man like any other gringo captain down on his luck who had a family connection in a very loose way with them and a host of others who kept stores or ran the chandler's offices, but by the time of his second appearance, there was a difference in Felipa. Her mother had died. Now she was a woman, a widow for the second time and the keeper of the purse strings, and it was as the keeper of the purse strings that she'd made that incredible journey to England. How the Mission Sisters would have been proud of her! See the waiters run in those squalid provincial inns. She had only to raise her voice and they came. There in the green gringo country where she had very wisely taken a little gold for gold made speeches all on its own – there she was a Madam and very pleased with herself for it was her idea to make the journey. The guano had originally been intended for North America. The old man would not go into North American ports and kept away from most of his fellow mariners but there was no reason why she shouldn't speculate. He had told her something of his other life, of an actual son and the port of Sveynton where there were always ships to be had – and it had all actually happened. How she had succeeded according to her own lights!

Grant her these thoughts asleep before the open porthole in the early hours before the dawn, still half aware of the anchor chain rattling and the wind beginning to moan in the rigging, the halliard blocks snatching restlessly. The rats, we may be sure, were long gone from the burning *Gazela* ashore as the fire ate at her bowels and all I am suggesting is that at this time in Felipa's mind, the legend of the *Caleuche* was reborn. It was an island story originally and in Chiloe where it began, there were soothsayers, wizards or *brajos* who made a living selling spells for warding off the consequences of just one sight of the ghost ship. The fishermen of the island did not want to see the *Caleuche* and they would hide their eyes like children at any bright light – if they could not see it, it was not there – but even though they hid their eyes, they paid a premium to the *brajos* just in case. One sight of it and you were done for, sure as eggs, man! But what was it like? Ah, the *brajos* said, that was a question that cost too. Everything cost. Well, it was bluff-bowed, high-sterned and square-rigged some days, or, depending on where you were, it could take the shape of a small coasting *galeta* with short stumpy masts, but always it was on fire, luminous in the black night with every spar and sail outlined by flames. Yes, man, on fire and sailing by guess and by God into the eye of the wind, sometimes far away, no more than a silver web in the moonlight with spars as white and fine as ivory. In Carelmapu they did not fear it if it appeared on New Year's Eve for they made special preparations for it, cooking clams in the sand and chanting in a semi-circle until the first ring of the midnight bell, for then it sailed out of one year into the next, leaving them free of its threat provided they paid homage to it. The bell was a sign of its coming and going, and the actual belief in it was important to your safety. Believe, the *brajos* said, believe and believe, and listen for the bell, so perhaps it was the distant ship's bell that Felipa heard before the shouts of fire. (When the *Gazela*'s woodwork perished the bell must have fallen.) A ship's bell was important in Carelmapu too but in the Golfo de Penas – the Gulf of Sorrows – there was another story. When the *Gazela* met a freak storm, the carpenter was sent aloft to repair a broken spar and then he had seen something which was never really disclosed and jumped to his death

155

screaming in his madness, shrieking that the light (of whatever he had seen) was too bright. And only the year before, one ship had put back into Pisaglea with not a man in the fo'c'sle prepared to go to sea again because of what they had seen, or thought they had seen. They did not go to sea again either since fever destroyed them ashore in the boarding houses, but of course there was and is no evidence of the connection.

All this Felipa knew and as she finally moved from the sleeping state into full consciousness, she drew a wrap about her and wandered along the companionway to the deck, and of course there was the *Gazela*, ablaze from stem to stern, fire crackling along the yards, flames shooting up her mainmast, her profile illuminated as if by electric bars. She moved at the precise moment, her bowsprit rising as she lurched forward with a hiss of steam into the mounting surf in the bay. Did Felipa scream? We do not know. Perhaps she merely froze with horror for there is no terror greater than one you have already predicted for yourself at the lowest ebb of your own imaginings. The light of the *Gazela* was too bright.

A few moment later, the striking of their own ship's bell roused all on board and within minutes they were near the centre of a spiralling gust of wind which marked the onset of a revolving storm.

"What is it?" Jack Hannah can be presumed to have said. He did not have time to say much because they had to make sail.

And her answer we may be sure was framed in one word that meant so much to ignorant and superstitious people.

"*Caleuche*."

It was a word he, Jack Hannah, had heard before, and would hear again, and ultimately, he would believe in it all.

Chapter Eleven

Before we left Mas a Fuera, wrote Evans, we experienced a williwaw or whirlwind of a minor kind, and although there was a mild tremor ashore, the severity of it was felt elsewhere and we put to sea in haste, the Captain losing the anchor, but we were soon into fair winds and there was day after day when the Creator of the Heavens and the Earth smiled upon us all. The islands we had just left interested me immensely even though we had not set foot upon the shore, and the Sailing Directory revealed that the larger island of Juan Fernandez was indeed the place where marooning was commonplace in times past. Not only Alexander Selkirk was abandoned there but, eighty years before, a party from Admiral De Witt's fleet landed a prisoner with a burial party, the deceased being encased in a coffin and after the burial the prisoner was left ashore to be marooned there. Within a day, however, the prisoner had dug up the coffin with his bare hands, removed the corpse and put to sea in the coffin, successfully using it as a canoe and overtaking his becalmed shipmates and begging for his life which was happily restored to him.

I told this amusing anecdote to Mr Waters who received it very curtly. Like a number of others he is affected by a mild lassitude, and the continual presence of the Captain in company with Senhora Salaverry once more has had an irritating effect upon him. I have again attempted to conduct a form of religious worship and have spoken several times to the Captain who continually retorts that the men have no appetite for it. He is not as short with me as he has been hitherto, but even in the days of fair weather when we rounded the Horn with all the signs of a fast passage, the Captain continued to be preoccupied and left the running of the ship to me.

The voyage back down to the Cape was made in flying fish weather, the flying fish darting out of the water in sprung crescents of silver, shimmering in the sun as they jumped, and perhaps the *Caleuche*'s legend was for them alone for the bonita ate the flying fish in the water while the bosun birds devoured them in the air, and that was their cycle of life. But the fine weather put all aboard in a good mood and it was Harry Grail who emerged the soul of joviality. Now there was often a song going and Harry Grail, a new re-born

Harry Grail turned entertainer, recited snatches of monologue in a flat monotone.

"Here's to the man that can heave the lead
Roar marks and deeps like thunder!
Send down a mast in a gale of wind,
And sing out, 'Stand from under!' "

"What's happened to old Grail?" they asked. "Very pleased with himself is Happy Harry. Look! I say! Is that a smile?"

The inscrutable eyes looked back at them, and now his small mean purse of a mouth was ever ready to join them in song, even on one occasion revealing further attributes of his character when Tommy Dance busied himself with the unending task of chipping rust from the exterior of the water butts. He appeared stripped to the waist with a set of spoons, reversing them like bone clappers and working them over his raised thigh, along his free arm, even the back of his thick pockmarked neck as he chanted like a workhouse inmate set up to do a turn for the master on Christmas Day. There was something about him that reminded you of a very sinister organ grinder's monkey.

"Chip, chip, chip!
With a hammer in your grip . . .
From the anchor to the cathead
To beneath the counter's deep . . ."

He went on day after day and from under that low-browed ferret's face, the eyes winked, the crooked mouth grinned, Grail poetry in a Grail summer, and no explanation for it. "That cat's been at the cream," the labouring ones said but they put it down to the weather.

There was a song going in the nights, too, hearty choruses slipping into lullabies. They sang "Ben Bolt" and "Clementine" and "Seeing Nelly Home", and once Evans remarked that when there was a song going in the dog watch, there was no need for the after guard to worry. Jack Hannah made a point of encouraging them in fishing with trailed long lines and once they caught a shark and tried oily shark steaks with apprehension but no ill effects, then a flying fish came aboard to save itself from pursuit and this, Harry Grail, using his re-sharpened knife, carefully filleted as a present to the Captain and his lady, touching his forelock as he presented it and suffering the gibes of the fo'c'sle in smug satisfaction ("Live and let

live, boys!"). They parted from a school of whales and Tommy
Dance was set to work as glazier, puttying and re-puttying the
windows round the poop, and once Harry spent an entire day
painting bird lime on a spar, farding as he called it, whistling and
cooing in an attempt to catch pigeons to add to the week-end's sea
pie. When he caught them he broke their necks between forefinger
and thumb, cooing sorrowfully to himself, supplying Evans with
the delicacy.

"A good man, that Grail," Evans reported. "He's come on a lot.
Mind, you've got to have a way with him. Give him his head and
trust him – there's nothing like responsibility to build up a man like
that. It brings them out, you see."

Cape pigeons made their appearance once more, a whole flock of
them hovering over the stern, their swoopings and divings somehow jolly after the weirdly screaming mollymawks, or the sullen
heavy flight of the albatross. Then sharks hung around for the day,
blue and gold pilot fish nosing alongside, but they were evidently
well fed, for their movements were sluggish and they soon disappeared. The Captain now posed in a deck chair, while the Senhora
painted his portrait. He seemed to have grown younger, had trimmed his beard to a neat spade shape and turned out in a linen jacket
which Tommy had pressed. He wore his uniform cap and the two of
them, the Senhora in a makeshift artist's smock with her usual
headscarf since she had ceased to oil her hair once more, made a
handsome picture aft while Harry Grail over the side on a stage in
calm days cooed at the sharks, screwing up his mouth and making
affectionate gibes at them. The handsome couple, unaware, were the
subject of speculation in the fo'c'sle. Willie Twomallow had given
his mind to it, produced an apothecary's diagnosis, comfortably
seated on his fat buttocks darning a sock, his apple cheeks rosy.

"My view, boys, is that he's falling for her all over again. He give
it to her once and thought the better of it, and now she wants a bit
o'courtin' again, that's the root of it. They're all the same, boys, they
want the smell of it, the smoke and powder, but they also want it
gentle with a fella that'll talk after. Like a bouquet to 'em, that is, a bit
of chat after!"

"You didn't get nuthin' extra in Shit Street for talkin' after,"
Morgan Morgan said. "You got exactly the same as me, a great
green blob on the end of it and a flea in the pipe all the way home!"

"No, but the Senhora's different."

"How d'you mean different?"

"I'm telling you, boys, love it is, you mark my words. Sorry he is for the meat he gave her on the way out, meat and lip, and chucked her out of the doss when her shimmy got in the way of his charts!"

Morgan Morgan couldn't see it, and Tommy Dance reported openly now. Talking, they were, talking all day, and not so much as a sniff of the how's yer father! She'd put the block on it, the hawse was tight.

While Harry Grail said nothing, but smiled all day, a dark secretive smile, now and again polishing a gold ring he'd got from somewhere.

"Where did you get that from, Harry? You ain't bringing presents home, are you?"

"My old mother's it was, boys."

"Get away!"

"Took it from that flying fish with a message."

"What's the message?"

"Going to fine meself up."

"Fine yourself up?"

"A company man from now on, that's me. Bosun on her next trip. Evans was only saying today."

"That come-to-Jesus . . ."

"A man like that remembers a willing hand."

Harry Grail's ambition had turned to gloating. Give a man a secret, he becomes an owner, and Harry, mindful of the pathetic upraised legs of his victim in that ridiculous position in the cabin ashore, had found a new spring in his step. He was a man avenged, the kin were avenged too, and now the *Avalon* bothered him no longer. The fire, the storm and the sudden leave-taking had fixed everything and made it a foolproof crime. He couldn't have planned it better, a weight was removed from his shoulders, and consequently the cracked smile of the contented ferret appeared constantly. "The lil ole world had took a shine on her lil ole self." And now what could he do to please his officers? He would have sailed with Jack Hannah for a lifetime, hugging that secret knowledge to himself. The Captain was so far gone on the woman anyway that he hardly noticed, and Evans had come to the fore in these palmy days of flying fish weather. Well then, he'd ingratiate himself with Evans.

Evans brooded over the *Gazela*.

"A copper ore man, that ship, or I'm a Dutchman."

160

"Well, you know a copper ore man when you see one, sir, I'll be bound."

"She was the *Avalon*, I'm positive. We should have towed her off."

"Salvage, sir?"

"Moral duty," Evans said.

"Well, there was no knowing how she was lying, sir. And very like, she'd broken her back. Must have. And the rot ripe in her. Otherwise she'd never have broke up like that, or gone that far up them rocks."

"The fire was very convenient," Evans said. "Not a trace of her left now, not a barrel, nor a spar." Everything was too right for his thinking.

"Well, you would know, sir," Harry said. "Pity none of us got ashore like – just to make sure."

Mr Waters meanwhile said nothing about that chance sighting of old Captain Josh ashore, nor gave voice to any of his suspicions. He did not feel quite up to the mark if the truth be known, feeling a heaviness in his legs, and daily he drove himself to complete the lightest tasks. There were subtle changes taking place on the ship. Grail too, he noticed, now began to hang back, having his chats with Evans, ceasing to be first aloft, sitting down more often, and a number of the others with him. As it happened, the ship seemed to sail herself to the Cape and there were none of the rigours of the passage out.

The big German and Billy Bones were making rope mats, the two of them busying themselves with scraps of rope, bent over their tasks like needlewomen, both with the sailor pox and both sheepishly teased by their shipmates on the other watches. They seemed to be relaxing too, preparing themselves for the worst the Horn had to offer. But the Horn had gone to sleep too, and day after day the *Whisper* sailed on in cruise weather on an ocean made friendly by constant winds, and apart from the lassitude that dogged some of them it was a balmy period when it was good to be alive.

For Jack Hannah, this was the swan song of the voyage and strangely, it had begun with Felipa's terror. She did not speak for a week after leaving Mas a Fuera and even after they had successfully emerged from the threat posed by the dangerous pyramidical seas and ridden out the blow, it was some time before he could get Felipa

161

to talk to him. He had a great wish for intimacy. Couldn't she forgive him his boorishness? Couldn't she understand his relief that his worries were over? An end, said he, to the *Avalon* affair and that seedy old man left behind to rot – he cared not whether he was alive or dead. For the first time in his life perhaps, a wish for gentleness had come to him, and with it a desire for routine and order. Couldn't she understand that? Above all, in view of everything that had happened, couldn't she forgive him?

But for weeks, it seemed, she did not even listen to him. She was indifferent to both food and company. There was a great weariness come upon her. One night in her cabin, he took her hand and held it, those great almond eyes looking at him limply. She seemed to be exhausted. He was puzzled and anxious. He had never had a day's illness in his life.

"What is it, Felipa?"

"Please . . ." she wanted him to go. There was a glaze over her eyes, a pallor to her skin. Her palm was cold and lifeless. He guessed it was a malaise of the spirit.

"Felipa, tell me?"

She gave a little shiver. It was still warm. She had a linen sheet drawn up around her, her hair clung thickly about her shoulders, but her face was without animation. "Think a thing, you show it." Perhaps she did not dare to think.

He frowned. He wanted her to laugh again, to tease him, even to play the Senhora. But she made no response. Then he did an extraordinary thing. He put her hand to his lips and caressed it, a Frenchman's kiss.

"You must tell me."

But it was another week before she mentioned the word *Caleuche* so that he had the physical evidence of her decline to check the smile that came automatically to his lips. People believed what it was necessary for them to believe. If it was serious for her, it was serious for him.

One night much later, there was a moon making a long pathway to the sea and shining from an unclouded velvet sky. He had insisted that she come up on deck. It was such a clear night that but for the motion of the sea you felt that your reflection could be clearly seen in the water, a time of night when such legends are not as absurd as they seem in the hard light of day. He had heard other such stories himself, and of course, there were strange sights at sea, unmanned

162

ships abandoned by their crews and sailing the seas for years on end, bumping off the pitch of the Horn, coming up and falling off before the wind, their wheels unattended, no soul about their decks, sailing on alone into all eternity because they took so long to sink. But she meant something else, he knew, and he knew better than to sneer, so perhaps his accepting silence did more for him than any words he might have found. She offered no resistance when he placed his arm about her and led her to his cabin. His desire was never very far away.

There now began a period which he never quite understood, a time when the mysterious blankness of her face and the emptiness of her eyes resembled a canvas waiting for an artist's brush to give it meaning – but it was also a time when the inscrutability of her face was not matched by the actions of her body and they resumed their love-making in a silence that was somehow made eerie and fraudulent by the absence of even the simplest endearments on her part. He would have a lasting memory of the eagerness of her mouth coming down upon his, of the incisive needle sharpness of her teeth, of the low moan which accompanied the arching of her back and the havoc wrought by her fingernails against his skin, but he did not have the wit then to sense a performance. There was still some part of her he could not touch and he had a sense of an area of pain and a depth of feeling so savage it could not be communicated. One performance gave way to another and he could not help watching her mouth (knowing in what forbidden places it had been) and being faintly amused at the vicarage garden game they now began to play in conversation. She would not stay in his cabin and their talks took on an air of respectibility once more as they stood on deck. The good weather continued and he had time now for idleness. He remembered a voyage he had made, as a young apprentice to the south seas where a man could earn a living in a climate that did not attempt to break you as these long voyages around the Horn so often did.

Had she ever been to the south seas?

"No, Captain." She kept up that pretence in public and had resumed her painting. "I am a traveller only for a purpose. Now, will you hold your head still. You will have to settle for a red beard, I cannot quite get the colour."

She was painting him a portrait such as might hang on a boardroom wall, but he did not see the humour of it. Instead, he tried to tell her that the world beckoned. He also wanted to show her how

163

broadminded and human he was. Whatever thoughts he might have had about dagoes, he was long past them now. Once he had been witness of blackbirding in the Solomons, but the capture of slaves did not interest him so much as the quality of life aboard the leisurely trading schooners who were not always engaged in that fiendish trade.

"It's a happy go lucky life there, most of the schooners are manned by ne'er-do-wells, runaways from the men o'war, a hard drinking, heavy-fisted crowd, but Australia's opening up. They need reliable shipmasters. It's a country with a future."

"Blackbirding?" she said.

"No, for trade. I often think of it, the climate's kind, a new country has its advantages."

"Do you mean a new life? Somewhere where you are not known?"

"Yes," he said earnestly. "We all have things to escape from. Surely, it is what we all want at some time in our lives?"

That drew a smile.

"Perhaps, but wherever we go, we take ourselves with us." She had a way of not entering into details, but he took her answer for acquiescence.

"Or, would you prefer Sveynton?"

She made some tentative brush strokes, considered them thoughtfully, pretended to be deep in thought.

For perhaps a day then, he actually considered her as a Captain's wife, notwithstanding the difficulties they would face, seeing such a possibility as an adventure. To be young was everything. What was life, if it was not a challenge with a partner to meet the world's ills head on? Well, he could dream. There were *Caleuches* and *Caleuches*, smiles that you would never quite forget.

She said nothing, as it happened, giving him that enigmatic smile and leaving him for an hour or two for his mind to race again, but even her silence appeared to be evidence that he had sown a seed. In these days, he became conscious of her moving confidently about the deck, a woman in control of herself, not so much his for the taking, but for the asking – he was sure of that. The fine weather brought out her fine clothes, the fine clothes showed off her figure, her figure arched his eyebrows, mesmerised him. But at the same time he was careful not to repeat what he thought of as his first mistake. When he touched her now, it was almost as if by accident.

164

He was courtesy itself. Perhaps she was somehow inviolate despite the things which had been done to her? Perhaps he did not know her at all?

Now there was another change in her as if she had wholly rediscovered a new propriety and she seemed to take care to come into the saloon only when there were others present. She did not, he noticed, complete the painting, and there were nights when he thought he heard her laughing with Mr Waters on deck, nights when he strained to hear what might be said but he could not. When they met, she would contrive to interest him, asking if she might try her hand at some savoury cake in the galley, and then she seemed to have fun with Morgan Morgan. He soon put a stop to that by imposing his own heavy presence on them both. But then she brought her savouries to his place at the saloon table and bade him eat them while they were hot, and it was again as if he did not know her at all.

The weather could not last, of course, nor could his dreaming, but they'd had the sun on their backs for long enough to stiffen them, and when it changed and they lumped into the great Cape Horn greybeards and had rounded Cape Stiff, leaving that bleak dreary looking coast, all black rocks and white foam, to westward, he noticed that one or two of the men were strangely limp, even hangdog in their movements. He put it down to the softness of the passage and the sun. He had, as before, only one focal point to his attentions.

During this period, Evans's letter progressed steadily, almost as if he had known that it would be preserved long after his days. He noticed everything about the Captain but less and less about the crew, including Grail who had brought his filthy bag of rings from the hiding place and lay in his bunk, playing with it. Now the crew were moving away from Grail, avoiding him.

After Cape Horn, we experienced a hard gale from the WSW with squalls and a high sea, but the ship, although labouring much, rode the sea well, and we had every hope of continuing with a fast passage.

At this time, the seaman Grail who had much impressed me on the return voyage, lay confined in his bunk, the lassitude which had affected him growing worse. Remembering the Captain's treatment of poor Samuel Scuse on the outward voyage, I did not at first report the matter, and here I must confess I was remiss. Very soon, he began to complain of "a light burning in on the eyes" and before long it was clear that he was in the grip of some malady which did not at first impress us with its seriousness.

165

The Captain was in his bunk when he heard the row on deck. Evans was belabouring the boy for taking the water from the butt.

"It's for Mr Grail, sir."

"Mister Grail indeed!"

"He's parched, sir, and crying for a drink."

"Crying?"

"Yes, sir. You'd better come and have a look at him. Please sir. He's trying to scream but he can't get the words out."

"Scream? Grail?"

"Yes, sir."

"What has he done?"

"I don't know, sir."

"Oh very well, but leave that ladle where it is."

In the fo'c'sle, the men had kept away from Harry Grail for days, simply because he did not want them near him and swore at them, clutching his bag of rings. At first, they covered up for him in his absences on deck, and Tommy brought his food down as usual, but his food was not eaten. Then he began to sweat at night and to call out in his sleep, but when they went to him to give him a shake, he struck out at them and they knew his temper well enough to leave him alone. Leave an awkward man to his awkward self, they said. He'd jeered enough at them when they got the pox, let him stew awhile. But then he cried for water and they could not leave a man without water. Besides, he was beginning to smell.

Evans went down into the fo'c'sle humming and hawing. In the dim light, the man's eyes were turned away as he faced the knotted wooden bulkhead and he seemed strangely hunched and small in the bunk. The sweat was standing out on his neck, the blankets were twisted as he gripped them in a frenzy and now a solitary hand lay over them, tightly gripping on to the small leather bag.

"Grail? What's the matter with you, man?"

No answer.

"You're not a man to shirk your duties."

The shoulders shivered, lay still.

"How long has he been like this?"

"He's been up and down, sir, since we sailed."

"He's done his work well. He was in good spirits."

"Not for a few days now, sir."

Evans did not want to touch him. The atmosphere of the fo'c'sle was rank enough at the best of times, but the man had obviously fouled himself. He continued to sweat and the sight of those twisted blankets spelt fever.

Then he turned in a writhing motion as if every muscle in his body had to be galvanised to make the effort to open his eyes. They were unnaturally bright against a death white pallor. Now he croaked hoarsely.

"The light . . ."

"Light?" Evans said.

"Burning in on my eyes . . ."

It was dark in the fo'c'sle. Evans licked his lips apprehensively.

"You've got a bit of fever, by the look of it."

They were alone in the fo'c'sle, the ship was bounding along, oilskins swung on their pegs and they could hear the swift onrush of water against the bow. Everything in the world seemed cleaner than that fo'c'sle. It had kept the land stink long after they'd sailed.

"You'd better wash him down," Evans said to the boy.

"He won't let anybody touch him."

"Get a bucket and a rag. Sea water mind."

Grail began to mumble. Evans spoke, keeping his distance.

"You've got a touch of fever. If you'd been ashore, I could understand it," Evans said. "If you'd been ashore, you might have picked up something?"

The eyes closed. There was a groan, a muttered curse that was incomprehensible. He seemed to be trying to kick the blankets off. Evans pulled at the blankets, lifted them and looked at the legs. They were shivering. He was about to cover them up when he noticed a red swelling above the ankle.

"Ah," Evans said, "That explains it." It was a bite of some kind, rats probably. Guano brought visitors. Whatever was wrong with Grail, it probably wasn't contagious.

But in the evening, Mr Waters did not make an appearance in the saloon and his eyes were definitely yellow. Evans went to see him, held a lantern up to his eyes as he leant over the bunk.

"Jaundiced," he said.

Mr Waters was sweating as well and said he couldn't keep food down. He didn't like the light near his eyes.

"Put it away," Mr Waters said, weakly gesticulating to the lantern.

"Let me see your tongue," Evans said, but he didn't quite know what he was looking for. They hadn't touched land, he kept telling

167

himself, not since Talcahuano, so it couldn't be fever. There was no fever in Talcahuano.

But it was fever of a most virulent kind. He got his answer from the Senhora's eyes as she looked into the cabin, a casual sociable enquiry as she was passing. There was a moment then when he sensed the gravity of it in the immediate recoil of her face. The pupils of her eyes were positively dilated. He could see terror in them. Then he realised. He had not himself seen the bodies drifting in the tide race ashore but he had heard of them. And she had been ashore, he thought, as had the Captain.

Waters grinned, a resigned grin, as if he knew already, then looked away, keeping the diagnosis to himself. He was beginning to dribble. There was an opaque sheen over his eyes that was more than resignation. Men very often know when they are going to die. Something in their bodies lifts them to their destiny.

The Senhora retreated into the companionway. Evans followed. "Does the Captain know?"

"The Captain?" he said flatly. He wanted to make a pointed remark then. The Captain knew only what suited him. If ever there was a man who had had his first command undermined from the outset, it was the Captain. He saw it all as a parable, a biblical story in which good and evil were as separate as sharply defined colours. There were no shades of opinion possible. But now her fear cautioned him. She was a dago. Dagoes knew about fever. "No more than a touch of fever. I'll inform him presently."

Her lips parted. He saw a pink sliver of tongue moisten them. She looked at the cabin door meaningfully. He enjoyed her fear, closed the door.

"You have an opinion on the matter, Senhora?"

Jack Hannah had remained in his cabin all day. He would blame Evans later for not reporting the matter, but Evans did not delay for long, and by the time Evans came into the cabin, Hannah was already feeling the same lassitude he'd observed in Mr Waters the day before. The edge seemed to be going off things. The trouble was, he thought, that he'd never been ill in his life, and this lack of edge seemed to be a state of tiredness which at first showed itself simply as a lack of will. He could have gone up on deck if he'd wanted to – but he didn't want to. By midday he had a dryness of throat and an ache behind the eyes that was more than tiredness, and it was an effort to do the slightest thing, even to cross his legs, and

168

the dull headache continued. Then, within a matter of hours, it seemed to get worse and his sense of time began to slip away. When did Evans begin to refuse the boy water? When had he last eaten? What was the meal he didn't want? And when had he last seen Felipa? He couldn't remember exactly. Had they quarrelled? Or was she just resigned to his silence? But when had he seen her? Was it one day away? Was it two? What was Evans doing locking up the water butts? Where was Evans? Why was no one standing the deck? Why had everything got so quiet? Was that mumbling coming from the sailors who stood around in little groups on deck? He had noticed that before and meant to do something about it, but hadn't.

He didn't feel anything wrong with his eyes until Evans came, and why, when he came, did Evans take so long to speak? He seemed to be standing there opening and closing his mouth, like a man trying to speak to you under water – there was a faint buzzing sensation in his ears. Evans's face seemed like a wooden carving.

"People can go down like ninepins."

"What . . . what?" He couldn't hear properly.

He was aware that it was a moment that Evans had been waiting for, and yet, staring at that sepulchral graveyard face, he felt reservations. Evans was doing the best he could. Why did he have it in for Evans? The man was a ship's housewife, no more, but he'd always known that. Why couldn't he like Evans? He was very unfair on Evans. And then a new feeling. . . . He had better like Evans. Evans might be all he had to rely upon. He felt light headed by the time Evans came. He could not quite hear properly and he did not want to move. And Evans gave no sign of panic. Evans was dressed for his watch, oilskins and body and soul lashings of yarn around the cuffs of his jacket and trouser legs, standing there like a gravedigger ready for bad weather – but the wind was dropping, he'd have a quiet watch. Trust Evans to get himself up like that. Foul weather gear for a fine weather watch, that was Evans.

Evans seemed to have been in the cabin for five minutes before he understood him; a black-garbed man like a dismayed vulture swaying in the heat haze.

"What . . . what . . . ?" He couldn't get the words out. He seemed to have been slumped in a chair for hours.

Evans held the lantern up to look into his face.

"Put that . . . what are you doing, Evans?"

"Yellow jack, sir."

"What . . ."

"One man in the fo'c'sle, and Mr Waters."

"Nonsense, Evans, not after all this time. We've been weeks at sea."

"Yellow fever aboard. Without a doubt, sir."

"No . . . not yellow fever. Can't be yellow fever."

"It's true, sir. Even your . . . the charterer confirms it."

"The charterer?"

"Those who have been ashore have brought it back with them. You went ashore, sir, and so did the Senhora."

"Not possible, Evans."

"It is, sir. Can you stand on your feet unaided?"

"What?"

"Now, sir. Can you get to your feet?"

"Evans. If I get my hands on you . . ."

"Unaided, sir."

And he could not. He could not? But how could a fever, yellow fever, hide itself, bury itself away all these weeks to break all the rules he knew about?

"Contact, sir," Evans said. "That's all I can suggest. Filth proliferates, I mean, it has its own tenacity like the weeds of the fields."

"Evans . . . Senhora Felipa."

"Filth is well and truly aboard, yes, indeed, sir."

He could not fully understand nor keep his eyes open. His limbs felt huge, his eyelids leaden. And he would remember Evans standing there ready for his watch, black garbed with a lantern in his hand, that bony face gleaming with the light of moral rectitude, his lips tight drawn, his satisfaction apparent. Fever aboard and raging! But it couldn't be yellow jack. He'd heard nothing of it ashore. And then he remembered those corpses in the tide race, and the insistence that they should have no contact with the fort above the cliff. His father performed services for the authorities. But what services? Was he the man, the only man, who was their contact with the mainland? And why was nothing said about those bodies? No, he was rambling. It was nothing to do with his father. It was just a spot of fever.

"You are very ill," Evans said. "It may be that nothing can be done. D'you feel a light burning in on the eyes? I understand. Let me assist you. Do not think of me, sir. I have every confidence it will not strike me."

And it did not.

170

Chapter Twelve

There were weeks now when the log was not written up at all. *A light burning in on the eyes*, Evans had finally reported, but by that time the lassitude had come upon them all, and later, Jack Hannah had difficulty remembering just how or when the malaise started. He would be able to remember only images and shapes, dog days drifting into recall like a part of childhood, the present and the past intermingling, scenes enacted woozily and without order, but nevertheless, continuing to run before his eyes, screened only by the bulkhead curtain as he lay limply in his bunk, sweating and sweating, the strength oozing out of him. And this was for the major part of their homecoming. The *Whisper* had ridden the greybeards so well. There was none of the battle of the passage out, but again, the images appeared like casual visitors in his delirium, among them the three-fingered hand of Jackie Breeze appearing, and disappearing as he remembered it rising on the crest of that one wave. His own feeling was of a kind of cottony weightlessness, as if he were drifting eerily in the confines of the cabin, quite free of the motion of the ship. Sometimes it was light, some days it was dark, but often he was awake, head lolling, eyes half open as he was made scrutineer of events, never remaining in charge of them. Occasionally, he tried to rouse himself to shout some abuse at Evans, but he never actually quite got it out and there was Evans's face like a mask on a bedpost seeming to be permanently fixed at the foot of his bunk, first the sou'westered figure staring gravely down, then in his shirt sleeves, sweating himself, with the pallor of the grave and always insisting that everything should be done exactly as he wanted it. Cutlery never left the cabin. Towels remained where they were. Now Evans was nurse, continually washing his own hands.

"You washerwoman, Evans!" he wanted to shout, but he could never get his lips around the phrase, and Evans by this time was a nut that could not be cracked. He tried to lift an accusatory finger at him, but the arm that held the finger would not move, and that made him cry and then he was ashamed of crying, ashamed of lying there – and

171

then, growing weaker, he was not ashamed at all and just lay there, witness of the procession of faces and listening to the sentences that meant nothing, like Evans saying, "He's got rat bites on his legs, but it can't be rat bites, it must be mosquitoes – it's always carried by mosquitoes" – and then there was something else that Evans harped upon to do with his father and the dead Chinese woman floating on the tide. And he had a moral for everything. "All races are the same under God!" Evans said, and then, as things got worse, "Fornication!" This Evans said every day for days and there was no checking him now and he was even driven to pleading with Evans, even crying, "Oh, please, Mr Evans," and Evans would reply, "Excuse me, sir, you are soiling yourself in your own filth!" and "The light burning in on the eyes, is God's light, Captain. All I hope is you have time to make your peace."

But even in the delirium of the cotton wool world, Evans still would not go too far, and the man was indefatigable, both with his accusations and with his attentions, including the constant washing of those pummelling fingers. He had long, lean, cruel fingers.

"Forget, Evans!" he shouted at him one night.

"The good Lord will not let me forget."

"You must forget, Evans. You can't carry it all in your mind, man." (But perhaps he was then addressing himself.)

"I have made a copious record, sir, and if you please, I have carried the ship this thirty days."

But that was later, so much later and by that time he had the strength to argue and to plead. Felipa made an appearance and came at last into the cabin when they were closer to home, but she never let up with her evil purpose, persuading him, working on him – and all the time he knew he'd agree even though it was against every principle he believed in, every rule in the book, but she didn't care about that, it was him she was thinking about, she said, and at the same time miraculously she'd got Evans on her side. When they thought he was asleep he could hear the two of them whispering in the darkness and he knew then there was nothing she could not do. He could even hold out no hope for Evans as well as himself. Well, that was how it seemed and Evans, reassured despite the enormity of what she proposed, went off like a blackbird in a new suit of feathers to clean the ship for the pilot, but that was much much later and there was a clarity to that. A clarity and purpose, one explaining the other.

What was not clear was the very beginning, that light burning in on the eyes. Try as he might, in the cotton wool world where he floated, he could not connect the spoon-playing Grail with the Grail who held his hand over his eyes and was too weak to scream. This Grail talked, he was well aware, but then they all talked and none more than Evans who went back to the very beginning.

"I remembered the man Scuse, sir, a very distended stomach. If you remember we got our slant just when you were going to insert the paraffin tube into his private parts."

"His arse, Evans . . pump him out . . ."

"Yes, sir, well you have your own expressions. If you remember, you left the actual doing of it to me. And sir, the way that man was treated left me in no doubt but that you should not treat another sick man on this ship, nor leave me to bury him."

"That was Breeze."

"No sir, it was Breeze you would not lower a boat for."

"I couldn't, Evans."

"It matters not now, except to your conscience, but I too have a conscience and Grail has told me things."

"He's playing the spoons, Evans. He's a village boy, a Grail, kicks and clouts from the day he was born – nothing goes right for them, they're Grails. Oh, you don't know, Evans. You can't handle men."

"Can I not, sir? Indeed, and perhaps you might ask yourself why? What have I had all the voyage but Bumscrew Evans and Parson Evans and Bo Peep Evans, humiliated by the Captain and ridiculed by the men – until they learned who it was that would bury them."

"How many dead, Evans? You said there were dead. How many?"

The voice went on and on. He grew to know it so well, it might have been his own voice.

"Humiliated and ridiculed while you lay with your seed spilling over the scissoring thighs of that wanton . . . I have seen you, sir, as have the crew through the lazarette. Yes, sir, Billy Bones made a hole with an auger and there's not a man aboard this ship . . D'you know that in the doldrums, they would give up their meat ration for a spell in the lazarette, sir? They got very bored with all the talking and they made bets as to which day there would be a resumption and what would be the latitude and longitude of it, each separate act of fornication. These men, you said you can handle."

"How many dead?"

173

"At first, I thought it was heat stroke but then I saw the rat bite – but it is not caused by rats. I knew very well because I was on the *Cobrero* in Santiago when five men died and it was the general opinion that swamp fever was caused by mosquitoes. In fact, the rat bite put me off, sir – just as the man Grail told me – everybody was put off the scent of the deposition of the bleeding heart of the *Avalon* mutiny. The removal was not a cannibalistic act made in frenzy of blood letting – it was a deliberate act of savagery ordered by your father so as to terrorise the men to do his bidding.

"Oh, well may you weep, sir, well may you weep, but ask yourself why it is that alone of all the able-bodied men on this ship, I remain on my own two feet? It is the Good Lord and my faith, sir, and fear not, I have cut away the topsails because I cannot reef them and we are sailing under lower courses because I can manage them on my own, sir. Yes sir, on my own!"

He understood then, the enormity of it. Yellow jack was raging. Evans was on his own. Oh, who would sail alone with Evans, or suffer the pains of being grateful to Evans? And his own weakness continued.

"How many dead? Please tell me. You must tell me!"

"Ah, that's a question, that is."

"Port watch, man?"

"Have you no concern for your officers?"

"How many dead?"

"Mr Waters was second after Grail, then Twomallow jumped overboard, far gone in delirium. Bones died this morning and Morgan Morgan has the light in his eyes, then there's the starboard watch, three men down and the worst thing you have not seen, sir, nor do you know it, Grail, sir. D'you remember his very high spirits, a man of low intelligence like that?"

"He's a Grail, Evans."

"And capable of murder most foul. Before he died, he showed me the knife, then a bag of rings in a little leather bag –filthy, sir, but even as he was talking to me, he had begun to decompose when alive, sir, that was the remarkable thing – with this complaint, they liquefy into death, and in the last stages, the rate of putrification is so great that . . ."

"Evans . . . Go away from me! Go . . . away . . ."

"Had you ever been near Grail, sir? Did you have any contact with him? Come sir, a little soup. You are giving me the greatest concern.

174

I do not think you can hold on much longer. Excuse me, sir, have you seen your own eyes?"

Lying there, day after day, there was only Evans. Evans reporting, Evans cleaning up, Evans trying to get soup down him, wiping him, moistening his brow, all the time talking. There was nothing he did not know, no one he had not listened to, and now, miraculously, they had drifted into a calm and Evans surpassed himself, even finding time to describe their predicament. Evans alone held up. Evans even found time for his letter. Evans too had his fears, but Evans conquered them. Five men dead, and all the rest afflicted. And Evans, surpassing himself, wrote his own private log for all history to see.

I had now the dreadful prospect of seeing all that remained in the fo'c'sle perish and prayed to God that I might not be the last, for I should then become an ocean solitary dragging on a life of hours in every second. A day became an age of misery. There was still no hint of a breeze, not even a catspaw, and the calm appeared as if it would last for ever and ever. I was in the presence of human dissolution and had never contemplated that so horrible a situation as mine was possible. Millions of living things seemed to ascend from the depths of the sea, or had been engendered from the stagnation and the heat and rendered the surface of the ocean and the decks of the ship, a plaything for their crawling snaky antics.

There was worse to come and there was silence for days now, it seemed to Jack Hannah, hardly a movement in the ship, and he was conscious of a great gap, a void when the heat was insufferable. The silence was like the silence of some great cavern and he began to have a recurring dream on which he saw himself hunched against the wind on the cliff above Ennal's Point, seeing himself standing there looking out over the cauldron of boiling water surging on the Hugo Bank. He was land-locked in the shelter of a wall as he looked, and he could feel the stubble on his chin for he was shabby in clothes that did not belong to him. He was aware of an embittered feeling of helplessness as he watched the never-ending curl of those breakers and also he had learned things about himself. He could not quite manage in this life. When he looked down, his boots were shabby and unpolished, one of the soles was detaching itself from the welt and as he stood there, children were laughing at him and he heard other voices. "Fingers to the bone," they said. "He was deep sea once. A guano man." And the voices laughed all the more. Then he was walking, down the cliff path to his cottage, those boots taking him

175

wearily to a shining brass rail on the step. But when he went inside, there was no one there. He was deserted, penniless, a man who could not cope, the solitary catch of a workhouse haul.

Three or four times this dream re-occurred and each time he awoke in a lather of sweat in the cavern of silence, and he could not understand why he was alone, and then he blurted out a name, the first strength in his voice in weeks.

"Felipa?" he said. "Felipa?"

Evans had returned by then.

"Ah!" Evans said. "I was wondering when you'd ask! Well, sir, it went like this, sir."

And that set Evans off again. At this time, there was a moment of miraculous clarity.

"You'd better hoist a signal pennant, Evans."

"I can't, sir."

"Can't?"

"The signal locker's been emptied. Any flag which might have given any indication of our plight has disappeared."

"Hoist . . ."

"There's no distress flag, only the ensign on the staff and that's in ribbons."

And that made him wonder. A ship in distress without a hand able to stand should indicate its plight by flags. But where were the flags?

"Why, sir? Ask Madam sir."

"Madam?"

"Your Senhora. She has not been seen in ten days. She did not even look in when you were shouting the name of that Greek Seaman. Yes, sir, you had your hands around your own neck and you were dribbling, sir. Who will tell me that the sins of the fathers are not visited upon the sons?"

There was one incident which Evans recorded! Felipa had paid some attention to Evans. He might be necessary. She had been alone in her cabin when Evans passed down the companionway carrying a lantern on his way to inspect the cargo. The cabin door was open. She'd been brushing her hair and heard him coming and for devilment thrown a brooch on to the deck outside the cabin where it would be obvious to him. What irritated her was that she could not get under Evans's guard, nor crack that formal mask of disapproval. She heard his breathing, his ponderous step, heard him pause, pick up the brooch and look in at her. It was the butterfly brooch.

She continued to brush her hair, aware that he was looking at her, then cast a sly glance at him, affecting surprise. She was wearing a lowcut gypsy blouse held by a string tied at the neck.

"Why, Mr Evans, you've brought me a present?"

"No I have not."

"Ah, you have found my brooch. Thank you."

He returned it. The hand that touched hers was coarse and trembling. You felt that those thin fingers would like to inflict a particular pain.

She moved the brush several times across the side of her head, smiled at him. But if he lusted after anything, it was not flesh.

"You are too modest, Mr Evans."

"Modest? What do you mean?"

"Did you know that there was a good deal of discussion as to who should have command of the ship before we sailed? It if it were not that your brother were part owner, I am sure they would have given the command to you. It was perhaps only his sense of fairness that prevented you . . ."

"Remember, my loyalty is to the Captain at all times."

"Of course, it is. But I wish he appreciated you more. For my part, I hope one day to see you where you rightfully belong."

"And where is that, if I may ask?"

"Why, you know very well, Mr Evans!"

But he would brook no disloyalties there.

"We depend on our ability, Senhora. We must let it speak for us," he smiled lugubriously and passed on. Only Evans could have used the royal "we".

But it was a seed sown, and perhaps Evans was made aware of her at another level that later she might build upon. She was making a friend of Tommy Dance again now and when the fever broke Tommy became her informant. From the moment when she saw Mr Waters's face she knew that it presented the greatest threat to all her ambitions, but she even had plans for that. She would either survive the fever or die of it. The fever made her more ruthless still.

At first, she brought Tommy Dance to her cabin.

"They're going down one by one in the fo'c'sle. It's the light, Miss, they can't face the light, Miss, Grail kept trying to tear at his own eyes as if the light was burning in on him. And there's a few off their food. Beg pardon, Miss, there's a few throwing up, and there's all black in it, and Mr Waters is far gone now."

177

After this, she began to eat from the preserved tins and jars she had shopped for at Talcahuano. There were stone jars of water and some wine and she got water from the reserve tank near the Captain's cabin. During this time, the Captain was strangely inert, feeling his own lassitude for a long period before he finally succumbed, and it was Evans who treated the sick. She had her own supply of water and food before the Captain's lassitude finally revealed itself as fever and the moment he showed his weakness and began complaining about the light, she locked herself away. This was before the full impact of the fever made itself felt and as they ran into the calm.

Then they threw Grail out of the fo'c'sle after he'd got Tommy to hide his filthy leather bag of rings. By now they had found out he'd been ashore. Jack Hannah managed one visit to him and it was then they all knew the most awful stage of the disease when the eyes began to liquify in the last hours of life with blood and water oozing from every pore of his body and even the corners of his eyes. This, a weakened Jack Hannah mistakenly thought, was dropsy. Felipa heard Twomallow scream as he jumped from the ship to his own death, grateful for the strength to do it, and she thought again of the *Caleuche* and its portent, but then as the Captain vanished she heard Evans squeaking.

"I think you'd better leave it to me, sir. The stench is worse than the guano. There's no question of burial, and you know I've not shirked my duty on that score. I shall have to use the shovel, sir."

It was then that Tommy Dance came running to her like a child to his mother, but she made him leave his clothes, every stitch, outside the cabin.

Now each event as each new day broke was strangely rooted in the past even as it happened.

"Bombas . . . Bombas . . . ," Harry Grail cried on the deck at the Captain. They were his last words, and then they shovelled him over. No one except she and the Captain knew what he meant.

The boy trembled in the cabin. She suggested he go to Mr Waters's cabin, but it was two days before they got rid of the body, and Billy Bones assisted with that, together with the Big German, and then Billy Bones went down with fever and at this time when she heard other men screaming and moaning and vomiting, she sent the boy at night to get the signal flags from the locker. If she could not have her cargo landed, she did not want to live. Three days Tommy lay in the corner of her cabin like a dog cowering. Who could blame him when they were shovelling men over, and now the wind dropped altogether and the silence of the calm returned to the ship and if ever there was a *Caleuche* ship, this was it. Evans alone tended to the yards, worrying about the Captain, attending to the Captain as if he wanted the Captain to live if only to suffer further pain and to witness all that he, Evans, was doing. Evans might have known that he would never be rewarded if there was no witness to his actions.

When Tommy became exhausted with the heat, she put him out of the cabin and finally finding his own clothes where he had left them, he dressed himself and went and found Evans who had thought him dead, another one jumped over, and she overheard their conversation too.

"I have been hiding, sir."

"What about your duty to your shipmates?"

"Yes, sir."

"Yes, sir. What sort of answer is that?"

"I'm sorry, sir."

"Very well then. The bogey stove is still alight. We want water, boiling water. Everything must be boiled, do you understand that?"

"Yes, sir."

"That is your duty, now. And then lime wash. The fo'c'sle must be lime washed. And the clothes shovelled over. First the water. When it is ready, bring me a pannikin to the Captain's cabin."

"Is he alive, sir?"

"Oh, yes, he's alive. The light does not burn in his eyes because he will live to burn in hell!"

"And the others, sir?"

"Five men in the shade on deck, not one left alive in that fo'c'sle, and the others weak, too weak to do their work, of course. Remember, touch no man with your hands, touch nothing."

"Yes, sir." (But Tommy forgot the chamois leather bag which he had hidden.)

"And sleep on deck – away from the others. Did you know Grail had been ashore?"

"No, sir."

"Then trust in your God and we will come through."

"The sails, sir?"

179

"I have cut some down – d'you think I can do everything? There is not a man who can climb the yards yet, but the halliards can be rove. Now will you pray with me, pray that the Captain will live to see this, and know why he has been saved."

It was clear that Evans had saved them. The calm persisted and the Senhora made an appearance once more, but then came the final *Caleuche* banshee, for then the locusts came.

They were now drifting, drifting, and no one was sure of their position, nor did anyone much care. She supposed that they were on the edge of the trades and there had been a slight change of temperature, evidence of wind in the offing, Evans said, but although some of the men were better, the Captain had not left his cabin. She was on deck alone, with some of the men lying on their blankets under an awning nearby, the yards banging against the masts, when she saw the cloud in the sky far off. It was a sign of a wind, she thought. Evans was not looking, there was no one at the wheel and as she looked, idling her time in an idle moment, the cloud got bigger and bigger. There was certainly wind over there, she thought, for the cloud was like a blue haze approaching them all the time, the haze and extent of it like the smoke of a distant battle murkily rising in the background of an ancient painting. She merely observed the change in the seemingly never-ending blankness of the horizon and turned to pace the deck.

The fever had brought another change. Now few of the men remaining on board spoke to her. While she might have tended the sick, she had not done so, with the result that she was probably more alone than at any time in the voyage. Her behaviour, as Evans said, not missing the opportunity, had exposed her for what she was – she'd heard him say that to the Captain. Satisfying herself that Jack Hannah was past the worst stages of the disease, she had at last paid him a visit, but had said very little. Some succumbed immediately, others did not seem quite so vulnerable. She gave Evans no credit for his nursing and there were days now when she spoke to no one at all and so it was quite natural that she should take up her painting chair and place it so that she could scan the horizon with no more than an idle curiosity. The winds must come again, and with luck enough men would recover to help them limp home to Sveynton. It was just a question of holding together. It was up to them, not to her. She could relax like a passenger.

Now the blue haze darkened and took on a shape as it approached, a spiralling motion just visible in the mass like sand devils whipping up dervish curves in the desert, but still she thought of it as a cloud, perhaps an optical illusion, well above sea level. She was still watching idly without any fear as at some natural, far-off movement of the wind. The haze extended for about five square miles across the sky, but in all the enormity of the horizon, it did not look much and she lost interest in it, crossing her hands in her lap and beginning to doze, and even when the sails flapped with the approach of the wind, it did not wake her. But then, the men on board heard a strange noise like the rustling of dead leaves in the wind, growing louder all the time. You could hardly describe it as a positive sound: it was an increase of just perceptible noise, like the fluttering of pasteboard, more like a subdued rattle than a droning and it grew louder and louder, still strangely lacking in definition.

It was Evans's voice which aroused her. He suddenly appeared on the poop deck staring at the cloud and now the noise increased once more, a more definite and eerie sound, but still subdued, a louder clatter like that of millions of tiny heads battling together, growing louder and louder, the haze now immense, blackening in a pall against the sun. At first, it looked as if it would pass over them but the wind increased, there was a coolness in the atmosphere, and she heard Evans's voice in a startled exclamation, 'Bless my soul!', opened her eyes and saw the darkness approach them, first distinguishing the swirling shapes like inanimate objects floating in the wind, all in haphazard flight, not seeming to approach with any sense of direction, but still towering in a whirling mass. It was as if the sky was gently cranking itself down upon them once more, but this time the eerie noise made it more frightening. The light continued to fade, but soon she could see the mass of tiny insects and again the noise increased, whirring and clacking, growing louder and louder until her claustrophobia was total. Then the first arrivals came, dropping out of the sky on to the sea, not singling them out but covering the whole area of the sea, at first slowly in limited numbers, alighting on the masts and sails, a half-a-dozen dropping on to the poop deck where she sat, others whirling around, the chattering noise now positively identifiable. At first, she thought they were grasshoppers or flies, but some, striking the mast, did so with a tiny plopping sound, falling directly to the deck, and then she saw their brown bodies had wings. She had got to her feet by now,

181

but the first arrivals were few in number, although they brought with them a smell like peat, and as every second went by more descended upon the ship and the whole area of sea around them. They seemed to take up space like sugar falling steadily out of a bottomless bag, first a trickle then a flow.

She stood there blinking her eyes, putting her hands to her ears, conscious that she was barefooted. She glanced up at the sails which had begun to fill and to her horror, she saw that the cords of the reef points of the lower sails were all covered with the creatures, the cords offering them a foothold, but it looked in that instant as if sentries of the swarm had been deposited in single file against the mass of white canvas. They were already dropping quietly in moderate numbers on to the deck and Evans, at last galvanised into action, began stamping on them. She went towards him unable to speak, a dryness in her throat and an itchy feeling of her own uncleanliness causing her to want to scratch herself. Now the swarm thickened, and appeared to be of an increasing density and suddenly there was no end to it. Evans, wide-eyed, stopped stamping as more and more descended, the noise increasing, and now the decks, the masts, the cargo hatches, the scuppers were beginning to be covered, and she followed his alarmed gaze as new arrivals seemed to make straight for the corpses of those he had crushed with his boots and began to devour them. It was getting difficult to put her own bare feet on the timber of the deck without touching them, and she saw Evans look across at her with his soulful eyes, for once not accusing but with a great and melancholy pity.

"Locusts," he said.

They were beginning to obscure the sunlight more completely as more and more came, and her immediate fear was that they would increase in such numbers that they would actually sink the ship. There were so many of them that it looked as if they would change the face of the sea for all around them the sea was covered – covered! – and still more came and it was like being in the centre of a grain field with clouds of chaff flying. She opened and closed her mouth to speak but could not and feeling her bare toes brush against them, opened her mouth to scream, but still could not and did not until they began to alight on her hair which offered a perfect landing place so that three or four descended and hooked on like may bugs. She began to tear at her hair, striking her hands against them, their hard shrimp-like shells brushing against her hands, but they were

182

securely hooked on and at last she found her voice, screamed and screamed and ran for the companionway below, her feet crushing them on the deck, on the stairs and even in the passage below. She felt one or two slip down the loose back of her dress and as she raced, writhing and tormented, tearing at her clothes, she finally got to her cabin and beat her head against the closed cabin door, the noise of the swarm still audible above the ship. As she beat her head, those she struck squelched there against her skull, and she actually thought she was being pursued by them. She tore her clothes off, stuffed them against the cabin door and took up a blanket to pummel her head, several now flying haphazardly about the cabin, and one which alighted on the mirror of her makeshift dressing table seemed to look at her and was thrown into relief so that she saw the long barbed legs, the shrimp like body and the curious hammer head with minute beady eyes as much larger than it was, and froze in a chill of fear as the noise of the swarm continued above her.

It was ridiculous, of course, her fear. This was the tail end of a much larger swarm blown out by the winds to torment her, born to die upon all that sea, and they would devour nothing on board save the galley jam for the wind that brought them soon took the *Whisper* well away – but she did not know that then. All she knew was that the ship – and she! – was alive with them, that the sea itself had disappeared under them, and then she had her own premonition of disaster, of life ending in a totally unforeseeable way, as if death would come, not with the violence of a storm nor the sickening grinding of timber upon rocks – she had heard that before – but from inside herself with resignations and weakness and the world pressing down and down upon her, scratching at her, a thousand pin pricks finally reducing her to a shivering, scratching wraith. That was worse than the *Caleuche* banshee; the one was a stream of fire and light, the other was weakness and nothingness, her limbs turned as now to jelly. People, she knew had scratched and itched themselves to death, and it did not bear thinking about.

She was kneeling naked on the deck of the cabin, trembling and moaning and swaying exhaustedly when she heard Evans crunching down the companionway heavy footed, then throwing open the door to see her there, staring at her abject nakedness. His eyes were bright, his face flushed, holy triumph written all over him. He had heard her scream but had conquered his own fear. ("No worse than grasshoppers – kerosene will shift 'em.")

183

"You'd better come," he said. "He is asking for you and we have the wind at last."

Was it that day or the next that the log-book was found and normality returned? As Evans recorded:

A plague of locusts was observed, momentarily covering the sky as far as the eye could see, but were apparently so exhausted in flight that their destiny was certain. The Chief Officer distributed kerosene and water over the decks, completing the cleansing of the ship.

And later, blessed normality.

p.m. Pleasant breezes from W.

The fever was over, the locusts had gone, no reference was made to the flags missing from the signal locker, and the scratches where Felipa had torn in terror at her own flesh, soon healed. And who is to say that the actress did not reappear newly clothed from the wings, ultimately playing the part she had meant to play all along?

184

Chapter Thirteen

LOG OF THE BARQUE WHISPER OF SVEYNTON.
Jack Hannah, Master.

Monday 28 June:
Lat. 51° 05'N, Long. 04° 53'W 3.30 p.m. Made Lundy Light
bearing NE. Took aboard pilot.

The sea covered everything, and what the sea did not cover, the
wind blew away. Memory could be the same and nothing that was
recorded could not be altered. What people did not know, they did
not mind. Neither did they have to be told. Men died at sea all the
time. Ships arrived short-handed in their home ports daily and no
questions were asked because everybody wanted a quick discharge
of the cargo for the simple reason that the cargo was the most
important part of their voyage. Was there a trace of anything that
had happened aboard the ship? No trace. Well, what was he worried
about? Felipa asked Jack Hannah. And with their feeling for each
other, and after all that they had come through together, why did he
hesitate? Didn't he believe her? (She asked that again and again.)
Well, if he believed her, the future was theirs. Say nothing. The fever
had blown itself out. It was a fact. So forget it. Anyway, didn't he
think it was dropsy originally?

But Evans?

Leave Evans to her!

The men?

What a fool he was! Seat the men in some dockside tavern and
who'd believe them? There was not a seaman left alive who bothered
about the *Avalon*. All who'd had relatives aboard her were dead. And
as for the rest, had anybody ever heard of locusts falling on a ship at
sea? Well, had they? And as for fever, was it all that unusual? If it was
fever . . .

"If it was fever?"

185

"Dropsy," she'd said again, seizing upon it. "That was what you first thought."

"Evans," he'd said again.

And then she'd repeated it. "Evans will do as he's told." The Senhora was herself again and the last act had begun.

Now it was Evans's turn to hide in his cabin, but the moment they'd made their landfall, Jack Hannah, weak, wan, drained as he was, felt well enough to stand a watch. And they'd actually managed a passage of just over a hundred and thirty days, not a fast passage, but a passage that was not likely to cause comment. There were five men dead, seven if you included Breeze and Scuse who'd gone on the outward run. When you came to think of it, it was not all that unusual. They'd had no desertions thanks to his insistence on keeping the men aboard in Mas a Fuera, but they might well have had desertions, and although they were short-handed, they could pick up a couple of longshoremen in Ennal's Point to help them work the ship across to Sveynton Dock. There were always men plying off there, and then, within half a day, the ship would be snugged down alongside. As far as Felipa was concerned, the charter was complete the moment the *Whisper* was alongside with her cargo safely aboard. The agents acting for her had probably re-sold it already, and later it would be re-routed – to Liverpool probably – but this was not all she wanted. Couldn't he understand? Now there was more than a seed planted in his mind. There was an actual declaration. If he was coming away with her, he should stop thinking about the *Whisper*. Once they were tied up, his responsibility ended. Evans would probably get the command. Well, Evans deserved it.

"Evans?" he kept on saying. His own fever although mild compared to the others, left him drained and woolly minded. He kept repeating things. "Evans?"

"Yes, Evans. And you understand what I said? If you are coming away with me . . ."

"Yes, yes," he'd said. "Yes, I understand, but Evans . . ."

The important thing was to get the ship alongside without fuss, then they'd walk down the quay into the future, just the two of them. Now let him answer her. Wasn't that what he wanted? Hadn't they discussed it for hours? Why then, did he flinch from the details? He should know that she was a business woman. She had brought a railway train timetable with her and carefully preserved it, knowing that they took pride in the regularity with which the trains ran.

There were trains from Sveynton connecting with the Great Western Express twice a day. They could disappear at Gloucester, from Gloucester to Bristol was no distance and Bristol opened to the world. She'd complete her business, he'd complete his, and then she'd put him to the test. Well, wasn't it what he'd begged her to do? He couldn't say she'd refused him anything, not one single thing; and with all that they'd discussed, if there was one thing that mattered to him, it was to be with her. Wasn't that true? "To be with me, my darling." Now the endearments flowed. It was as if the authoress had let herself go in a final purple patch. And the hero had replied.

"Yes, oh, yes," he'd said.

And there was also the matter of a ship of his own. So where was all this talk of another life now? Oh, why did he hesitate? Wasn't she providing him with everything he asked for in this life? A clean break, a ship and her? What was the matter with him? It was every wish he'd expressed and he'd talked her into it. *He* had! Well, what was stopping him?

"Two things."

"What things?"

"When I was ill . . ."

"I prayed for you!"

"Where were you?"

Now she grew eloquent.

"I tried, oh, my darling, I tried. I tried and tried. But you know Evans? He hates me! Can't you understand what Evans tried to do to us? No, he did not try, he succeeded. He told me he had bored a hole with an auger to spy on us on the passage out. He's mean and filthy. He lives like a vulture on other people's unhappiness. He does! There is a special part of him that welcomes other people's misfortune. He despises, disapproves, forbids. And he preys on all living things. He is a blight on human happiness. Don't you remember you had to strike him? Well, he hates you, and says the most terrible things.

"How d'you think I felt trying to get into your cabin, hearing you groaning in there, groaning and retching – and he wouldn't let me in to see you. He even said I had caused it all. Me! Oh, I know it hurts, but it was Evans's fault. He even spied on me in my nakedness. When the locusts came, I was terrified – and he laughed! And you must know the things he's said about me. Listen . . . I'll tell you the way to judge a man like Evans. Ask yourself how he speaks of other people? Is there any charity in his heart? And then, ask yourself how he might speak of you when you are not present? Can you imagine? I tell you, men like him last for ever by destroying others. They are the locusts of life itself.

"Well, I can deal with Evans. Yes, I can. I am not without influence. How d'you think you got your command? Well, I can do the same for Evans. Don't you realise? Thanks to you, I am a wealthy woman. Yes, wealthy! A person of substance. Thanks to you. And after all that you've done for me, you will not take the reward! Have we endured all we have together – for nothing? So that we shall go off alone along our separate ways? – for nothing! Well? Why don't you say something?"

There were days of this. Her face haunted him. She grew precise, passionate, spelling it out. Now the almond eyes were sharp with intent. They looked at no one but him.

"Yes, that is nothing. And I thought we meant something different to each other now, at long last? Oh, my darling, if it is only Evans, look at Evans as he goes round the ship muttering to himself."

But it was not only Evans that made him hesitate, Jack Hannah thought; it was that dream he'd had, the vision of himself ashore standing in those leaky, poverty-stricken boots and staring at the sea, the boots ever going before him, making their drab way into a drab future. Dreams and locusts, he thought – it was as if an Old Testament presence had come upon the ship, Evans's world pursuing them and becoming reality. But he could not smile at it, nor laugh it away. Somehow, the vision *was* the future projected, he felt sure, and then in his delirium there were the awful hallucinations springing from the past, the face of the thick-necked Greek at the gallows, and the shrivelled sniggering presence of his father in that filthy cabin and worse than anything else, Grail's shimmering eyes in the last hours of life. There were moments when he could not distinguish what was true and what was hallucination and Jack Hannah felt the weight of it all, a weight in all its extremity that was perhaps more than any one human being could bear, he thought.

But Felipa could. Of that he had no doubt, and he looked at her wonderingly. Perhaps a part of her strength was that there were always things she wanted. Her mind was never idle. Her wishes were never simple either and she could turn everything to advantage. Sighting Lundy Island reminded her of what he had been on the

188

passage out, she said ruefully, a simple boy. But he was that no longer. So much for his ambition. He had not the strength for it.

"*Your* ambition," she said with a sure smile. His, not hers. And now she questioned him daily.

"Tell me exactly what will happen from the time we will pick up the land?"

"We'll sight Lundy, that's the first landfall in the channel."

"And then?"

"A pilot?"

"A pilot, yes. And what does he do?" (At last there was something she did not know. Or said she did not know!)

"He pilots us in."

"To the dock?"

"Yes."

"Does he ask questions?"

"Only in a sociable way."

"What questions?"

"Where we are from, what cargo, days in passage."

"And you tell him?"

"Of course."

"And what else?"

"News, news of shore."

"Ah," she'd said. And her eyes sparkled.

He thought then of Beatrice Trevoake for the first time in months. They'd spoken to other ships in passage and had themselves reported a dozen times, and the owners would know of their homeward passage, of course, and ashore there would be the expected stirring in the port. Beatrice would know within the day when they were sighted coming up channel and their cargo was probably already being given a price that would only alter when the tonnage was known. For Beatrice, as in times past, it would mean a special rising in the morning if she still had any interest in him. She had described it often, how the sight of some homeward bound ship sailing full rigged up channel would cheer them all. But that was in the past when her interest, like his own, was declared.

"When the pilot comes aboard, he does not inspect the ship?"

"No, he is sailing it."

"And then, after he has brought you into the roads?"

"We're short-handed. We'll need to pick up some hands to help us in."

"That is not unusual?"

189

"No."

"And once in the dock?"

"The owners will have been informed."

"And will come aboard?"

"Perhaps. There will be instructions about the cargo. It's the cargo they're interested in."

"And the seamen?"

"Paid off."

"But the authorities?"

"In our case, we shall declare fever and may go into quarantine."

She smiled. "If you declare fever?"

"If?" he said. "With five deaths? We must declare it. We have had five deaths in passage."

"Dropsy, you said."

"Fever!"

"Isn't it true that quarantine means interminable delays? They will not thank you in the port. All Sveynton ships will face delays."

"They will not thank us if we bring fever in."

"It's blown itself out."

He hoped so. But he wasn't so sure. The big German, Flohr, was not pulling his weight. Little Tommy Dance, made silent by the enormity of events, was pale and thin, shivering whenever you spoke to him. But they'd been on hard tack for a month. Three-quarters of that watch was gone.

"When we are in the dock, who will come aboard?"

"The rummagers, first the Collector of Customs. He'll ask the usual questions."

"What questions?"

"Port of departure, date, the cargo, bonded stores – he's looking for smuggled goods."

"Anything else?"

"Well, there are routine questions, the pratique."

"Pratique?"

"A clean bill of health from the port of departure."

"Ah, but we have that, stamped at Talcahuano."

"But . . ."

"The pratique is valid. There'll be no delays. Not for dropsy."

"But Evans?" he said again. He knew exactly what she was driving at. When the time came, he could blame no one. There were too many facts. If they'd had men sick of yellow jack at this moment,

190

they could not have flown a plague flag because the flags were missing. The log-book had been missing too, but then that was found with his large legible entry relating Grail's death of dropsy, his first mistake, a mistake without rhyme or reason. But all he could think of was Evans.

It went like this with Evans.

"Any violation of the quarantine laws," said Evans wet-lipped with pleasure, "and you are liable to a penalty of three hundred pounds and six months' imprisonment." He'd found a book of rules and read from it in laborious tones. *"Not to quit such a vessel, either by going on shore or by going aboard any other vessel with intent to go ashore until regularly discharged from quarantine . . .* it's all here, Senhora. Break the rules, and there is a penalty."

"Quarantine might take weeks, Mr Evans."

"And if they quit the ship, they may be compelled by any persons whatsoever and by any kind of necessary force to return on board, and are also liable to a penalty."

"But only if quarantine has been declared. It's not cholera, Mr Evans. And if dropsy only is declared . . ."

"You cannot expect me or the Captain to be a party to any deception. The Captain . . ."

"Within a day of our docking, Mr Evans, the *Whisper* will be looking for a new Captain, but this is told to you in absolute confidence."

Oh, she knew him! What a gift she had of knowing the useful people!

She smiled. Evans smiled. There was nothing Evans liked better than a confidence.

"Like father, like son," Evans said yet again. "If you'll allow me the familiarity, Senhora."

All this was reported. "Leave Evans to me," she'd said. "I'll deal with Evans." And then the land was upon them, the decks cleared, the only problem their being short-handed. Evans had retreated entirely. Of course, he'd talk, but when would he talk?

"When we've gone," Felipa said. "Don't you see? Within twenty-four hours we'll be gone."

Evans hugged that phrase to himself. "Told to me in absolute confidence," he said to himself. His smile was cruel, but now for the

191

moment there were things it was better to leave for a while. He had only one request.

"A clean discharge, Evans?"

"That is my right, Captain."

"When we dock."

"In the event of your rapid leave-taking, sir, I thought it prudent to ask now. Excuse me, sir, I am a party to certain confidences."

("Watch his face," Felipa said; "see him smile!")

He smiled!

And so he received his testimonial.

This is to certify that the bearer, Handel Evans, has proved himself a most capable Chief Officer, a sober, honest and trustworthy man who has every qualification for command.

It was brief, but it was enough. Evans would not be present when the Collector of Customs asked his questions and examined their pratique. And that night, Evans resumed his letter:

No mention was made of the days when I nursed the Captain in his sickness, nor of the long weeks when I alone carried the ship, and although I repeatedly asked to see the log-book this was denied to me on the pretext that it was mislaid and was only finally produced for me to sign as a matter of routine.

Evans cleared Evans, and Evans continued his retreat, fulfilling his earlier promise to complement his Captain, "one accustomed to follow", as he had said. Like the locusts, everything was come to pass.

All of which was before the pilot came aboard and when the cutter approached Jack Hannah stood watching it, a gaunt, hunched figure, Felipa beside him, her eyes sharp and watchful, never leaving his face. Now was the moment of decision.

"Trust me," she said. "Have we not come this far?"

He could have pulled back then, but he said, "You mean it? – everything?"

"Would I have brought a railway timetable to sea if I did not?"

Jack Hannah could not decide exactly when he had ceased to think for himself, but it seemed as if they had suddenly arrived at this precise moment in time entirely through the actions of others and so he felt he had no choice in the matter. Choice was long gone. She was not asking him, but instructing him, and he had no wish to disobey.

"Answer me!" her eyes were narrowed, her voice abrupt.

"Very well."

He saw the pilot come over the side – Evans and a seaman had to busy themselves without the Captain's instructions – and then he found himself looking at a new face, the first in months, that of a bluff young man in an open-necked shirt below his reefer.

"Where from, Captain?"

"Talcahuano, a hundred and thirty days in passage. Guano for Sveynton."

"And a passenger, I see?"

"Yes, and we are short-handed. We may need your boat to help us with a couple of lads at Ennal's Point."

The pilot nodded, turned his eyes to the passenger.

"I'm so excited," Felipa said. "How long will we be?"

"You've brought a fair breeze in a windless month," the pilot said. He was grinning already. "A regular heat wave. There's been nothing like it for years."

"Splendid," she said. "Take care you do not lose the wind."

The pilot cast his eyes over the two of them, grinned once more, and began to busy himself with the ship. No more questions. Normality was returning as if blown by the warm southerly breeze. Flaming June had cooled the *Whisper* down. Felipa went below satisfied and when eventually the familiar outline of Ennal's Point came in sight and they hailed an oysterman to take on two hands, she did not bother to go on deck. She was already packed and she knew they had but to wait for their tug. She heard Jack Hannah come below, heard his footsteps heavy upon the deck, waited for his knock and then saw him enter, his shoulders stooped, eyes bloodshot, deep drawn shadows etched below his eyes, put there by fatigue and hardened now by shock. He had not said a word more than was necessary to the pilot. She took his hand carefully.

"What is it?"

"They've come aboard."

"Who?"

"The longshoremen, two of them."

"Well?"

"They're both Grails, village boys. They're asking for Harry. They were waiting for us."

"So?" she said. "Died in passage." She shrugged her shoulders. They would have to know sometime. Why did he stand there so wretchedly? Did his resolve allow itself to weaken by the presence of a family of hobbledehoys? Did he think his luck was theirs?

193

"You don't know them."

"You'd better forget them and compose yourself for the Collector."

She could see she'd have to hold him up until the last rope was thrown to the bollard on the jetty.

"You will not change your mind," she said. It was an instruction. "And neither shall I! Now then, once I am ashore we will be apart. For one night. That is necessary. But I shall have to know where to find you?"

.But he could only stare at her. Why was there not a mark on her face? She was as cool, as self-possessed, as in command of herself as when she had first come on board, whereas he – he could hardly utter a command. He blinked, feeling his tiredness. He could hear Evans muttering aloft. The two new men had tried to question the big German, but he could only shake his head dumbly. Then they went to Evans. They wanted to know about Harry Grail's effects.

"Effects?" Evans said incredulously.

"They should be entered in the log," Ephraim Grail, the elder, said.

His brother Samuel, barely sixteen, stood beside him.

"By rights," Samuel said.

"Disposed of with the deceased," Evans said, then sent them packing.

"Bless my soul!" Evans said, but Jack Hannah could see their faces, both cast in the family stamp, low-browed, dark-eyed and accusing. He had seen them on deck and he could actually imagine them taking the tale ashore, "Gone, and all his effects with him." They would tell it to the moustachioed Louisa, basting washing with her brawny arms over the tub, and he could just imagine it. "Died in passage, but somebody got his effects." That was a Grail sentence.

"I will see you in twelve hours," Felipa said. "Don't forget to be ready!"

And then, finally, a rare endearment in Spanish, a muttered *querida* and a laugh. "Do you think I am – what? *Abuje?*"

"What?"

"A parasite," she said. "Not me. I have earned my egg! Now then, tell me once more. Promise me you'll be ready? The Great Western Express! Doesn't it sound exciting to you? Just think. Clean linen and fresh food."

He heard the clanking of the steam tug approaching, then the

194

tramping feet of the men laying the hawser out along the deck, but he feared to move, even to go on deck at all.

"You have lost your tongue?"

"The Collector," he said.

"We will make him welcome," she said. "What else?"

And they did. Indeed, they were lucky with the Collector. There were a number of ships just put in, he was busy and it was very hot. A copper ore barque was nothing unusual except that she wasn't carrying any copper ore. He dropped down on to the deck from the lock gates. Felipa had found sherry in the saloon, making the visit pleasantly social. Evans kept out of the way. The pratique was on top of the manifest, the ship's papers ready in the normal way. She insisted on being introduced.

"Senhora Salaverry – in passage."

"Sherry?" she said. "This weather!"

The Collector was a junior collector, a young man. He had eyes for the rippling swell of her bosom, the sheen of her hair, the multiplicity of her jewels glistening in the filtering sunlight. It was unusual to see a woman in a ship, still less a wealthy woman who leant attentively towards you when you spoke. And her perfume . . . Well, the Collector could dream, couldn't he?

"Are you carrying any mails, Captain?"

Jack Hannah shook his head, feeling that his every action said liar.

"The manifest?"

"In front of you."

They had nothing to declare. A few deaths, weather and dropsy, but that was normal.

"There's been a run of smuggling from the American ports, cigars and the like," the Collector had the obvious on his mind.

"If you could give me a cigar, you'd make a friend," Felipa said.

"You, Senhora?"

"Are we not to be allowed our vices, sir?"

"Vices, Senhora?"

"Come, sir, you do not think me perfect?"

And that was how it had gone, a horny young man with a wet mouth and his eyes falling out of his head. How she sparkled, how cleverly she made Jack Hannah seem a boorish everyday nonentity. No dishonesty there. And nonentities ruled the sea because the imaginative could not last. That was the Collector's view. No romance in it either.

195

"I'll put the rummagers aboard, Captain," the Collector said. "If you step up to the long room with the cargo manifest, we'll see to your clean bill of health."

Jack Hannah could feel his stomach heaving, but Felipa showed the Collector off, taking care that she should pass him in the narrow doorway with a rustle of skirts and a bold stare just in case she might come this way again. A real whore never forgot her trade.

"Not much unpleasantness in that young man," Felipa said.

They tied up at midday. Belasco's carriage was waiting on the quay, postillions and black fellow in attendance, and a little to one side of him, not permitted the dignity of the carraige, the Reverend Elias Evans and Cornelius Lewis, the painless tooth extractor, like two black beetles but clearly beside themselves with excitement. There was no sign of either of the Chauncey-Vernon brothers. Baron Belasco did not come aboard and Felipa went straight to his carriage as she said she would, little Tommy Dance struggling with her baggage, barely able to carry it. She said she did not want to waste any time until the financial arrangements were settled. The cargo was short of the expected weight but she would settle for whatever she could get. In the necessary haste of the transaction, they would lose of course, there was no denying that – but this was expected. For his sake, it was better that everything was cleared up as quickly as possible. What she did not want, was him changing his mind. They were conspirators now and the longer they were separated, the greater the risk. Oh, she knew him all right! But there was another thing, she did not want either of the Chauncey-Vernon brothers poking their noses into the *Avalon* affair. That was as dead as mutton. A man of Henry Chauncey-Vernon's wealth and standing could put obstacles in their way. So there would be no accusations. He must put them right out of his mind and she must know that in order to assure Belasco. Then they'd get their cargo discharged at once. And when she said at once, she meant at once.

So . . . no threats, just normality. The *Avalon* affair was closed. The *Whisper* arrived home with her charter: end of passage.

Jack Hannah watched Belasco hurry to remove his hat, bowing low as he welcomed her, the black fellow manhandling the baggage. Tommy Dance did not even receive a tip, he noted. He kept on noticing things but they did not register, that was exhaustion.

"You'd better see the longshoremen," Evans said. "There's two who won't take no for an answer."

"In the saloon."

He took off his hat and went down to sit behind the table, the mouldering bag containing the ship's money ready for him where she had put it. She had attended to everything.

Now the boy, Samuel Grail, took up the role of spokesmen, the two of them soon standing before the table, both aggressive and accusing. They'd got no satisfaction out of Evans.

"Our Harry?" Samuel Grail said. "He had gear with him. Where's his bag?"

"He had a knife."

"A knife?"

"A knife his brother gave him."

"All his effects have been destroyed."

"A knife – burnt?" Samuel said.

"I don't know," Jack Hannah said wearily. "It was all bundled up, all his gear."

They looked from one to the other like inspectors of deceit uncovering a vast fraud.

"His money?" Ephraim said.

"His money's for his mother."

"She don't get about much now."

"She'll get his money in due course. Anything else?"

`Ephraim shifted his feet uneasily. Their own money was still to be paid to them. They seemed to be balancing prudence with the desire to make accusations. Ten shillings each was due. You could live for a month on that.

"Fever, was it?" Samuel said.

"Sick," Jack Hannah said. "And others with him. He was a good seaman."

"And Willie Twomallow?"

"Gone."

"Billy Bones?"

"Gone."

"Morgan Morgan?"

"The same. Died in passage. If there's nothing else, make your marks and you'll be paid."

Finally, they did so, and nothing more said. Then he heard the cadences of the Reverend Elias Evans talking excitedly on deck to his brother. Now the vultures are really aboard, he thought, but when the Reverend Elias Evans descended, his small dark eyes glittered

197

with excitement and his face was wreathed in smiles. Clearly, his brother had said nothing untoward and he soon confessed his pleasure. There was every indication that their cargo would fetch a good price, but this was the vulgar stuff of commerce, he implied with an airy gesture. He had other news, and prattled on effusively. His sixty-fourth share had brought him up in the world.

"I bring you the warmest possible greetings from Miss Trevoake – she made it her business to send for me to convey her greetings and apologies. She could not be down herself to greet you as her employer has taken her away for the day. But fear not, there's a letter awaiting you at your lodging."

Jack Hannah stared at him. No parish priest could have conveyed such an air of knowledgeable familiarity with intimate personal business, and the reverend gentleman began to nod and smile with the assurance of one who is party to the most intimate of family secrets. He was hearing wedding bells.

Evans paused in the saloon doorway at this moment, his face drawn and disapproving, undertaker to the goodwill bubbling in his brother's heart.

Jack Hannah made no comment and presently after a solemn hour when he paid off the crew, hardly registering their faces as they filed in one by one, he took up his rule and laid it in the dog-eared page in front of him.

LOG OF THE BARQUE WHISPER *OF SVEYNTON.*
Jack Hannah, Master.

2 p.m. Moored up ship and paid off the crew. Began discharging cargo.

Ultimately, only the heat of the shore was abnormal and he gave the gruffest of farewells to the men as they left. He did not see the package which Tommy Dance gave to the Grails. The voyage was over. If there were any surprises still in store, they could only spring from the continuing emptiness which had accompanied his own dazed state, he thought.

Everything else had been arranged.

Chapter Fourteen

Extract from a report by the Medical Officer to the Privy Council

During this period an almost tropical heat prevailed in Sveynton and no rain fell. Probably the climatic conditions of the South American seaboard had never been better imitated in Great Britain. Sveynton Dock, it should be said, is situated along a low lying island at the mouth of a river. Copper smoke from the nearby works adds to the existing health hazards.

It was the heat which had led Beatrice Trevoake to a remote beach further along the coast that day in the company of Mrs Chauncey-Vernon and her two children. The knowledge that the children would have been disappointed had she asked for the day off to meet the returning *Whisper* persuaded Miss Trevoake that she could not do so in all conscience, but she had seen the *Whisper*'s white painted spars off Ennal's Point and fervently hoped that the copious letters which she had written to Jack Hannah had been received by him. She gave no thought to the possibility that they might still be lying in that remote Chilean port unread and the strength of her feeling had long ago been demonstrated by the fact that the single garnet stone of her engagement ring now lay once more upon her finger, she having gone shamefacedly to Jack Hannah's aunt who supervised the house on the waterfront. She'd said she'd left it there by accident! No other action so aptly summed up her change of heart and she had grown more and more to regret the circumstances which had attended the *Whisper*'s leave-taking.

How she had rued her lack of understanding, and as for that wretched woman, Miss Annie S. Swann, she had been responsible for further homilies which Beatrice now reminded herself of as she lay fitfully in her governess's room. The heat brought out the smell of the beeswax polish on the heavy furniture, all substantial leftovers or unwanted items from the other rooms – leftovers like herself, Beatrice thought dismally. And her follies had continued. Receiving no letter from Jack Hannah, she had taken it upon herself to ask for further help, penning a letter under the pseudonym Booby. She felt it described her wan self aptly. And the reply had been cryptic, causing her further discomfiture. (Nothing had changed in Sveynton.)

Booby is quite well pleased with herself, but she suffers from lack of friends and admirers. How is she to attract them? It is passing strange that at twenty-four she has no friends after having lived in one place and been connected with the same church for so long. Perhaps she is not amiable or expects too much from her friends? I would only ask Booby to remember that the happiest people are those who have the most friends, or those who give out affection, service and gracious kindliness without thought of self or self's reward.

So had Booby been put in her place, thought Beatrice. She could not blame the penning of the letter upon the heat, but she could blame the heat for her non-appearance on the dock and she only hoped that the letter which she had sent to Jack Hannah's lodging would leave him in no doubt of her affections. What depressed her more than anything was that she had appeared to be lacking in her understanding of his difficulties, and worse, in the empty months which followed his departure she had been nothing less than a simpering idiot in consulting the likes of Miss Annie S. Swann at all! She was neither idiot nor ignoramus, and while she had penned page after page of lady-like affections to Jack Hannah, nothing she had said or done revealed her real understanding of him. In a sentence, she was sure that he was a man who needed a leash, and she had been markedly wanting in the provision of it. He needed handling, in short, and the management of him ought to be the core of her ambition. Oh, there was no end to her thoughts and the most important of them did not belong to Booby at all.

She had better take care on the morrow, she thought. She could only hope and pray that he still had a morsel of interest in her. One mistake and a year to regret it, was an apt summing up of her predicament. Perhaps in all this life you had but one chance to find the right partner and this chance, coming once only, was as elusive and imperceptible a thing as a note of music, or the barely discernible rustle of a leaf upon a tree, not so much a physical act as an intangible stirring inside herself which, once risen, must be grappled. Perhaps, too, it was not so much Jack Hannah she had offended against, but herself, the self that bridled when her mother, looking disdainfully up at her angular six foot daughter, tartly remarked, "Simper a bit and don't be so pushing!"

So much for her mother, as avid a disciple of Miss Swann's as might be imagined. Beatrice felt such a mass of confusions and disloyalties and her final hope was that her letter would provide that most undeserved second chance which she craved. It was all she could hope for and led as usual to more and more questions. Why did everything in life seem to conspire to dispossess her of the calm patience and langorous elegance of the heroines she read about? Why, oh why, had she not been at the dock to greet him? Why did duty call her when the obligation to a sense of duty so easily evaded others? And why had she not heard a word from Jack Hannah in all these months?

And in this mood, so full of doubts, what hope was there for her? She could not sleep, and she would be like a wraith in the morning.

So her thoughts continued as she perspired in her shift, that last classic remark of her mother's returning, "Simper a bit and don't be so pushing!" It was typical of her mother, but now for the first time she gave her mind to the uneasy thought that her mother might be wise, and her last surviving hope was that the letter she had so recently penned might put everything right.

The heat too had affected Jack Hannah. The moment he left the ship, it caused him to take a hansom cab to his lodging. His aunt who had the habit of the family women of making herself scarce had left a cold collation covered over with a wet tea towel for him on the kitchen table. Propped against it was Beatrice's letter, the firm copperplate handwriting boldly announcing his name and title. He did not feel like eating, but took up the envelope and rested it unopened on his lap as he sat there before the mantelpiece from which his garnet ring had so long ago disappeared. He was of a mind not to open it at all, and stayed slumped there, a tired man drained of energy as the evening light faded. Presently, he could see the beams of light from the lighthouse and one or two of the lights of the oyster dredgers as they came up to their moorings in the bay. From what the Reverend Elias Evans had said, he could guess what was in the letter which was perhaps why he did not want to open it. He had a firm instruction on his mind, only hours to prepare, and the envelope was a distraction to a man with thoughts of leaving everything he had ever known.

"Stronger cabin trunks," she'd said, and so much else in that honeyed voice made firm by the intensity of her conviction and purpose. It was the one detail which stuck in his mind. You could not mention a detail like that unless you had planned ahead.

He looked upwards and saw his face reflected in the dull light of the brass shell canister, the shape elongated by the curve of the metal. It seemed to look back at him wonderingly, a stranger's face. He put the envelope down still unopened and went upstairs to rummage in the loft. There the heat was doubly oppressive, the heat of an oven. There was an old cabin trunk in the corner. It had belonged to his father and he saw the faded initials upon the worn and scratched surface. Full circle, he thought, and he recalled his year-old phrase, debts paid by the foresail. Would a hurried leave-taking bring a solution to all discomfitures? And when he kept their rendezvous, where would they go? Could anything be more vague, more unsatisfactory? The Great Western Express beginning its journey at Gloucester was not a magic carpet which would whisk them into oblivion and a guaranteed happiness. And what was he to do with his life thereafter? But she had her answers as pat as an advertiser's slogans. They would decide that when the time came. What was more exciting than uncertainty? In Bristol there would be time to look around. In Bristol they would be anonymous and there they could recuperate from the exhausting effects of the voyage. He had nearly died, she reminded him. He was in no condition to think for himself even. Wasn't a partnership a relationship where the stronger helped the weaker when necessary? Oh, she was a modern woman! Leave it all to her.

He could hear her voice still and parallel to it, he saw another life for himself, a repetition of things past, of hurts and grievances and slights, the drab monotony of the sea itself, of constant journeying in the service of others. Where were his wits? She had asked that too. Look at Evans. Evans would go by the book of rules and Evans would die by the book of rules. Evans was everyman, touched by the narrowness of his little life, a prisoner of the ghetto of his own dismal world and puny expectations – she had said all she was going to say about Evans. The question was, would he risk all on a promise and pay his debts by the foresail? It was his phrase as it had been his father's before him. But never mind that. Let him live by it. And she was holding out her hand. He could please himself whether he took it or not.

And of it all, he thought one word which he repeated many times? "Liar! Liar! Liar, liar, liar!"

But he was tired. He did not have the energy even to open his letter. Wearily, he extended his arm below the rafters to the worn handle of the cabin trunk and dragged it to the door, his hand belying the one word he continued to repeat to himself. But then that hand had sought hers, had imprisoned him where no conscious thought or deed had ever led him before, to that intimacy and dependence which all his life he had dreaded.

The heat was also blamed for Tommy Dance's strange lassitude, although there were other contributory causes.

"The boy is beside himself with excitement," his mother said. "It's his first voyage, and look at him – as thin as a rake."

She had made a special tea with tarts and pikelets and *tieson lap*, or flat cake, light as a feather and made from sour milk, with ham sandwiches, farm butter and freshly baked bread, the crusts removed for this special occasion. The table was laid with a white cloth. Father, brothers, aunts and neighbours congregated in the passage of the little house. The whole street was waiting. But he had not come back with a swagger and his bag on his shoulder, although he had indeed been "all over" in the words of the blue water men. To everybody's consternation, he wanted to lie down as soon as he got into the house.

"He wants feeding up," his mother said. They had received only the briefest of details of the *Whisper*'s voyage, but it was enough to have him safely back. The cooper round the corner was looking for a good lad to bind apprentice and Tommy Dance's mother, like Beatrice Trevoake, had plans.

At the edge of the docks, there was a public house called the Cuba with two low-beamed bars which did a thriving trade from the jacks off the ships. It served beer from the wood and stout by the jug and was kept by an octogenarian one-legged veteran called Callous Ned, who had been one of Nelson's bosuns and had the reputation of being the best cutlass fighter in the Royal Navy. He had been known to keep order with his wooden leg when there was any difficulty with any of the lads who got beyond themselves in drink. One of his oddities was that he would let no women of ill-repute into the house, a custom rare in a dockside tavern. You might get struck on the head by Callous Ned's wooden leg, but you wouldn't get rolled or crimped, and the only danger was if your tongue or temper got the better of you. There were very few women who went in there at all unless they were working around the docks. One of these was known as Sawdust Sal and although she had undoubtedly walked the paves at one time, now in her late thirties she earned a respectable living selling sawdust to publicans to lay on their stone floors. She collected the sawdust from the timber mills and trundled it around in a handcart, a big, open-faced countrywoman whose only affliction was a severely arthritic arm around which she wore a copper band. It was this band which the big German seaman Flohr wanted to buy.

He had gone straight into the Cuba from the *Whisper* but once there complained by pointing to his forehead of a headache, and Sal, seeing the pallor upon him, rare in a deep sea man, had tried to talk to him, but, of course, he could not speak. Later, out of the kindness of her heart, she had recommended a sailor's lodging in Welcome Court, a burrow of back street dwellings nearby. She would not part with the copper band, but she noted the big German had difficulty in raising his elbow as well as in speaking.

"They'll see you right in Welcome Court," Sal said; and to the landlord, Callous Ned, who was keeping a baleful eye on her, "Lovely boys them big Dutchies – as long as they got money on 'em!"

She actually followed the German with her handcart and pointed the way to Welcome Court. Now there was a well set up man she could take a real fancy to, especially as he couldn't answer back! However, she was now in another business and – as she was grateful to recall – she didn't let her generosity get the better of her that day. She went on trundling her handcart, the idlers noting the usual presence of Sawdust Sal, a familiar figure, while the big German went the other way, head down with leaden footsteps and with scarcely the energy to wipe his brow as the sweat poured from him.

Ephraim and Samuel Grail had delayed before going home and had fortified themselves before calling in to see Louisa and her mother in their cousin's house.

"Buried his effects with him," Ephraim said.

"Not right," Samuel said.

"A good job I went down to the fo'c'sle," Ephraim said grinning.

"What d'you reckon happened?"

"They wasn't all buried."

"How d'you mean?"

"Harry must have been ashore and done a bit of trading."

Ephraim said. And then he showed Samuel the chamois leather bag with several gold rings still in it.

"Little Tommy Dance showed me where they was hid. He reckoned they was Harry's property, but he was frightened to tell the Mate."

Henry Chauncey-Vernon was in his club, the Exchange and Commercial and he too like the other members present felt the heat. He had come there in the early evening since the reading room was situated in the basement, making it one of the coolest rooms in Sveynton. Here, with the *Gentleman's Magazine*, *Punch*, *Fair Play*, *Judy*, *Moonshine*, *Illustrated Bite* and *The Pink 'Un*, he proposed to spend his entire evening. Far from being the ogre of Jack Hannah's imaginings, he was a red-faced little man in his late forties who suffered from the effects of over-eating and lack of physical exercise. Having devoured the Club's three shilling supper, which consisted of a chop, a small mound of sautéd kidneys and a slice of grilled ham as long as a good sized shoe, he suffered all the more and the news of the *Whisper*'s arrival affected him but very little. He had no special reason for fearing the resurrection of the *Avalon* mutiny – that was long past – and his offer of a command to Jack Hannah had no sinister undertones. His wife had constantly reminded him that their governess was bespoke to the young man in question so that when the *Whisper* arrived, he merely noted the event and reminded himself of the probable loss of his governess. When a prominent docksman arrived with certain information later that night, he merely grunted. Ships were more trouble than they were worth. He was very glad that his major interest was in the smelting of the copper, not the carriage of the ores. Guano he knew little about but gave it no thought, and when one of the doctors who was playing billiards in the club was sent for by messenger, he was also very glad that he was in no way at other people's beck and call. He remained perched in the comfortable hide chair, his paunch as round and taut as a football, his short little legs dangling on the floor, runnels of sweat standing in the creases of his podgy jowl. Even in the reading room, there was no permanent respite from the heat. Jamaica weather, he called it.

The events of this day and subsequent days were to be documented and bare facts would emerge. As every minute went by, it was ceasing to be a matter for the *Whisper* and her sixty-fourthers alone or those who had been aboard her. An official pen would recapitulate.

205

The Whisper *entered Sveynton harbour showing no quarantine flag and giving no indication that sickness was on board. A good many people went on board her as she entered the dock. Within an hour of the ship's arrival, the passenger was landed with her baggage and the crew paid off, dispersing themselves over the town. Then the hatches were removed, a stage rigged and gangs of men began discharging the cargo.*

There were also a number of isolated incidents which would later be seen to have a connection. The pot boy of the Mackworth Arms got a half sovereign that night.

"Where did you get that from?"

"The ostrich."

"Ostrich?"

"Her with a feather in her hat in Number Eight."

"What did she give you that for?"

"Train time-tables. I told her there was a new time-table this month."

"A half sovereign for . . ."

"I went up the railway station special and took a note to her bit o'fancy."

"Who's that then?"

"Ah, that would be tellin'! That's what she give me the half sovereign for."

"You can tell me . . ."

"No, I can't. Oh, all right, he's here now anyway. Booked into Number Nine and his carriage blocks half the yard."

"Not . . ."

"Not a word, mind!"

"Of course."

At midnight, Beatrice Trevoake still could not sleep. She lay restlessly on her specially lengthened bed. Her fear now was that she would look even more dreadful in the morning, shadows marking her eyes when she wanted to sweep coolly and imperturbably to the dock a picture of wraith-like gentility under a parasol. Well, she'd bought a parasol and the weather had come to match it.

That night the Collector of Customs had his last undisturbed night of sleep for many weeks, so did Sawdust Sal, Callous Ned, and whole gangs of men who had worked along the dock. For the medical practitioners, it was ever a busy time and now they began to get the first of what later became a flood of calls to the poorer dwellings. Tommy Dance slept fitfully, moaning occasionally.

Excitement, Mrs Dance continued to think. But it was not excitement, although no one quite knew what it was.

When Miss Trevoake went down to breakfast on the following morning, she was aware that she had interrupted a conversation between her employers. Mrs Chauncey-Vernon, who was a small birdlike woman, smiled at her, however, while her husband who had got himself home at midnight was decidedly liverish. He had stayed in the Club long enough to speak to one of the more astute general practitioners and now there was certain definite information.

"Your young man's caused a cufuffle and no mistake."

Beatrice's mind was still embedded in the circumstances attending Jack Hannah's leave-taking and she thought at first that some news of his father had been received. She had not mentioned one word of his reported reappearance.

"Captain Hannah?"

"Come in with fever aboard."

She thought that he might be ill himself.

"Fever?"

"A couple of lads down and one dying by all accounts. The Mayor has called a meeting of the port authorities, but fear not, it's only the fo'c'sle crowd. Captain Hannah and his passenger appeared quite well to the Collector. It seems they made a prosperous voyage. At any rate, his passenger went straight to the broker's!"

"Is the fever serious?"

"Just a few cases."

So it was little more than talking point.

"Should've been reported though," added Mr Chauncey-Vernon.

"It was not reported?"

"Too much in a hurry to dispose of the cargo, I expect."

"The heat helps no one," said Mrs Chauncey-Vernon to her cinnamon toast. She pecked at her food while her husband gorged. Now he nodded and began a weary attack on two poached haddocks.

Beatrice attempted to compose herself. It didn't sound serious fortunately, and perhaps might even be the cause of Jack Hannah spending a longer period of time ashore.

Of this period, the offical pen would write:

It was not until midday of the following day that the sanitary inspector came to the Mayor stating that a sick seaman was suspected to be suffering

207

from a virulent fever at Welcome Court. Dr Griffiths was sent on the Mayor's instructions and found him lying in bed in a wretched room of a small dirty house, dying of exhaustion from fever, his body tinged yellow. His landlady informed the doctor that the deceased was a German national who could not speak "as he had no roof to his mouth". His body was later put into a tarred sheet and burnt within an hour of death, his bedding and clothing destroyed and the house treated with limewash and chloride of lime. The Mayor sent the police to find the passenger and crew of the Whisper *but the passenger could not be found.*

Later, there were detailed notes made, names passing down into history.

Dance, Thomas, ship's boy, aged fifteen. Seen by Dr Griffiths on the first day of ailment. Began to complain of intense headache at seven in the morning and complained that he could not stand the light in his eyes! Dry tongue, great tenderness of the abdomen. Much black vomit. Skin dry, distinctly yellow. Very restless and unmanageable. Kept crying out the names of his shipmates in delirium. Mother thought he was "passing on".

Jack Hannah slept half the night in the chair. At the foot of the landing below the entrance to the loft, the cabin trunk lay where he had removed it in the middle of the night. Then, returning downstairs, he had dozed off again, awakening in the early hours of the morning when he had at last eaten the cold salad put out for him. Only then had he gone to bed properly, so to speak, passing the cabin trunk, another reminder of his intention. He had not opened Miss Trevoake's letter and it lay upon the mantelpiece exactly where his ring had lain. When the front door bell rang at ten in the morning, he thought at first that it might be her, come to plead with him. That was how his thoughts were running then. Even if Beatrice had broken off her engagement, she was still a sensible person and there was no doubt what any sensible person would try to prevent him doing, what, in fact, he was now about to do.

But the caller was not Miss Trevoake, nor indeed was it Senhora Salaverry. The squat, black bearded and black garbed figure of the Reverend Elias Evans stood there, his prominent adam's apple bobbing above his clerical collar at a pulsating rate. He was simmering with news, but there was fear and accusation in his eyes as he began with a pulpit announcement on the front doorstep.

"She has gone!"

"Gone?" For some reason, Jack Hannah thought he meant the ship.

"On the train with Baron Belasco. And none too soon either."

"Gone?" Jack Hannah repeated. He spoke like a man jilted, one of Miss Annie S. Swann's victims, left at the porch of the church.

"The man is in debt up to his eyebrows with creditors everywhere, but I have not the slightest concern with him or her. Why did you not declare the fever on board?"

"Fever?" He blinked. It was incredible that he could have forgotten it. Sleep, he thought. Now even sleep was part of the conspiracy. She would not even let him sleep!

"There are two cases reported ashore and more suspected, suspected what is more amongst persons who were not even aboard."

He looked past the Reverend Elias Evans across the street where there were already a crowd of longshoremen beginning to mutter amongst themselves, one or two looking across the street at him. Talk, he thought. He could feel their animosity. Perhaps this was also a part of the life his father had rejected, the gossiping voices, the accusing eyes, the endemic resentments of poor people against those who took their fate into their own hands.

He showed his visitor into the little parlour room where the Reverend Elias Evans's eyes flickered at once to the unopened letter prominently displayed upon the mantelpiece. Sheepishly, Jack Hannah took it and placed it inside his pocket, suddenly conscious of a great emptiness. Reality was returning like fog lifting in patches to reveal broken water where only grey headlands and a lumpy swell were visible.

"Gone?" he said stupidly. "Who has gone?"

"Senhora Salaverry. Did you really expect anything else, Captain? Indeed, I must tell you that I have been up half the night with my brother Handel and he has told me everything – every single thing. But this fever – it is apparently serious. You did not mention fever, not yellow fever?"

Again, he avoided giving an answer. He could imagine Evans and his brother closeted like bugs all night, ferreting out his misdeeds, scavenging upon every imperfection. But there was so much upon which they could feed. Give them a chance, they descended upon your life like flood water, dampening, then drowning every spark of rebellious spirit. And yet they called themselves nonconformists.

209

Evans rattled on.

"Naturally, the matter is out of our hands now. Mr Chauncey-Vernon has been informed as Chief Magistrate. You must realise that any meeting is quite impossible."

"Meeting?"

"With Miss Trevoake. Not for the length of the quarantine period."

"Gone?" Jack Hannah said again. "Where did she go? When. . ."

For a moment it looked as if the Reverend Elias Evans did not know or would not answer, but he had all the answers and bristled with importance as if he knew the event was to be the making of him. But he would not have spent half the night rabbiting away without a reason. He was unwittingly party to a deception, but deception might well lead to profit as well as disaster, and so the two of them, Elias and his brother, must have chewed over the affair like maggots at a carcass extracting what they could. Their sole concern, of course, was the ship and her cargo.

"Where has she gone?"

"All I can tell you is that very strenuous efforts have been made to find her. Belasco and she took railway tickets to join the Great Western Express at Gloucester for London. That is all we know. They apparently left at seven this morning, having cohabited in the Mackworth Arms last night."

"Belasco and she . . ."

"Have absconded with a very substantial purse. But that is not the half of it. Don't you understand what I'm telling you? There is talk of the ship and the cargo being burnt. You are to return at once with my brother and must not communicate with anyone on shore. Handel is aboard now."

He saw the Mate's gravedigger face in his mind's eye and swallowed. Now a constable had joined the watchers on the other side of the road and he could just see his helmet through the window.

"Is he ill, your brother?"

"From what he has told me, it is a miracle he is not. Captain, the police have instructions from the Mayor to put you aboard. You must stay aboard with Handel for at least the period of the quarantine. Fear not, we'll fight to save her from burning."

"Burning. . ." Jack Hannah repeated. His thoughts were in a remote place which he had never visited: Gloucester. "She'll not burn!" And yet the sense of the betrayal stabbed at him like a physical pain.

"Any belongings which you have brought with you must be returned aboard the ship, or burnt. My brother is waiting for you."

"Your brother is . . ."

"Handel is aboard. He can be relied upon to do his duty always. He is preparing for at least a six-week stay."

"*Six-weeks?*"

"I am afraid so. We will agree to anything to placate them."

For this he had crossed the world, Jack Hannah thought, to be closeted with Evans once more. He still did not properly understand what he had been told about the fever. How could it have lingered this long? And then there was Evans. "Leave Evans to me," she had said. But she had not. She had left Evans to him!

She had also left a problem for the port authorities.

The Mayor convened a meeting of the magistrates to consider whether there was any power to remove the vessel from the dock. The Captain and Chief Officer went aboard after some persuasion but no shiphandler or seaman or rigger could be found who would go near the vessel as by this time other persons were reported sick of the malady and it was only upon the Medical Officer's insistence that food was thrown aboard to the two officers. Instructions were given that no bilge water was to be pumped and the dock was sealed off. There was some acrimony between the Master and Chief Officer but it was only to be expected as they faced the prospect of close confinement for many weeks after an already prolonged voyage. Offers by clergymen to go aboard and join them had to be refused, but prayers were said regularly. All efforts to trace the passenger failed.

Aboard the *Whisper*, sinner and saviour stared at each other daily, and now it was Evans's turn to crack.

"She promised me! I demeaned myself to converse with her, that slut! And she promised me!"

"Promised you?"

"The command. You were to leave. Don't you understand, neither of us will get another ship here? She's even taken half the profit of the cargo and the cargo might have to be burnt. What are the owners to do? Belasco and she have swindled everyone. Every penny of profit gone – when there will very likely be no profit at all."

Then Jack Hannah smiled.

"Belasco will not get far with her."

"Is that an answer?"

"If you are asking on whose neck all this will be laid, Evans, it is mine." He already knew. How else could this shabby adventure have ended but in disaster and disgrace?"

211

"Well, don't say I didn't warn you. You are lucky to escape with your life. Other fornicators have not been so fortunate. If only I had forcibly removed you and taken command myself."

"You, Evans?"

"There are parallels. I would not have moved one inch from the chosen path of my duty."

"I thought she promised you . . ."

"That was in the circumstances prevailing. Those I had to adapt to. Don't worry. I have told my brother everything. There will be no repercussions about my conduct."

"What about the log, Evans? She got you to sign it too?"

"You were sick. I had no alternative. I nursed you for weeks."

"Thank you, Evans."

"At last! But it is too late. How the Good Lord allowed you to recover, I do not know!"

"You nursed me."

"Yes, I was His instrument. I think we had better take up our respective positions on separate parts of the ship. Oh, when will it rain?"

"When the wind comes, Evans."

"Yes, but all the winds that blow cannot alter what you have done. D'you know there are still dead locusts in the bilge? I inspected it this morning. That was another thing. Locusts! Locusts! Does anybody ever dare to tell me there is no God? Oh, yes, the winds carry seeds, I tell you, the locust winds carry seeds. The Good Book is right."

"I'd keep away from the bilge if I were you."

"Is that all you can say?"

"What else is there to be said?"

"I will tell you," Evans said. "As God is my witness, I will tell you . . ."

And he did – endlessly. It was as if the whole voyage had been for no other reason than to give Evans his unwilling captive and audience, forcibly kept there by all the recently hastily invoked majesty of the law.

The major bone of contention ashore was the cargo.

At a second meeting between the Mayor and the magistrates, the medical officers present recommended the destruction of the cargo but Mr Henry Chauncey-Vernon, representing the shipowners of the port, presented a tabulated list of vessels arriving from South America in the previous year,

212

stating that one in three ships had members of their crews infected with fever. Twenty-four Cuban vessels had also put into the port in the same period, fifteen of whom recorded deaths of yellow fever in passage, and none of these ships or their cargoes had been interfered with. All agreed, said Mr Chauncey-Vernon, that the vessel should not have come into the port, but having entered and discharged her cargo, the law did not permit either her removal nor the destruction of her cargo. Indeed to do so, would set a very grave precedent in the destruction of private property and he hoped that wiser counsels would prevail.

You throw a stone into a pool, Jack Hannah had once thought, and the ripples continue to the very edge. But the ripples which accompanied the *Whisper*'s homecoming followed no logical pattern and now that precautions were taken, they were seen to be too late, for the fever which should not have survived, did survive, and other deaths occurred, some with logical reason, others not. Other names passed into history.

Ephraim Grail, longshoreman, living at Ennal's Point, aged thirty. Began to ail at 5 a.m. feeling dull pain in the head and lower part of the belly, vomiting and complaining that he could not stand the light. Had been aboard only in passage from the lighthouse across Sveynton Bay to the dock. Said he had searched the ship for his brother's effects. Died within three days. Autopsy not permitted.

Louisa Grail, his cousin. Visited by him on the day of the vessel's arrival. A strong healthy young woman until she was taken with sudden headache which got speedily worse and became so intense that she raved with it and had to be forcibly restrained from attacking the attending physician. Collapsed and died. Autopsy not permitted.

Samuel Grail, cousin of the former. Sixteen years. Had also been aboard the Whisper *in passage across the bay. Collapsed in the Sailor's Safety tavern and was cared for there by a relative and survived.*

There were others less fortunate, however. Old Callous Ned was callous no longer and then there were riggers, longshoremen, persons who had been aboard and persons who had not been aboard, twelve in all dying, including those whose contact with the *Whisper* could not be traced, and as the deaths increased in number, there was popular talk of a march to the dock to burn the ship, but she was moved by tug and placed against a remote pier east of the dock with Captain and Chief Officer still aboard. There she lay unwanted and untouchable, a pariah.

"What ship is that?"

"That ship is no man's ship. Don't you see the sign? 'Keep Off!' "

Day after day, Jack Hannah was closeted with Evans and Evans raved, growing stranger, sometimes refusing to eat what was cooked for him, sometimes welcoming, sometimed hiding from, the daily visits of the guard boat. His biggest rages were usually about inconsequentials. He grew leaner and more gaunt, harping on trivialities.

"Dropsy? Why did you think it was dropsy? Because you can press your fingers into the bone – is that it? Well, you can do that with dropsy, but what about the yellowness? Didn't you notice the simplest thing? And the black vomit?'

"Does it make any difference now, Evans?"

"And that woman, that foul, filthy, half-caste heathen? She stripped naked when she prayed, you know? But to what God? I caught her grovelling and chanting some wretched curse. Said she was English or half-English – but she couldn't have been. I'm surprised she didn't have tribal marks. She believed in spirits, she told me, spirits of the air and the water, she said. D'you know she rubbed oil all over herself when the locusts came? I wouldn't be surprised if she didn't drink her own urine, I wouldn't. Some of them do, these heathen, I've seen it. They eat their own young and make sacrifices of a kind that decent people should never have to learn about. But there, I suppose you joined in with her? Oh, why did I ever allow my good name to be besmirched with the likes of . . why? Oh why?"

It was a question to be hurled to the winds when the winds came at last and by now they were getting letters and news from ashore, but Evans remained obsessional. They daily examined each other for any signs of fever, but with the bizarre lack of logic which characterises such outbreaks, neither the pilot, nor the customs men, nor Evans suffered. It was the disease of poor people. There was no reason for that either, but it was.

"She even took the flags. At the height of the fever, she took the signal flags. She did not think of herself for if we could not signal anyone, she would have gone down with us. We nearly did, you know?"

"Perhaps she wanted to die if she did not succeed."

"Succeed! 'Daughter of the Chaldeans,' I said, 'Lie down.' I knew. Did she not defile herself with idols and never give up her harlotry? And Grail told me things. Why did your father put into Buenos

Ayres? And did you know that Henry Chauncey-Vernon was implicated? I can tell you, I know everything!"

"Then keep it to yourself, Evans. If it wasn't for him, the ship would be burnt."

"Grail told me . . ."

"Grail's dead."

"Your father . . ."

"Dead."

"Mr Waters even saw her with . . ."

"Dead."

"And where is she now? Laughing at us!" said Evans wild-eyed once more. "Laughing at us – at what fools she has made of us all."

It was what Jack Hannah thought himself. By now, he had worked it out for himself and had begun to read what he thought was a kind of perspective. He had been victim for every hour of that voyage and everything she had said was a part of her pretence. She was there for profit and profit she alone had. There was no action of hers he could recall which did not lead to this final disappearance of hers, clutching a bag of gold. He had been skilfully used and was now ruined, for the deaths ashore would brand him for ever as the man who brought yellow fever to Sveynton. But at least, here at the bottom of his luck, he felt the beginnings of the calm that comes when even despair is seen to be pointless. He could fall no further, and in all this quarantine period, there had come packets of letters from Miss Trevoake, including some of the letters returned from Chile so he was aware of Beatrice Trevoake's feelings, and presently had little else to think about as the weeks drew on. In her polite way she hoped that he was holding up in this difficult period of trial. She sent him daily encouragement and assurances that they would be together soon if they kept faith with each other. Then there were the endearments, the backlog of longings, and the formal politeness turned to more positive things.

For his part, he could not, of course, reply for they were still isolated and everything that was delivered on board remained there, nothing being allowed on shore, not even a letter. At first, he had thought himself so unworthy of Miss Trevoake that any relationship seemed out of the question, but he soon became aware of a change in tone apparent in her letters. One thing was clear and that was that she knew a good deal more than he'd suspected. The Evans faction had not been idle ashore and he began to realise a singular fact about their relationship. In a bizarre way, he was more desirable to her as an outcast to be picked up from the floor at the bottom of his luck than he was as a confident young master of his own future. Trapped, he did not threaten her. Victim, he was still helpable. Pariah, she would scorn the prejudices of the ignorant. It was as if she had always wanted a victim of her very own! And she was not without influence. Sveynton remained a Welsh port despite its energetic intruders and a quiet word here was so much better than a loud bray there amongst the clamour of vociferous nonentities. Property ruled, and property would triumph.

You will not want me to hide the truth from you and will have realised that there is a good deal of animosity felt towards you in the village as a result of the deaths of Ephraim Grail and his cousin Louisa who was the cause of such a commotion in the London papers last year. But Samuel Grail has recovered, as has the boy Dance. There is now some talk of you putting into a remote island which was not afterwards declared to the Collector of Customs. Mr Chauncey-Vernon, however, has been an absolute brick and says that the matter is now closed, and that it is in the interests of the shipowners and work people that Sveynton should not be declared a source of yellow fever, otherwise all outward bound ships from this port will be quarantined upon arrival at their destinations. If this happened, all responsible people are sure that the copper works and the coal exporting yards will come to a standstill as they cannot be expected to pay wages to idle hands.

So if Mr Henry says the matter is closed, you can rest your mind upon it. The official report will say that there has been a great irregularity and neglect of the usual precautions but the persons concerned appear to have acted in ignorance and Mr Henry agrees. He also told me to tell you that as you must naturally be concerned about your own future, he is desirous of finding a superintendent to supervise a patent fuel works which he is building on the site of the Coppermen's Arms. He is anxious to recruit someone with a knowledge of the loading of vessels as a great trade with foreign ports is envisaged, patent stove grates being all the vogue as far away as Stockholm. A position of trust of this kind will, of course, mean a change of your ambitions, my dearest . . .

"My dearest," it was now -- bold liberty! But the letters told him more than he could have expected. If he had ignored her, she had thought of nothing else but their engagement and he even predicted what might be described as a happy outcome to all this affair then – a simple marriage from which all the turmoil of the past might be completely erased.

Whatever motives he put on the offers of assistance which came from Beatrice's employer, he knew he would very probably accept them, and indeed, his acceptance of all things came in perceptible stages. The sea, the iron-fastened sea, fastened him no longer. He was finished there, a beaten man, he knew, as perhaps his father had been finished long before his time came. There were currents at work once more, he felt, currents of feeling which amounted to an untypical resignation – no, it was a capitulation – to the fate that awaited him. Beatrice, it seemed, had his future planned, and so had her employer. There would – or would there? – be further things to confess, but then those with things to confess often made the mistake of believing their confessions were wanted. (Witness Evans daily moving towards a dementia of his own making.) Even the events Beatrice knew about were tumultuous enough – and what she did not know, she could probably guess. But for the future, there it was, he thought, already encompassed in the suggestions revealed in that firm copperplate hand upon her employer's thick parchment notepaper. He could see it all and it was so normal. Indeed, further images came to mind, of a greystone terraced house, a patch of lawn and a dockyard job with a superintendent's stove pipe hat.

He scratched his head ruefully as he considered it, alone for once as Evans slept fitfully in the saloon – he still would not use the Senhora's cabin. So no more landfalls, he thought. He was a shorebound man, one like others for whom that life upon the waters had become too much.

He could hear them talking ashore already.

"What did you say his name was? Hannah? Swallowed the hook after that yellow fever business. Bad business that. They say he had bit of skirt on board and his john willy got in the way of his compass."

So it would be remembered. Well, he was not the first and doubtless would not be the last to have quit, and he would be lucky to find a berth ashore. The chapter was closed and he had better settle. He informed Evans of his decision, and then, to his astonishment, Evans, who was still instructing him to gird his loins and mumbling about harlots, brightened up. Now Evans discovered a new rubbery quality as he moved one step towards his command. Evans got rid of his doubts and anxieties by foisting them on to other people and their last conversation saw Evans sitting there in the saloon, his cadaverous face nodding omnisciently, survival written all over him.

"Very wise to recognise your limitations," Evans said. "Size is not everything. Take myself, I've always been on the lanky side, but I've always known when to stand back, d'you see? It is a captain's task. Any fool can pulley-hauley."

When the guard boat called the following day, he asked for starch. He meant to cut a figure when he got ashore, had kept his best linen unused for that specific purpose.

"Mistakes have been made but we must go forward," Evans said. Oh, Evans was a survivor and there was now a wooden obstinacy about his face, a new set of the mouth, a glint of the eye. Having purged himself, the shell of the man was filling up again. He had been forced outside the ghetto of his own mind and meant to succeed if he could. He would go on, fearful, worried, a mumbler along the waterways of the world, the kind of man who, in the longevity of an ocean life would ultimately have seen everything and people would eventually come to respect him. It was a sobering thought that Evans was the better owner's man, a man who would last, small fry made large and with all the durability of grass. Such men conquered the sea and went on conquering it. Their ambition never over-reached itself. They never fought tides, they rode them. Above all, they did not dream and could not be lured.

"All I hope is, that you've learned your lesson," Evans said with his queer lopsided smile. "And fortunately you don't require me to write you a good discharge."

When the quarantine ended, they took Evans off first with a fuss of doctors and officials and then came back with a nervous watchman and a gang of workmen armed with more chloride of lime, and finally it was Jack Hannah's turn to stand, a solitary figure, in the stern sheets of the harbour cutter. It was not long before he saw Beatrice waiting for him at the jetty beside the Custom House. She wore a smart toque hat of strapped velvet and felt which he had never seen before. As the boat drew near, he realised how tall she was, how well set up, a monument of a woman, but perhaps that impression was heightened because of his own feeling of frailty. He was down to a mere fourteen stone. She towered above Henry Chauncey-Vernon who stood fussily beside her like a small apoplectic frog, but calmed no doubt by the certainty of his silence, Jack Hannah thought. Beatrice waved happily as if her charge had been released only by her

218

personal guarantee of his good behaviour. That welcoming hand was the future, he thought, not the shabby boots of poverty but the lowly propriety of a starched collar and goods brought on approval to the house. He could see it all again as he looked towards them. He did not give his mind to any other detail, but yet somehow, her smile was that of a contrite woman.

"My dearest . . ." her lips framed the words in a picture of simpering gentility before he could hear them, but he did not delude himself into thinking that only tenderness awaited him. One day, no doubt, there would be a day of reckoning. Those twelve deaths ashore would make him enemies for life. Like his father, he had secured a reputation, and like his father's it would last. Children unborn as yet would point accusingly to his issue, and even Evans's letter like that of the unknown Scranton seaman's concerning his father, would find its way into dingy cupboards, forgotten memorabilia awaiting a researcher's pen.

"Well," he said. "Well . . ." He had to mind his step on the slippery stones of the jetty.

"Jack," she answered, corrected herself with a fonder more maternal, "John."

They could not, of course, embrace in public, but she had boldly removed her glove so that the solitary garnet stone was visible. She it was who took his hand first.

"Miss Trevoake," he countered. It was the best he could manage as they were observed.

"As to the voyage," Mr Chauncey-Vernon said later when they were seated side by side in his carriage, their joint weight buckling its springs on the corners, "a closed book, I'm glad to say."

"Yes sir," he said, and added a gruff, "Grateful to ye."

And that – at last – was the beginning of the end of it, since all he had guessed at fell into place and it was not until they were safely married and he neatly shunted into an office where he could not see the sea save from behind the towering steam crane, that Mr Henry's dissolute brother Roderick Chauncey-Vernon took it upon himself to call. He too was back into the fold since Belasco had also swindled him, but the news he brought concerned neither. Now he addressed a serge-suited Jack Hannah whose brown dust coat looked incongruous below the stiff wing collar which Mrs Hannah obliged him to wear. He was not, as she pointed out regularly, a tradesman! Neither was he allowed to sit in his shirtsleeves in the house. A superintendent of works simply did not do that! There were standards to be maintained. If he did not know them, she did.

"Glad of a chance to get you on your own," Roderick said. His brother Henry was safely away taking a spa cure for his gout. "I thought you'd be interested to learn some details of Senhora Salaverry."

Jack Hannah felt his pulse race.

"She attempted to come back here, you know?"

"Come back?"

"She did not join the Great Western Express at Gloucester that day, she entrained for Bristol where she thought she could get a steam packet directly across the channel to Sveynton. She waited several days, but by then, the news of the fever had reached Bristol."

"Bristol?"

"It was her intention to return to see you."

"How d'you know this?"

"Belasco told me. He followed her. She had misappropriated certain monies belonging to him. When he eventually caught up with her, it was too late."

"Too late for what?"

"She was far gone in fever and died in Bristol later in the week."

"No . . ." Jack Hannah said. It was almost a protest. "No yellow fever was reported in Bristol or any other channel port?"

"It was not reported as yellow fever, Belasco did not want complications, nor indeed did the tavern-keeper. A local apothecary recorded the usual 'Death by visitation of God.' In his opinion, she was some months gone with child."

The wing collar seemed like a noose suddenly. He could not speak. Then he swallowed, forced himself to be casual.

"She . . . she was a wealthy woman."

"Belasco has repaid his debts."

"How do you know she was coming back here?"

"She told Belasco, but she was feverish, of course. It was very courageous of him to stay with her, especially when she had robbed him. Apparently there is a great brightness of light in the closing stages of the disease. She was hallucinated and thought she saw things."

"What things?"

"I have no idea."

220

"A ship," Jack Hannah said. "The *Caleuche*."

"I beg your pardon?"

There was belief and there was what you believed, and what could happen to you, given time, Jack Hannah thought. She had said all these things. There were also said to be spirits that came from the sea and ate the lips of liars, and once there was a girl who crept away from her mother and ate manioc raw, sitting naked listening to a native story-teller by the head waters of a forgotten river. There was this girl, then there was Seraphina, then the woman staring at the slowly turning body of an Indian in the water, then the actress, the incredible actress who remembered everything, who had a capacity for listening and twisting things to her advantage, who knew exactly when to disappear, and having disappeared, when to return – to haunt you. And her name was Felipa, but what her true nationality was, or who her father was, or where her husbands lay buried, or whose child she carried, or why she had finally decided to return for him, he would never know. Except that she had promised to, and in a strange way, she had kept all her promises save one, and death had put a stop to that.

But what if she had come back? Would he have gone? Why hadn't he packed when she had been so specific about a stout cabin trunk, her own being so worn? He had found the trunk but he had not filled it.

And if he had gone, it would only have been to see the brightness of light in her eyes, perhaps even in his own once more. But she had kept all her promises, he couldn't forget that.

"It must have been an extraordinary voyage, Captain?"

"Well," Jack Hannah said – it was a year later, there was a comfortable spread of paunch below his waistcoat after a year in a desk bound job. His future lay in patent fuel stoves and Mrs Hannah's attentions were turning to a nursery and even moving house as there were Irish riff-raff ever moving up from the docks and thick-tongued yokels swarming in from the country. Normality, like a blueish haze, blanketed his life, but he had prospered like a blinkered carthorse plodding away, his role in life now demanding fatter fingers to ply to more ordinary bones.

"Extraordinary from the beginning?"

"From the beginning, there were complications," Jack Hannah said.